THE BETRAYERS

PARRIS AFTON
BONDS

THE TEXICANS

The Brigands

The Barons

The Bravados

The Betrayers

The Banshees (2021)

OTHER WORKS

THE BETRAYERS

THE TEXICANS · VOLUME FOUR

NEW YORK TIMES BESTSELLING AUTHOR

PARRIS AFTON

BONDS

LAGAN
PRESS

an imprint of
THE OGHMA PRESS

OGHMA
C R E A T I V E   M E D I A

Bentonville, Arkansas • Los Angeles, California
www.oghmacreative.com

Library of Congress Cataloging-in-Publication Data

Names: Bonds, Parris Afton, author.
Title: The Betrayers/Parris Afton Bonds. | The Texicans #4
Description: First Edition. | Bentonville: Lagan, 2021.
Identifiers: LCCN: 2021934701 | ISBN: 978-1-63373-629-0 (hardcover) |
ISBN: 978-1-63373-630-6 (trade paperback) | ISBN: 978-1-63373-675-7 (eBook)
Subjects: BISAC: FICTION/Romance/Historical/American |
FICTION/Romance/Action & Adventure | FICTION/Romance/Western
LC record available at: https://lccn.loc.gov/2021934701

First Lagan Press trade paperback edition May, 2021

Jacket & Interior Design by Casey W. Cowan
Editing by Mari Mason & Kelly Sohner

This book is a work of historical fiction. Any references to historical events, real people, or real places are used fictitiously. Other names, characters, places, and events are products of the author's imagination, and any resemblance to actual events or places or person, living or dead, is entirely coincidental.

Published by Lagan Press, an imprint of The Oghma Press, a subsidiary of The Oghma Book Group.

Dedicated to Vicki Stiefel,
The fantasy author whose imagination is boundless

and

With gratitude, to Bob Mapes
For the Card Lessons

THE TEXICANS
GENEALOGY

THE BETRAYERS

Alejandro de la Torre y Stuart
6th Baron of Paladín

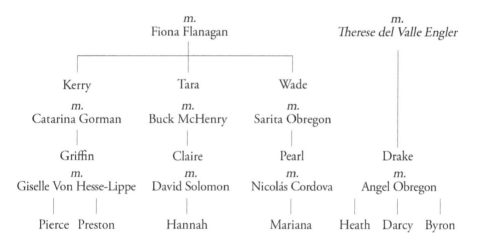

m.
Fiona Flanagan

m.
Therese del Valle Engler

Kerry
m.
Catarina Gorman

Tara
m.
Buck McHenry

Wade
m.
Sarita Obregon

Griffin
m.
Giselle Von Hesse-Lippe

Claire
m.
David Solomon

Pearl
m.
Nicolás Cordova

Drake
m.
Angel Obregon

Pierce   Preston

Hannah

Mariana

Heath   Darcy   Byron

Karl Von Hesse-Lippe

m.
Maria Elena Gunter

Maximillian
m.
Ingrid Dreschner

Giselle

Amarillo

Red River

Brazos

Fort Worth • • Dallas

Nacogdoches •

El Paso

Brazos

Trinity

Rio Grande

• Austin

Houston

San Antonio

Galveston

The Barony

Corpus
Christi

Gulf of Mexico

Rio Grande

TEXAS

Rio Grande City

Brownsville

Nueces

1

THE BARONY
SEPTEMBER 1917

In forty-four-year-old Drake Paladín's opinion, 1917 clearly ushered in a stellar year of fighting.

After Great Britain intercepted a German telegram to Mexico, offering to recover its lost territory of New Mexico, Arizona, and Texas, the United States at once declared war against Imperial Germany.

Drake didn't take too kindly to Germany's idea. His father, the Baron himself, had fought and won the right to their land at the battle of San Jacinto.

The Mexicans were fighting already. Pancho Villa had waged a civil war lately on what Drake considered his own turf through his wife, Angel's, legacy—the Lone Star Smelter Company, as well as its El Paso environs.

But of more immediate concern to Drake was the riot and mutiny in Houston. The fighting had erupted between the city's police officers and the soldiers of the all-negro Twenty-Fourth U.S. Infantry Regiment.

Only the month before, the regiment had been posted to Camp Logan on the newly opened Houston Ship Channel. It was a vital connection between the Port of Houston and the Gulf of Mexico fifty miles away.

From behind his late father's desk and domain of The Barony Enterprises, he faced a roomful of females wearing their war bonnets while he wondered what had happened to his roaming days. Of course, it was a female Texas tornado that had happened to him. The irresistible Angel had lassoed his reckless heart and ultimately dragged him, along with his oil empire in southeast Texas, back to The Barony's ranching empire.

He often yearned to have his father at his back once more, frugally doling out sought-after advice, as spare as his inordinately tall frame, about running the business side of ranching, The Barony Enterprises. But Baron Alejandro de La Torre y Stuart had died in his arms eleven long years back. Old age had taken a life whose pistons had always stroked full out.

Since the Great Galveston Hurricane of 1900, he and his father had come to affectionate terms. Well, as much as his old man's strong temperament ever could bend. Drake was the prodigal son returned home to replace his late half-brother Wade's run of The Barony.

Even after four years, the loss of Wade in a freakish water well collapse he had been repairing on his own was still a painful memory Drake kept behind steel doors. Of his three half-siblings, Wade's disposition most resembled his own. Maybe that was why he was finding the business of ranching, even from behind a desk, not the burr under the saddle he had anticipated.

With Angel to help guide him through the ranch's business maze, he found himself enjoying wrangling its new challenges. And if it wasn't oil or ranching challenges, then it was his Angel. She had both rope-bound and spellbound his bleak, soulless self, and now it was he who meant to bind her to him forever.

Arms folded, his niece Pearl, a mere two years younger than he, paced before the window of his office. Absently, her fingers rubbed at the elbow's lace sleeves of her yellow frock. She possessed Wade's dark good looks, as did her and Nicolás's daughter Mariana.

The sixteen-year-old Mariana sat in the Campeche chair's sling seat and riffled through the documents in her folder. She had accumulated police reports, newspaper articles, Houston's mayoral response, and Colonel Cress's report to the Commanding General—among other documents—to substantiate her defense for her best friend, Daniel.

His thirty-four-year-old beauty of a wife, who had bewitched his heart and badgered his body, did most of his reading for him since he barely could. Not that Angel hadn't done her best to get his Word Blindness up to literacy par, even committing herself to studying ophthalmology at Galveston's medical school.

Pushing back a swath of sun-golden hair that had tumbled forward, she adjusted the reading glasses perched on the end of her pert nose and looked up from the paper she held. His never-ending craving for her had resulted in three sons, so far. Heath, Darcy, and Lord Byron, named for her romantic literary heroes. "Drake, according to this County Sheriff's account, it proves that Daniel was in the county jail during the riot and mutiny. No way he could have participated in it."

Drake knew that Daniel had just returned from serving with the Pershing Expedition in Mexico and, if anything like his father Mandrake who had served in the Spanish American War, Daniel would never mutiny. So, naturally, Drake raised a dark forbidding brow at Mariana. "And exactly why was Daniel in the county jail?"

Pearl's daughter wasn't intimidated. The slender Mariana was mature far beyond her years and had skipped several grades in school. As a law student at the University of Texas, and the only female in her class, she was quick to the defense. "Because Dan was sitting in the 'whites only' section of a streetcar!"

Becky, Daniel's mother and Pearl's longtime friend, raised a tear-dampened face that had been buried in her hands. As an eight-year-old, she had served as a slave. After Drake's half-sister Tara had rescued her—or maybe it was the other way around—from the Paladín's longtime enemy Liam O'Brien Obregon, Becky had faithfully served Wade's family. And as a forty-one-year-old emancipated woman, she had served proudly as a nurse in Cuba during the Spanish American War, where she had met Daniel's father, Mandrake. She was still proud and comely at sixty. "Two mounted police officers beat him and sent him off in a patrol wagon."

Pearl spun from the window's view of the giant live oak on the hill, from where The Barony Ranch unrolled across Southwest Texas plains and desert. "The problem is all 118 soldiers are represented by a single attorney working on a mere two weeks' preparation. Major Grier has no trial experience. He's not even a lawyer—he only taught law at West Point."

Drake reared his scuffed, dirt-crusted boots, spurs and all, atop the large desk—incurring a black look from his beloved. With the cards stacked against Becky and Mandrake Jarvis's son, the young man would need the best representation possible.

Reaching for his cigar, he turned narrowed eyes back toward Mariana. "Then the Paladíns will just have to grease the palm of the best attorney money can buy." If nothing else, Drake had learned at least that from his father's business scruples.

SAN ANTONIO
SEPTEMBER 1917

Drake had to concede that Roger Clarendon certainly qualified as the best attorney money could buy. He earned wealth and fame getting big names off the hook. That night, all Drake bought were drinks for Roger, Angel, and himself at the Menger Hotel bar.

Not that money was any problem for Drake. He made an embarrassing amount. Between his oilfield gusher in Conroe, The Barony Enterprises, the patents for his various inventions, and his wife's inheritance of Obregon commercial properties in both Brownsville and El Paso, he had more money than God.

After the Galveston hurricane, it had taken him a while to recover his finances. His oil derrick in Conroe had been blown to bits.

With imagination and determination, his half-brother Kerry had taken the reins of a devastated Galveston and created a new strong centralized control to handle the economic recovery. Kerry's son, Griffin, with his invaluable architect contacts, had ensured Galveston reconstruction was under way rapidly, branding his name deeply in the minds of Texicans everywhere.

Drake doubted his half-sister Tara had ever recovered, not fully, from the loss of her husband, Buck, in the hurricane. These days, she divided her time between her own ranching spread and visiting her daughter, Claire, in Dallas. Claire and David's Dallas Emporium had donated mass amounts of clothing to the hurricane victims and had since gone on to open new Emporium locations internationally.

For that matter, Sarita had not fully recovered either, following the loss of her idolized Wade. Growing up as she had on the Rio Grande, it was only natural that afterward she had sought out the familiarity of their old home on Buffalo Bayou, but even there, on the times Drake and Angel had visited, Sarita had seemed despondent and not in the best of health. Without her Wade, she seemed a tortured, broken soul.

Roger Clarendon, who was in the best of health from playing tennis, usually mixed doubles with his father. Sitting with Angel and Roger that night around the small table in the mirrored and cherry wood bar, something about the high-priced attorney annoyingly circled Drake like a whining mosquito.

True, Roger Clarendon won in the courtroom every time. Even on the lawn tennis court, Roger was formidable. His colleagues stood in awe of him, clients clamored for him, and his father, Brighton Clarendon, was a Supreme Court Justice and close confidant of President Woodrow Wilson.

"Should I decide to take on this case, you should know I command astronomical fees, Mister Paladín. As a civilian lawyer, I have no chain of command. I don't have to obey the rules like military defense attorneys. With my autonomy, I can challenge high-ranking military personnel for misconduct without concern for reprisal."

A white-jacketed waiter set another Gillette cocktail before the fair-haired Roger. "I trust the bartender didn't bruise the mint?"

"No, sir," the colored man bobbed his head and departed.

Roger swilled a deep draught. The more he drank, the more often one eyelid blinked a half-beat behind his other, like a doll's broken lid. "It's that easy, Paladín. Daniel Jarvis's free military lawyer can remain on the case. Your nigger friend doesn't have to choose between me or the other, should I take the case."

Drake's hackles raised, and Angel intervened. She did not look at all her thirty-five years, having that perennial air about her of a mischievous child, but at that moment it was difficult for him to miss the unholy gleam in her eyes.

He could visualize her upswept hair ruffling at her nape. The very spot he took great pleasure in dropping feverish kisses when he wanted to possess her, body and mind, both joy and fury. Right now, it was her fury that predominated—at Clarendon—which let Drake off the hook, for once. "Should you take the case, Mister Clarendon, just who would be in charge?"

Carelessly, Roger draped his arm across the back of her chair, already swathed with her stole, and shifted his supple weight slightly toward her. "Of course, the assigned military defense would assist me—but their legal counsel would not impede me with the military counsel's usual ineptness."

His words, Drake noted, were slurring slightly.

She arched a brow and, with her linen napkin, patted dry luscious lips that he knew were bared in a humorless smile. "Well, should we decide to retain you, we'll keep that in mind."

Clarendon's metallic eyes glinted with arousal. "Given your piquant charm, Missus Paladín, I am finding myself inclined to take on this case, after all."

"It's getting late. We'll mull this over later." Drake's voice rumbled like summer thunder in his ears. "I'll take care of the bill."

He knew if he didn't haul himself away from the table, he'd wind up taking the starch out of Clarendon's pompous ass—and if Drake had learned nothing else over his lifetime of sparring, it was to choose his battles wisely. Once that road was taken, there was no going back.

The man irritated—and bored—him, but it was more than that. It was the man's assumption to a proprietary claim on whatever interested him. He reminded Drake of the war going on in Europe… of countries taking the opportunity to seize what they wanted, regardless of the hundreds of thousands of lives, not just bodies, but lives, maimed by doing so.

Chin high, his beloved rose to stand as stiffly as a soldier at attention. "We'll wait outside."

She couldn't be any more eager than he for the agonizing evening to end. Summoning the black-tie waiter, without glancing at the numbers at the bottom of the bill, he peeled out a Ben Franklin—more than enough to tip the staff magnanimously.

Stalking toward the restaurant exit, he spotted Angel's frilly wrap on her vacated chair and retrieved it. He got no further with her stole than the Menger's portico, where he saw Clarendon forcing Angel against one stone column as she swung wildly at him.

If a man's *cojones* had a sound, it was the roar Drake let loose.

————————————

ROGER CLARENDON HAD ESCORTED ANGEL from the restaurant out under the Menger's portico. While they waited for his motorcar to be brought around, it was all she could muster in civility to evade his grasp. Gradually, it had wandered from her elbow to the back of her waist, and from there downward ever so slightly to rest lightly on the upper curve of her hip.

"I wonder if your husband fully appreciates your… *attributes,* Missus Paladín."

Subtly, she shifted her slender torso away. Her tight smile was just short of a snarl. "Enough that no one else needs to." Just get through the next few moments without causing an outright ruckus. After all, his father *is* a Supreme Court Justice.

"Ah, but every female appreciates extra attention, do they not?" His hand returned to her waist, steering her up against one of the portico's nearby stone columns. When his fingers slid beneath her arm toward the fullness of her breast, she whirled and swiped at him with her beaded handbag.

At that same moment, Drake appeared out of nowhere, as if part of a magic act. He launched a fist into the younger man's jaw. The punch spun Clarendon's shoulder toward him and, dropping her stole, he landed a crushing blow with the other fist to the man's nose. Blood splattered out like a violent sneeze. Drake attacked the attorney in a primitive beating that would have made the boxer Jack Johnson, the Galveston Giant, look like a schoolboy.

A late-night crowd gathered to watch her hero in full lethal force. Drake, in her passionate perception, had been her hero from the time he won her, a seven-year-old, as a marker in a poker game. She had known he might not yet love her, but he was hers. She had known this with a certainty that stubbornly defied any contradiction from Heaven or Hell.

His raw, harsh masculinity had called to some disturbing need in the child she had been—perhaps that masculine appeal reflected her childhood's absentee father. Yet it was more than a mere connection of the flesh, what she and her ferocious lover shared. More than a complement of their weaknesses and strengths. It was the fierce tenderness with which they both protected one another from all life's hurts, large and small.

But, at the moment, Drake's protectiveness was going a bit too far. "Stop! Drake, stop! You'll kill him!"

If he didn't, the green Peerless Motorcar being brought around would, because when she tugged on his bicep, Roger took the opportunity to escape—fleeing right into his motorcar's oncoming path.

And in that same awful instant, the thought slammed into her—Heaven and Hell might not let her lifelong defiance off that lightly after all.

ALSACE-LORRAINE, FRANCE
NOVEMBER 1917

Over there. Over there. The Yanks are coming.

The propaganda-ridden song snagged sixteen-year-old Heath Paladín and his twin cousins, once removed, Pierce and Preston. The war was an emotional contagion of the nation. After a German U-Boat sank the British Lusitania with 128 Americans aboard, submarine warfare escalated, and fever-pitched fury took over America.

Heath had felt as if he were missing out on some grand but elusive adventure. He wanted to get over there—over to the fighting where all the excitement was.

Yet nothing had gone right since the three of them got "over there."

Unbeknownst to both sets of parents, the three had lied about their ages and joined the fledgling U.S. Army's 120th Fighter Squadron at Kelly Field in San Antonio. All three had the patriarch Alex Paladín's inordinate height, so no questions had been asked.

Not that questions would have been asked anyway. They were at war. There was a way to get around anything.

But after signing on the dotted line and shouldering his duffel bag, Heath was dismayed to find that they had been transferred to the 1st Aero Reconnaissance Squadron that had served in the Pancho Villa Expedition. The squadron's mission was merely surveillance. What a disappointing come down—from fighter squadron to mere reconnaissance squadron.

While the war raged in northern France, he and his cousins had started training at the French Amanty Airdrome in Lorraine. The Blériot Penguin used for training was a flightless aircraft that gave the sensation of flying while still on the ground.

Classes were held in radio, photography, and machine gunnery while ground training was conducted by French officers. Fortunately for him, he had acquired passable French from his Grandmother Therese. She had died when he was ten—only weeks after the passing of his Grandfather Alex. His cousin Giselle, the twins' mother, claimed she had died of a broken heart, but he didn't believe that.

A romantic notion is what it was. God knew he had it up to his ears with romantic females, their sighs of "Handsome Heath," and their never-ending comparisons to Heathcliff. He might have Heathcliff's dark gypsy features, but never would you catch him eating his heart out for a female. What had his mother been thinking when she had named him and his brothers?

Even his cousin Mariana teased him unmercifully about his name. One summer, when they had been wading in the Nueces shallows, trying to catch a crawdad—they couldn't have been more than eight or nine—she quipped, "Heathcliff, Heathcliff. He has dark hair and eyes, and he'll never catch a crawdad, though he tries!"

Fed up, he shoved her hard. She fell on her butt against the mud-slick bank and damn it if she hadn't come up laughing—and with a crawdad squirming in her hand.

The romance thing had gradually escalated since he joined up. While at training school, a number of squadron observers were sent to the front-line trenches. True, with his proficiency in machine gunnery, he was lucky enough to be sent on a bombing mission with a French squadron.

However, unlucky for him, he became the first American in the U.S. military to shoot down an enemy aircraft. Somehow, his mug wound up in a French Film newsreel. When off duty, he couldn't go into the farming village of Amanty, one mile away from the aerodrome, without being recognized and besieged by girls.

One, in particular, was relentless. Bernadette Brummel accosted him at every opportunity.

Come the five o'clock "green hour," when off duty doughboys consumed the highly intoxicating absinthe, he and his cousins would adjourn to an Amanty that reeked of pipes, anise, stale coffee, and cheap Pinard—the essence of turpentine. The café was almost as good as the canteens, with their chocolate and cookies dispensed by American girls volunteering to help maintain soldiers' morale.

That particular afternoon, a gorgeous autumn day, only he and Preston sat at their usual sidewalk table, as Pierce was out on a reconnaissance mission. Back home, the Paladín clan would be celebrating Thanksgiving.

An old mustached man wearing a jaunty red béret was breaking out his accordion. Nearby, in the horse-chestnut trees, sparrows squabbled. An elderly woman pushed a flower cart.

Bernadette sashayed past, paused beneath one almost denuded tree, and winked at him. Dark-haired, she was pretty in a blowsy looking way, but for the proof on her round face of a lost battle with either chicken pox or acne. She took the brown paper cigarette from between her lips and rubbed it out on the stone pavement with her shoe. *"Vous voulez baiser,* Yank?"

He glanced over at Preston, who was about as tipsy as himself. His cousin's newly shorn dark red hair clumped in spikes from his foldable overseas cap. Likewise, his face was clean shaven. Shaving was required to get a proper fit and seal on their gas masks. "This your stalker?"

Heath sighed and rolled his eyes. "Yup."

He always thought of Preston as the more hotheaded of the twins, perhaps because of his fiery hair. Charming but quick on the draw, as Heath's father would say. "I don't have to speak French to know what she asked." Preston doled out a Franc for another pint of beer. "Go for it, cuz. I'll guard the fort."

Maybe he acquiesced because of the absinthe that fogged reasoning. Or maybe he acquiesced because he had yet to have bed a woman and now seemed as good a time as any.

As he followed Bernadette around the corner into the alley, he broke out into a sweat. What if she laughed at his ineptitude? What if Preston learned of his ignorance about such matters? He and the twins were the same age, but the twins had experience with girls. Or at least they talked as if they did.

The good-looking twins had always been wild-spirited and charming, in some ways a personality mixture of their parents—Heath's Uncle Griffin and Aunt Giselle. However, he felt self-contained and intense. Perhaps a reflection of the young man his father had been and still was, but his mother was totally different. Angel Obregon Paladín was a direct, head-on, full blown dust devil, whirling full tilt at her objective—and her primary objective was always her beloved Drake Paladín and sons.

He didn't know who he was, but he was sure as blazes setting to find out.

His knew his moods could be as dark as his coloring, inherited from his father and grandfather, the larger-than-life, Alex Paladín. Perhaps it was because so much was expected of him, the first born of three sons, whereas the golden-haired Pierce and red-headed Preston could always play off one another—although Preston was the more devil-may-care of the two.

Heath shouldn't have worried. Bernadette took him in hand… literally. Tugging him through the backdoor of a cobbler's shop, she nudged him down atop a pile of smelly leather hides. Immediately, her small, plump hand palmed his crotch. "It is your first time, *non?*"

Had his anxiety, his awkwardness in dropping his drawers, given him away? "Hell, no!"

He latched onto her waist, feeling the fat rolls, and pulled her beneath him. His hands were all fumbles, and she giggled. *"Non, non. Laisse moi."* She took control. Efficiently and expertly, she proceeded to divest both of their clothing.

He was so worried about performance that sweat pooled underneath his arms. Then his breath whooshed between his lips as she drew over her head her batiste blouse to display a boned corset, her breasts nearly overflowing its top. He swallowed hard. This was his first up close and personal sight of those female attributes. No need to worry about his cock wilting. And then soon after, another first—feeling himself inside a woman. Holy shit it was glorious.

His first experience was over almost as quickly as it had begun, and he practically swaggered in his new manhood back to the table and a widely grinning Preston, who had idled the time by peeling the label off his beer bottle.

Heath ignored his cousin's smirk. He was in love—and he hoped he gave during that wondrous time in the cobbler's back room as good as he got.

Which was exactly the case the next morning when he awoke and discovered he had gotten a bad case of the crabs. Yet another reason, he resolutely decided, for him to scorn "romance." It only led to annoyances—like this, furious dousing his pubic mound with gasoline to kill the vermin.

That morning heralded yet more bad news. He and Preston stopped by the bureau to check the daily list tacked on the bulletin board of killed, wounded, and missing airmen—and learned that Pierce's French observation aircraft, a SPAD 11, had yet to return.

SAN ANTONIO

The Cavalry and Light Artillery Post Addition of Fort Sam Houston contained the barracks, mess hall, bakery, latrines, stables—and the stockade.

Mariana Cordova marched past the various buildings, the towering fence, and, lowering her striped parasol, stopped to sign in at the guardhouse of the stockade, a medieval ambiance of an institution with its native stone and brick walls constructed by long-forgotten inmates.

The parasol was a roost, as was her saucy hat, to make her appear older than her seventeen years. Well, almost seventeen. Her father argued she wasn't even dry behind the ears yet, but at seventeen, Nicolás Cordova had been boxing his way out of Galveston's crime-ridden alleys.

That Thanksgiving Day was sunny and bright. Once inside the stockade's bleak visitation room, she stared, somewhat dazed, at the half dozen tables provided for family and friends. She made her way to the table the clerk had designated as hers and sat… and waited.

She was the only white person in the sparsely furnished room, other than the two provost guards with their Colt M1917 sidearms. The other tables were occupied by colored families and friends visiting the inmates.

She felt uneasy, fearful even. She could feel her shoulders rising to meet her ears. A prison could make one feel uneasy. But the fear... it had to do with being the only one of her kind in the room. Not fear that these colored people meant her harm, but the fear of being different. That was how Dan must feel. How he must have felt on the streetcar that horrific day.

Within minutes, he was admitted into the room. Tall and ropy like his father Mandrake, Dan's carriage was, likewise, the military's ramrod straight. Hands cuffed for the visitation, he crossed to her table and slid into one of its chairs across from her. His inky black curls had grown out. He could have been the noble jungle savage Tarzan—except Tarzan had been an English lord and Dan was two generations of slavery removed from the jungle. And yet, weren't some of Charlemagne's royal descendants of African blood?

"Where are you staying?"

He asked as if there were no other concerns—as if in ten days, he would not be going into a courtroom where his fate would be settled before a trio of all white officers, where the verdict was virtually already in and the penalty was death.

Unless Dan had the only defense attorney in all the country who could save him—and that attorney lay recovering in the hospital, crippled for life.

The attorney's father, the Honorable Justice Brighton Clarendon, had telephoned merely to say, "Politics is dirty business," and then hung up. Doubtless whoever might have been on the party line would have been puzzled by the cryptic remark.

Uncle Drake and Aunt Angel weren't.

"Mom and I—and your mom—are staying at the old Gorman Ranch House. Your mom is coming to visit later today."

He nodded. Above high, slashing cheekbones, his brown eyes, so dark they were almost black, beseeched hers. "Give up on this, Mariana. Go back to Galveston."

Dan had always been like that, considering others first. His life hung in the balance of Lady Justice's scales, and yet he was concerned for her.

She remembered the summer at The Barony when, at eight, she had burned her hand badly on the branding iron. She and her cousins, along with neighboring kids, had been horsing around at the spring roundup, but it had been Daniel who had noticed her distress and grabbed her wrist, pulling her over to the trough to plunge her blistered hand into the cooling water.

And she remembered his parents' periodic visits—climbing pecan trees with him, spinning around, giggling, and falling down, dizzy. They took turns swigging from the garden hose on hot summer days, catching fireflies in a canning jar in the evening, and slept on the screened-in veranda on sweltering nights, listening to the crickets.

It had been shy Dan who had made sure both his mother and Mariana's Grandma Sarita received bouquets that first national celebration of Mother's Day, three years before. After all, it had been Grandma Sarita who had bought Dan's grandparents from a sugar plantation owner and set them free.

Mariana knew he had been smitten by a girl whose grandparents had worked the same plantation in Sugarland on which his own grandparents had slaved. But two years ago, the Ku Klux Klan had scared the girl's family into moving away, and he had never heard from her again.

She shook her head. "No. I won't. I won't give up on you."

But she, too, knew the outcome of the court martial appeared hopeless for the 118 colored soldiers. Already, three brutal lynchings of colored men had occurred in Texas, a rigidly segregated state. Three years before, a young colored man in Marshall was accused of kissing the daughter of a white farmer. A mob had sheared off the colored man's ears, slit his lips, and mutilated his genitals.

"You never gave up at chess or billiards or poker either." Dan gave a rueful half-smile.

His mother had kept house for her mother, and she and Dan had played together as toddlers and into teens. She had even dragged his scrawny prepubescent body ashore when a riptide had almost swept it out in the Gulf.

She had shared with him her darkest secret—that she was in love with her cousin Heath, and he had advised her how to attract Heath's attention—ignore him. Instead, she had simpered like a ten-year-old. That ploy had failed miserably.

All these years later, Dan was still her best friend. She held for him the deepest affection and admiration. They were merely two young people, trying to figure out life together.

In her mind, Dan had been the one who had obeyed the rules. She was the one who had been kept after school so often for defying authority. Yet he was the one who had landed in trouble now. Big trouble.

Heath and the twins were in big trouble, as well. If the Germans didn't kill them, her uncles, Drake and Griffin, would when their sons got back stateside. *If* they got back. She bit the inside of her mouth and was surprised by the coppery taste of blood. Heath had to come back. She couldn't imagine her life without him at its center.

She reached across and capped Dan's big knotted hands with her small gloved palm. One of the provost guard's head whipped toward their table.

Did the guard think she was going to wrest the handcuffs from Dan, or was the guard simply stunned by the sight of a white woman touching a black man's hand? She was all too aware that Texas miscegenation laws exacted as much as imprisonment for intermarriage.

Worse, in Texas, marriage with a first cousin was a criminal offense. As her own mother had been at one time, she was infatuated with a cousin, even if this time Heath was a cousin once removed.

"My Uncle Drake himself delivered directly to the military defense's office proof you were in the hoosegow during the mutiny and riot, evidence there was no way you could have participated. We'll find you a good civilian lawyer yet."

She hoped.

Because it seemed that all Uncle Drake's money or the contacts her Uncle Griffin had made when mayor of Galveston, could not circumvent both public opinion and politicians' power—at least, not this specific politician's power.

Word was that Roger Clarendon was now wheelchair-bound. Undoubtedly, Justice Brighton Clarendon was waging his own war against the Paladíns.

She squeezed Dan's hand. She sincerely believed in America's judicial system, that the Declaration of Independence's immortal statement—that all men were created equal—was not a passel of extraneous words. Her great grandfather, a founding member of the Republic of Texas, was half Spanish. Her great grandmother Irish. Her father half French. Was Dan's African ancestry to be deemed any differently by the Declaration? She could not bear to think that was the case.

"I promise you, Dan. Justice will prevail."

———————————

ALSACE LORRAINE, FRANCE

Bad weather, clouds at four thousand feet, and engine trouble had plagued the two-seater SPAD biplane, with Pierce Paladín in the back seat. But at the moment, it was the dogfight with the German Empire's Albatross fighter that endangered the French reconnaissance plane.

With the Albatross's stellar rate of climb and lethal pairing of synchronized machine guns, the fighter easily outmaneuvered the SPAD. Using sun and altitude, the Albatross launched a surprise attack from above.

Although British high command had ordered all reconnaissance aircraft to be supported by at least three fighters in tactical formation, the French were so harassed on their own soil that their pilots were flying on a wing and a prayer, as the saying went.

The SPAD French pilot, Guy Lennoir's, job was to get the reconnaissance plane behind enemy lines. A wide strip of desolate, bomb-scarred landscape marked the trench lines.

Pierce's job was intelligence-gathering—identifying German activity along roads and railroads, ammunition dumps, and airfields. through both visual and photographic means with a high-altitude camera.

Even at that altitude of 15,000 feet, the rat-a-tat-tat spit of the machine gun could be heard, and the SPAD vibrated with the impact of bullets. Tracers puffed smoke blossoms. Guy, older than Pierce by three years, flashed him a harelipped grin and turned to meet the threat.

Exhilaration zinged through Pierce, with fear whipping bat's wings not far behind, puddling sweat beneath his arms and at his crotch. Still, if he died at that moment, he doubted he would miss out on anything so grand as the thrill of flight and fight that he was feeling now.

Maybe a dozen times, the SPAD and the silver-bellied Albatross, with its black crosses, circled one another. Each tried to get behind and above the other, but the newer-designed Albatross, with its Mercedes engine, was superior.

And the German pilot was no beginner. He and Guy began a waltzing pattern. The helixes the two planes made were so narrow that Pierce got a vivid look at the *Boche,* wearing a soft leather helmet and goggles over a long blond mustache, its tips fluttering backward in the wind.

Unable to climb any higher, Guy stalled the plane, dropping it down in a slip-wing through the cold mist cover to about 2,500 feet, then leveling out in the sunlight. The Albatross followed suit.

From his cockpit, the German pilot waved insolently. In the same instant that he opened with a spat of bullets, Pierce aimed his Colt and fired once. He plugged the *Boche* in the forehead. A nearly impossible hit, considering the speed of both planes.

Pierce's exhilaration was short-lived. The SPAD shuddered violently from the Albatross's bullet damage and dove into a spiral. The struts and wires were whining as they sliced through the air. A stream of oily, black smoke unraveled past the wing to his left.

"Merde!" Guy shouted above the rush of wind and the roar of the motor. His French uniform, horizon blue, was flecked with red. He fought to recover control of the SPAD, but the ground and its woodlands were coming up too fast.

Pierce took a deep breath. It was Thanksgiving Day. The Paladín clan would be gathering at The Barony around the dinner table, and he would not be there—not now or ever again.

How could so much go through a mind in those last fleeting seconds? He had never bedded a woman, nor been in love. But he had felt the love of his family, known the joy of their holiday gatherings, experienced the conviviality of the tug-of-war rope-yankings with his twin and his cousins, the shoving of one another off the limestone cliff into the Nueces River below. Felt the soul-deep love of his mother when she touched his cheek or hugged him and his father's deep abiding love delivered with a mere wink or clap on his back.

As his plane plummeted, he wondered why he had ever enlisted, though he knew the answer. Because he and Preston were a team, both brats growing up. What Preston did, he did, and vice versa.

But now his twin would have to carry on alone.

SAN ANTONIO
DECEMBER 1917

The court martial, the largest in American military history, convened at Fort Sam Houston's Gift Chapel, which possessed the only space on post large enough to hold a trial for the first of sixty-four men on dock for charges of disobeying orders, mutiny, and murder. All maintained their innocence.

As the right to a public court martial hearing was not absolute, the military deemed the trial involved material not appropriate for the public, and the court martial was closed.

So, Mariana only learned at its finish that the evidence supporting Dan's innocence was never introduced.

As she stood there, along with the condemned and those with families waiting outside, she learned of the verdict and sentencing a mere two days before the actual executions.

Because the U.S. was at war, the swiftness of the executions was backed by the Articles of War. No time was allotted to seek clemency.

No immediate notice was given to the newspapers or the public of the sentences handed down—five soldiers acquitted, forty-one others received life in prison, and a most unlucky thirteen were to be hanged at Camp Travis at dawn, December first.

That dark morning, frost vaporized her breath as she, Dan's parents, and her own, along with her Uncle Drake and Aunt Angel, made their way toward Fort Travis's Salado Creek. From the cottonwoods lining it, an owl hoo-hooed. Hastily constructed gallows not far from the creek were enveloped by its mist, as if the mist wished to hide the skullduggery about to take place.

The execution site was securely guarded to prevent the intrusion of unauthorized persons. All family members had been warned that no demonstrations or unseemly conduct would be tolerated. Mariana wondered if crying until one's heart broke was deemed unseemly conduct.

The doomed men had been taken off the trucks, and the troops stood at attention as the hanging detail of Company C approached with its colored prisoners. Before she even saw them, she could hear their melancholy voices calmly singing the hymn, "Lord, I'm comin' home." Only when they came into sight did she note that all decorations and insignia had been removed from their uniforms.

As Dan drew near, a weeping Becky reached out a hand to touch his arm. "No." Mandrake cautioned and captured her hand, but tears also glistened in his eyes.

Dan appeared not to notice. His eyes were fixed on something far beyond.

With a mournful wail, Pearl buried her face in Nicolás's shoulder while Mariana's Uncle Drake and Aunt Angel watched with stony countenances as the unlucky thirteen shuffled by.

Mariana was shivering, and it was not from the cold, nor fear for Dan. It was past the time for her to fear for him. Paroxysms of rage roared through her body, rendering it uncontrollable, as if in a grand mal seizure.

That a politician and his attorney-son could damage so many lives out of bitterness... perhaps it was fear she was feeling. Fear that the common man had no recourse.

Thirteen ropes dangled from the crossbeam of the scaffold. Thirteen chairs sat in front of the ropes.

The knotted ropes were fastened about the young men's necks. A chaplain and medical officer stood ready. Even the eyes of the hardest of the soldier's present were wet.

At this point, seven seventeen—exactly one minute before dawn—family members were ushered away. But Mariana turned back and thrust pass the escort. Crossed bayonets rushed to halt her, but not before she saw all thirteen soldiers hanged simultaneously. Even as Dan's body swung convulsively, swift disassembly of the scaffolds was beginning.

Pain, hurt, and the rawness that was life backed up in Mariana's throat. As if in the throes of an epileptic fit, teeth sank through her bottom lip to stifle her outcry. Tasting the blood's copperiness, she swore that, though Dan did not get justice, she would get vengeance. To do so, she would use the weapons of the foes of her family as her own—the American legal system.

2

METZ, GERMANY
JANUARY 1918

Since Charlemagne's rule, the borders of the province of Alsace-Lorraine, which straddled France and the German Empire, had shifted often. Over the last few centuries, the province had become a geo-political prize fanatically contested between the two countries.

On that particular day, the part of that province in which Pierce Paladín awoke—the ancient city of Metz—was part of enemy territory. Just east of the Western Front by a few miles, Metz now served as the capital of the German Department of Lorraine.

Not a good place to wake… and not a good way to wake—missing part of one's leg, seven inches below the right knee.

Grappling with the wood-and-metal appendage, he gave a hoarse scream that nudged the back of his drug-warped brain, whispering that he must have been screaming a lot. The first—and last—thing he remembered feeling when his plane barreled into the ground was the excruciating snap of his ankle… and then nothing.

A roughened hand smothered his scream. *"Chut!"* hushed a male voice in French. Then, in German, *"Du lebst noch. Seien Sie dankbar."*

Horror skated through his veins. His neck muscles were bow-string taut. He blinked, trying to focus on the foggy image above him. His gaze slammed into intelligent eyes staring down through a gold rim Pince-nez. A thatch of salt-and-pepper hair framed an energetic face. An equally grizzled mustache drooped down both sides of tightened lips.

Pierce's recollections of childhood exchanges in German with his mother were vague. Even her Von Hesse-Lippe family had been only passable in the language.

The middle-aged man hovering beside him had said something about being alive and being grateful or maybe, should be grateful.

In English, Pierce demanded in a raspy voice, "What happened to the rest of my leg?"

Brows darker than the hair or mustache met again in another frown. The man said something over his shoulder to someone out of range.

Another visage soon replaced the man's. Auburn hair smelling of lavender and fluffed about a young woman's classical features was caught up in a bandeau of red ribbon. Thick, artist brushes of brows knitted, as if in concentration.

Her wide mouth, bereft of rouge, spoke haltingly in English as bad as his German. "Tell me... slow... what it is you say."

He jammed a finger in the direction of the rudimentary contraption fastened at his leg's stump and tried again, this time in his rusty German. "What happened?" Disbelief hammered against his brain. A bad dream. That was it. A nightmare. With the growing realization that it was not, fear shell-shocked him. Chilling sweat broke out over his face as he began to understand that even his adept imagination could not make up the pain—or lack thereof—in his lower appendage.

She nodded her understanding and through her English. "A farmer... he found you. A plane. In a tree. Carried you to my father."

"How long have I been here? What day is it? Where am I?"

She tilted her head, as if considering how to answer. She could only be, at the most, a year or so older than he. "Two months, maybe? It is January. Our home."

"What?" Two months! From the sieve of his memory, a haze of pain mixed with blurred imageries dribbled out. The trees zooming up. Guy's curse—or was it a prayer—simultaneous with the impact. An inferno erupting around him.

"You were sick. *Beau coup* sick. We worry… infection. The doctor… animal doctor?"

From an energy-sapped, drugged stupor, he supplied, "A veterinarian?"

She nodded rapidly. "*Oui.* Yes. He feel for the French. No one else to trust… to save you. Then you get the plague… influenza. A farrier—French feelings, too—he make the leg for you. He puts it on when you are… *beau coup* sleeping."

"Fuck!" A vet and a blacksmith for surgeons. Hell, could it get any worse?

"You must be… no noise… at all times." She alternated between English, German, and French, her index finger raised to her lips. "The Reichsstatthalter… the military governor… their office are—is—close, around corner… at Kaiser Headquarters on the Place d'Armes. Its rooms beneath ground the Tower of Hell."

Hell just got worse.

———————————

WORCHESTER, MASSACHUSETTS
MARCH 1918

Existence at last appeared to have a purpose—being accepted for the coming fall semester into the second oldest graduate school in America, the prestigious Clark University.

For fifteen-year-old Byron Paladín, the youngest of the Paladín progeny, the possibility of studying in the physics lab under the world-renowned Dr. Arthur Webster made bearable all the years of frail health that had gone before.

The Paladíns were a robust family, yet Byron alone appeared to have inherited some mutant gene of physical fragility. Tall, thin, and gangly, growing up at The Barony he had constantly suffered from all sorts of ailments—pleurisy, colds, bronchitis, and tuberculosis, much to his mother's anguish.

Byron might have inherited his father Drake's predisposition for inventing, but from his mother he had inherited her voracious love of reading. Forever he had importuned her to find him books on physical sciences. Whenever he accompanied her to the Gorman Ranch House in San Antonio, she would work on The Barony Enterprise's division of Gorman Transport files while he devoured books borrowed from San Antonio's public library.

Shy and socially inept with a rationalist's approach to life's ironies, he was as far from his namesake Lord Byron's irreverent and romantic image as possible. At the library, he sprawled his lanky body at an unoccupied desk and buried his face between the pages of a book, all the while praying no one would plop down at his desk.

One day, as all the other library chairs were occupied, a girl had been forced to share his desk. Pulling out the chair across from him, she had given him a nod and asked, "Do you mind?"

He couldn't stutter out a word, merely a curt nod—and all the while thinking how goddurn pretty she was, with her hair curling in disarray on her shoulders and freckles dusting her pert nose. His heart galloping, his guts clenching, he shoved back his chair from the desk and fled the library.

The same went for the school playground. When the guys hustled out of class after lunch to play baseball, rather than subject his ungainly height to ridicule, he would hide out in the library to wrangle with the Dewey Decimal System.

Yet when Byron climbed the tall oak tree on the hill overlooking The Barony's sprawling hacienda, he was an entirely different boy.

Sitting on a limb at night, his imagination would soar. The tree would transform into a Jules Vern space gun, propelling Byron not to the moon but to Mars. From boyhood, the problem of escape velocity had plagued him.

Today, at Clark University, his mother sat like Queen Victoria on the other of the two armchairs facing Dr. Webster. She was on one of her missions—this particular one was to get Byron accepted for the fall semester. Umbrella still damp from the rain and sleet earlier that morning, she held it in her small hand like a scepter.

"This past year, while working on his engineering degree," Angel Paladín informed the old man. "Byron patented the tri-cone rotary bit. Commonplace gadgetry, I grant you, Doctor Webster. But his research could be applied to military applications like field weapons and torpedoes. My son is a child prodigy, and I assure you his intelligence far excels that of most adults."

This was not stated in a bragging tone, simply a matter of fact. Nevertheless, Byron wanted to slump down in the armchair. His mother considered her third-born son as brilliant as Albert Einstein.

He had done his father's two-cone rotary rock drill bit invention one better. When Byron received the patent for his tri-cone, his father promised to guide him, upon being graduated from college, through the ropes of creating his own company, the Paladín Tool Company.

But a drill bit was no longer challenging enough. His childhood interest in aerodynamics was leading him to a field of science that might just help the United States in its war effort—rocket research.

Apparently, Dr. Webster was not as impressed as Byron's mother with her son's genius. The head of the physics department glanced down at a letter in his hand and then back at Byron. "I am sorry son, but, your qualifications, while excellent… uhh… fall somewhat short of what we're looking for."

Byron did not know which stunned him more—Dr. Webster's rejection of his college application or the glimpse at the velum's letterhead.

SUPREME COURT OF THE UNITED STATES
WASHINGTON, D.C.

METZ, GERMANY
APRIL 1918

So many questions… with the answers parceled out over days and weeks while Pierce struggled to regain his strength—while he struggled to regain his balance on his badly fitted and painful prosthesis and while he struggled to regain his sanity and lose his bitterness.

And his fear.

What kind of life would he return to, damaged as he was? If he even made it back home.

He eventually learned the girl's name was Aubrey Clermont. Her father, Jules Clermont, had taught metallurgy at the University. She was studying to be a ballerina. They were Jewish. Ashkenazim or something, although Pierce noticed no ritual observances. His cousin Hannah's husband, David Solomon, was Jewish, but that was about the extent of Pierce's exposure to Judaism.

The Clermont home, he learned during his long convalescence on a plump feather bed, was a narrow three-story building squeezed among others with red slate pepper-pot roofs—and it was also a filter for French intelligence. People came and went. Common people—laborers, delivery men, dog walkers—but the conversations were always hushed and hurried.

Clearly, they brought information regarding the enemy. But how was the information relayed back across the dangerous western front to Paris and Allied headquarters? The latest information had been delivered by the milk man, no less. The Red Baron, the German combat pilot ace, had been shot down. His last words were reported to have been, "Kaputt."

Metz, a cultural center, was the cradle of the Gregorian chant and the Knights Templar Commandry. The city had been built three-thousand years earlier as a garrison on a place where branches of the Moselle and Seille Rivers created several islands.

From the moment the German army moved quietly across the border into

Alsace Lorraine in 1914, the fighting on its Western Front never stopped, though there were ominously quiet periods. Despite four years of waging war and all the lives lost, the battlefront had shifted only a few miles in one direction or the other, as ground was taken and then lost and then retaken.

"At once," Aubrey explained in English that had gotten progressively better, *"Boche* soldiers, their leaders start rules to… to make French things smaller. Before, street names, they were in both German and French. Now, only German. They confiscate our homes."

She was explaining this as they hiked across a wheat field of a farm owned by her cousin. Or rather, she hiked. He limped with the aid of a cane. The loose earth was an impediment to any kind of sustained rhythm for his metal-and-wood leg. His stump was raw and so were his emotions.

The loose earth also harbored dozens of unexploded mortars, grenades, and shells, some containing still lethal poison gas leftover from a battle the year before.

Where he was awkward, she was graceful and lithe, but her ballerina's delicately curved body was too thin. "Your face, your smile, reminds me of an elf's."

Her light laughter was the sound of champagne cascading against cut crystal. "My name comes from Alberic, king of the elves in German mythology."

She was prone to wearing simple black skirts and jersey blouses with flats. Today, she had also donned a black-and-white harlequin-patterned headscarf that she had knotted in some stylish fashion.

He wore one of her father's denim shirts and corduroy britches that barely clung to his hipbones and were far too short. Heavy, lace-up work boots called gadillots pinched his long feet. Well, at least, his one foot. A black béret topped off his feeble wardrobe.

As this was his first outing, Jules had cautioned him to refrain from speaking with others.

"Only German can be spoken," she explained further. "We are used to mixing our words in both French and German. Now, even to use *bonjour* can cost a fine. Some of our neighbors, they listen closely. To show their patriotism, they will tell the police. So…" she splayed her hands, palms up, "only few of our Messines are *beau coup,* very much, powerful, while the big part of us… the *bourgeoisie* and the peasants, we keep our fists in our pockets and wait."

She glanced around, as if to make certain they were alone, then turned her gamine face up to his and bestowed upon him a shy smile. "Before we walk any farther, we show we are *amoureux.*"

He canted his head. "Sweethearts?"

Eyes cast down, she nodded. "Ya. Put your arm around my waist. Lean on me. We walk. We talk *un peu*… we kiss *un peu.*"

For the first time in a long time, he grinned. "Only a little?"

She nodded again, looking up at him. "Always, eyes are watching. I have something to show you. Not for other eyes."

He put his arm around her slender waist. She was right. Hampered from the use of his cane, he had to lean into her. She was taller than most women, but of course, still far shorter than he. She smelled good. Fresh. Of lavender fields and almond milk soap.

"What I wish you to see is my cousin's wine cellar."

"I can think of nothing better I'd like to see than wine right now."

Yes, he could think of something better. His right leg and foot as it once was. Texas. His family. His mom and dad, Griffin and Giselle. His twin, Preston. And, at that precise moment, Aubrey, beneath him, naked. For the first time since awakening in the Clermont home months ago—eons ago—he felt a stirring of desire.

When he was making that confusing transition from youth to manhood, a married woman, the thirty-nine-year-old wife of a Galveston city councilman, had seduced him—and, as he discovered later, his twin as well. Following that initiation, he and Preston had goaded one another into a dalliance with a pair of most eager sisters, but that had been the scope of his own amorous forays.

But not so for Preston, with his dalliances continuing to occur here and there. Preston and he were not at all alike. Fraternal twins, he would say he was more the dreamer, the visionary, while Preston was the doer with a magnetic appeal that capitalized on opportunity. But both were risk-takers. He supposed it was in the Paladín genes.

"The wine, the German soldiers drank it all."

His arm about her waist halted her steps. She glanced up at him quizzically.

"We kiss a little." His hand slid up her spine to cup her nape. He grazed his lips against hers just firmly enough to share her sharply indrawn and heated breath. He wanted to deepen the kiss, but her trembling lips told him she was nervous.

And he was hideously maimed. He stepped back. "We walk a little."

Head ducked in a skittish but charming manner as they made their way across the field, she was talking, a quick and chatty mixture of all three languages, which he was grasping with less difficulty these days.

"Our soft chalk and limestone ground, it is good for more than just storing wine." They had come upon a ramshackle farmhouse, obviously abandoned. Adjoining it was a cellar, its doors gaping on broken hinges. "Let me go first." She held up her hand to help him down the set of stone steps.

He hated that, hated having to be helped. This was what the rest of his life would be like. He had better damned well get used to being an invalid.

Save the shaft of sunlight, the room was dark. And musty. She moved away and flicked on a single overhead lightbulb. The room was a shamble. Wine racks had been broken. Magnum cases torn open. Diamond bins smashed.

"Watch your feet," she warned, gesturing at the shards from shattered bottles that littered the stone floor. At that, she looked up at him and grinned. "Watch your foot."

For that singular remark, he could have kissed her again. She hadn't avoided looking at his stump or referring to it, as if it were something repulsive and unsightly to her—which it was to him. Instead, she had treated him as if he were a regular person and his stump merely one of his components.

She crossed to the back wall, lined with double-deep racking and pulled. It swung open to reveal a narrow tunnel with dusty chalk walls that sloped away down into the darkness. "Behold—your route to adventure, Pierce."

A route, also, to escape. But escape to what? Back to a mundane life? Escape after flying had taught him that he liked living on the edge.

3

It was not until after Pierce made seven or eight missions, transporting maps, surveys, messages—even at times invisible ink and a full set of tiny picklocks in the hollow of his wooden leg—that a thought began to niggle in the remote regions of his subconscious.

That insidious germ of misgiving wormed its way to the front of his brain with sickening, yet not quite identifiable feelings that he kept pushing back.

From the farm's wine cellar, nine miles of tunnel labyrinthed thirty feet beneath the trench lines of the cratered Western front—No Man's Land—to emerge by way of a rickety ladder up through a hole not much bigger than an animal's burrow.

Concealed by brush and tangled barbed wire, that end of the main tunnel opened within a short distance of the village of Vandières and but fifty miles from General Pershing's A.E.F. headquarters. A scrap of fabric on the barbed wire signaled messages, pickups, and drop-offs.

Electric lights powered by a diesel generator, insulated by concrete against sound, lit the tunnel's limestone ceilings through which roots had grown down. On the chalk walls, troops of the 26th "Yankee" Division had inscribed their names and regiments, caricatures, and sketches, one being the insignia of the Free Masons.

Nearly a dozen stenciled guidepost designated various underground passages shooting off the main tunnel. These were strewn with bottles, shoes, shell cases, and steel helmets.

He learned that many underground caves carved into the chalk under villages in the province, normally used as the famed champagne cellars of the region, provided shelter for the locals as well as the French, British, and American armies—and the Germans.

Aubrey accompanied him on his first trip. By now, he was walking without a cane. The journey was more harrowing than he had expected. She had explained that muffled voices through the chalk walls or scraping of shovels meant that an enemy mining unit might be tunneling only yards away.

In the underground war, British and German tunneling units were constantly detonating mines so that the landscape above was often cratered or riddled like Swiss cheese. Trench warfare had made traditional cavalry operations outdated and inefficient. Where a troop might have only a single grenadier, now every soldier was familiar with grenades.

Every so often, she would raise a finger to her lips and halt in her footsteps. "If you hear what sounds like bags or cans being quietly stacked," she whispered, "the German, they are laying high explosives."

He would come to a standstill. Despite the tunnel's cool temperature, he was sweating like a field hand in the nerve-racking silence that ensued. At any second, charges might detonate and blow him and Aubrey into bits or bury them alive.

During his first venture below, they had been in the tunnel less than an hour when the lights went out. A hand-railing fastened to the walls assisted in the dark, except where passages intersected with the tunnel. At once, she struck a match and lit a candle she carried.

"Ah, light finally."

She gave him one of her pixyish smiles. "I think your Boy Scouts say, 'Be Prepared.'"

He didn't know what prompted him, but he retorted, "Shakespeare says, 'Let not light see my black and deep desires.'"

With that, he blew out her candle. The scents of lavender and almond soap signaled that Aubrey still stood in front of him. The faint murmurs of the land above accented the constrained silence between them. He groped and found her waist, pulling her into his embrace. Clumsily, in that utter darkness, his lips skimmed her cheekbone and, searching, moved down toward her lips.

Her hands came up to frame his face and her lips, soft as suede, meshed with his. A thrill, both like and unlike the exhilaration he felt when flying, shot through him. His sharp inhalation of surprise at this feeling came simultaneously with the hard throbbing at his crotch. Could she feel the lengthy knot mounding against her stomach?

Her lips parted and instinctively his tongue responded, slipping between them to taste her. He wanted, *needed,* to taste more of her, but unsure of himself, unsure of her, he hesitated.

Her breath rushed out in a half pant, half gasp. *"Oui."* Her hands deserted his face and dropped to his forearms, lightly pressing. He needed no coaxing and levered her down with him onto the carved-out tunnel's damp dark floor.

Blindly, he fumbled for blouse buttons and, driven by a primal urgency, ripped the last few. Her soft laughter fanned his face. Even as he thrust up skirt and wedged himself between thighs, her hands were slipping between their bodies to loose his fly's buttons.

Their intimacy was awkward, both because of the absolute darkness and because his maimed body lacked its normal fluidity. Yet, this coming together with her was sweeter than anything he had yet experienced. He wondered if it was always like that—if when faced with danger and death, things were sweeter.

Was he in love with danger or Aubrey—or both?

He didn't know, but he did know that all other normal interests of life after this would seem flat and stale.

Later, brushing back his old-gold locks of hair that had grown out, she rained kisses on his face. "When this war is over," she whispered, "so shall the thrill you take from it be over, yes?"

She understood him all too well. But he wasn't sure he understood her. What did she want from him? What did she want from life?

She spoke little of her past. Her mother, Baroness Maria van Arnhem, was a Dutch aristocrat who had fallen for professor, Jules Clermont. Their marriage began to falter after Aubrey's father discovered his wife in bed with a British diplomat. Aubrey's mother eventually left the family abruptly to settle in London following the divorce.

Other than that—and the obvious fact that Aubrey was both brave and beautiful—Pierce knew only that she had attended the Metz Conservatory where, in addition to the standard school curriculum, she had trained in ballet and that she sometimes secretly danced for groups of people to collect money for the underground spy network.

She also sometimes served as a courier.

And this knowledge brought him full circle—back to that insidious thought jangling back there in that nether region of his mind only to sneak forward at unexpected times.

His ankle had snapped, had needed attention. But if Aubrey and her father were so dedicated to the cause, might they have amputated his foot needlessly—as a means to keep him there to help them in their spying?

He had nothing to substantiate his suspicion, except the fact that the wooden part of his prosthesis he had been fitted with while unconscious had also been conveniently hollowed out.

———————

KARLSRUHE, GERMANY
OCTOBER 1918

The small, motorized hornet comb made of thin strips of wood, linen cloth, and wire was all that kept Corporal Preston Paladín aloft in the clouds. The average amount of time for fatalities was one for every sixty-five hours of flight time—and that was for non-combat flying.

But the French Lafayette *Escadrille* and, later, the Lafayette Flying Corps, were both combat units, and their flyers were given scarcely a couple of weeks' longevities.

When Preston learned of Pierce's death, his own longevity mattered not. Realizing he would never see his brother again, he had collapsed to his knees, doubled over with gut pain, and sobbed amid his retching. Bitterly, he swore then to avenge his twin's death.

He volunteered for the duel-to-the-death in the air by joining the French Foreign Legion. Its SPAD combat monoplane was a remarkable means of achieving revenge. The machine gun trigger dealt out his revenge in staccato bursts of death. His hot-headed, devil-may-care attitude seemed to shout, "Bring it on!"

He scored his first victory on March thirty-first, shooting a tri-wing Fokker out of the sky. He soon got two more, this time Gothas, over Verdun's Fort Baux on April eighth.

With a pause in the rainy summer season, July the eighth had been the first good flying day in a long time. He made the best of it, adding up another victory by bringing down an observation balloon.

It was a propitious start for the new, determined pilot.

A few days later, he added more victims to his count. He was going from success to success, winging three or four sorties a day. The death count mounted, but with each aerial victory, somewhere in the far accessible recesses of his mind, a niggling twinge of regret lurked. Was the pilot he shot down someone's brother or boyfriend? Did he have a wife or children? But, following times like that, the thought would at once slam against the forefront of

Preston's brain that the pilot he just shot out of the air might be the one who delivered the same cruel fate to Pierce.

He became the natural and undisputed leader of the group. Each pilot had his own insignia painted on the top wings of his plane. Some were merely initials, others were a palm tree, a girl's image, or a heart.

His was the Grim Reaper.

Of course, word of his prowess reached the French newspapers, especially *Le Temps* and *La Parisienne*.

The latter featured a column, *Les Marraines de Guerre*, the Wartime Godmothers. Its objective was to sustain soldiers' morale—to comfort those men cut off from any news of their families and deprived of any emotional support or parcels. Anything that might give meaning to the fighting.

The weekly review published two full pages of small ads from lonely godsons seeking adoption and godmothers who felt it their patriotic duty to open both their hearts and their beds. Following the ad placements, amorous letters were often exchanged and meetings arranged.

Pilots were looked upon as nobility. They were chivalrous and gallant. Without even soliciting, Preston was bombarded by perfume-laced letters from adoring females. He was indifferent to the adulation.

Over time, though, one persistent correspondent piqued his interest. Fabienne Allaman would write in her precise, almost school-girlish strokes thought-provoking passages. *"You have courage and confidence, Corporal Paladin, but I wonder if you have a heart?"* ... *"Your exploits are daring, Corporal Paladin. Do you do it out of patriotic duty or solely for your own gratification?"* ... *"I should think you are so self-sufficient, you would find that people intrude upon your space."*

Somehow, her insight had generated moments of self-assessment during the long periods when inclement weather made combat duty impossible. Although he never responded to the perceptive letters, they were the only ones he bothered to continue to read. That is, until she revealed she was only twelve. What the hell!

Maybe it was sharing the womb with Pierce, older by three minutes, but Preston didn't want to share anything with anyone anymore, most of all himself. Was it selfishness? Or worse, fear of being crowded into oblivion?

As it was, on July the fifteenth, he ended up sharing a German prison-of-war camp at Karlsruhe, in Baden with about two dozen other Americans, along with Russians, Brits, Australians, Canadians, and Frenchmen.

After his SPAD's engine had been jammed by a Fokker's unexploded bullet, he had managed to wing-slip onto a field near Ville-en-Tardenois, where he found himself in recently acquired German territory.

Suffering only a broken nose, twice its normal size, he was promptly surrounded by *Boche* soldiers and hustled to a prison camp that squatted in the heart of the Karlsruhe. He was pissed as hell that his string of aerial combat victories had been abruptly ended, but he wasn't particularly afraid. The prison camp didn't reach horror-story proportions, but its commander, a no-nonsense major, took no chances with prisoners escaping.

The camp was enclosed by two high fences, one of barbed wire and one of wood. Guards were posted every forty-five meters on both sides of the fences. In between, the area was brilliantly lit, and prisoners were forbidden to approach on pain of being shot.

Wearing the same bloodstained and dirt-smeared khaki uniform in which he had been captured—his warm, woolen helmet, fur-lined boots, and, of course, his military bracelet with its ID disc—Preston faced the porky major.

Dressed in the German field gray uniform, the major removed his monocle, cleaned it with a black silk handkerchief, screwed the monocle back in place, and gave a genial smile. "Germany is a very civilized nation. Our prisoners are given the most humane treatment."

"Oh? The grapevine telegraph disputes that."

The major shrugged meaty shoulders. "Regardless, risk escape and you will most assuredly be executed when captured."

He grinned amiably. "If captured."

"Granted, a few prisoners—three to be exact—have escaped beyond these walls, but every single one of them was re-captured and either hanged or peppered by bullets."

Despite the major's warning, the prisoners constantly formulated escape plans both in the barracks and on the recreation grounds. While boxing or performing Swedish drills to keep physically fit, or studying languages to keep boredom from setting in, they also covertly put plans into motion.

One, a harelipped French pilot named Guy, attached himself to Preston when he realized Preston was Pierce's twin.

"Mon ami, I am telling you that your twin, Pierce, he is alive. The *Boche* were all around us when we crashed. The trees, they saved us. Your brother was unconscious when a farmer took him down from one. Me, I hid in shrubbery. I had only a shoulder wound." Guy spread his palms in that gesture French did so eloquently. *"Hélas,* the *Boche* found me!"

Pierce was alive! Relief, followed by soaring exhilaration, nearly staggered Preston. He blinked fast, clearing suspiciously damp eyes. When he had thought his twin dead, he had begun to experience something akin to what soldiers who had lost limbs termed phantom pain—a part of him had been missing.

Renewed hope surged through him. He was now determined more than ever to escape. Nevertheless, he refused to heed Guy's importuning.

"We will always be prisoners unless we take the chance," pressured Guy, who seemed never to sleep. Preston could drop down anywhere and be sound asleep at once.

"I know the region well, once we get out. We'll want to head not to France, the closest, because the borders are too well guarded, but to Switzerland."

Quickly, quietly, he outlined his plan to the others in the recreation yard. It involved escape by hiding in a rubble bin that would hold as many as four prisoners. *"Eh bien?"* he inquired of Preston. "Are you in, *mon ami?"*

Occupied in repairing the sole of one boot, Preston, seated on an empty gasoline can, did not even look up. "Nope."

Guy and his two fellow would-be escapees never made it out of the compound. They were apprehended while still in the rubble bin. Shackled to each other and blindfolded, hands cuffed behind their backs, the three were lined up in front of the rest of the prisoners, summoned to the exercise yard.

Just before the five guards raised their rifles, Preston saw the tell-tale wet stain of fear spread from Guy's crotch and dampen one pantleg. One of the other condemned man's legs buckled,000000 and he fell to his knees, sobbing.

During the rat-a-tat firing, Preston closed his eyes. A great sadness overwhelmed him. Jesus Christ Almighty, please let him go down fighting, whether for the lives of others or for his own, but not trussed up like a turkey in a slaughterhouse.

After the summary executions, the monotony of prison life resumed. The bells of the town clock chimed every quarter hour, reminding the other prisoners that life was swiftly passing them by. Word filtered to them that it was rumored the great French pilot Roland Garros, the inventor of the fighter plane and the first man to fly a loop-the-loop, had been shot down.

Three weeks later, a Brit captain broached his plan—dig a tunnel out. All dinnerware was collected and accounted for after each meal. Shoes were also taken from the prisoners each night. No one would get far barefooted. Not with nearly 120 miles to the safest border.

But tunnel they did with improvised tools. Once again, Preston was asked to join the escape group. "How about it, old man?"

"Nope." Not only was he keeping his boots in shape, he was keeping a tin of leftover bacon grease for his feet. Two hundred miles was a long way to walk.

Unfortunately, the Brit lacked engineering skills, and he and two others burrowed too near the surface. It caved beneath the weight of a Badger, a German flamethrower tank, which had rolled into the camp. That evening, at sundown, the three faced the firing squad.

Other such debacles continued to take place. Each small group plotting a means of escape was eager for Preston to join them. He merely bided his time.

Instinct, he figured, was better than deliberation.

Then, when an opportunity appealing to his instincts presented itself, he hopped on it like a coyote on a rabbit.

In this case, he hopped on an NSU military motorcycle replete with sidecar and, best of all, a mounted gun that had been left unmanned while the careless soldier, tossing off his helmet into the sidecar, checked in at the guardhouse.

As Preston kick-started the motorcycle, released its clutch, and throttled up, shots from the guard's Krag-Jorgensen rifles began to zing through the air. He laughed exultingly.

What a glorious way to go!

4

METZ, GERMANY
NOVEMBER 1918

Pierce learned a lot about intelligence work. Wiretapping, encryption, deciphering, and other more devious tricks of the trade, like cyanide poisoning, distilled from the seemingly harmless almond.

He was passed off as Aubrey's cousin from Flanders, which accounted for his appalling accent in either French or German. Expecting at any time to give himself away by some foolish slipup, he felt the iciness of panic every time he spotted German soldiers.

His body became a tattoo artist's dream. Invisible ink quite often written on his back or stomach carried elaborate messages or detailed maps. Over time, the inks used for the invisible tattoos corroded even steel pens, which did not bode well for either his mental or physical health.

He also learned that it wasn't living on the edge that loosed the daredevil in him, as he had supposed, but the thrill of flying. He missed it. He missed his family. He missed his twin.

At times, he thought about leaving. He knew enough now to escape through enemy lines. But he felt he could be of more use here as a courier rather than in France in combat, given his debility.

Or, maybe he was rationalizing. Because there was always the image of Aubrey's luminous, arresting features that haunted his dreams by night and dogged his footsteps by day. And so, he put off leaving by one more day. And then one more.

How much longer could the war go on? True, the day before, on the tenth, came the depressing news that H.M.S. *Britannia* had been sunk by a German submarine in the Atlantic. But then word also had it that on the same day, the Kaiser had decided to abdicate.

Could it be true what Aubrey had overheard—that only the day before, German armistice delegates had reached Allied General Headquarters in France?

Pierce might have lost a foot, but he could have it worse. He could be fighting in the trenches. Even the most obedient of soldiers had suffered enough shells rained down on them, without any means of fighting back, so that they lost control. The ear-hemorrhaging sound of anti-aircraft shelling was enough to drive one crazy. After months in the mud and snow and ice, many soldiers, both French and German, deserted.

He could recognize them on the few occasions he passed them, wearing that thousand-mile-off, vacant look. Shell-shocked, their eyes expressed the madness of the war. Their bodies trembled uncontrollably from concussions and disorientation. Four years of fighting… and for what? A stalemate existed. The battle lines had shifted little, and the fighting was still as fierce as ever.

Using the last of the citrus juice, he scoured the vestiges of invisible ink from his skin, towel dried, and, wrapping the wash-worn linen about his lower torso, limped down the short hall to his third-floor room, more a garret.

The cramped, cold, and musty living space was lit by a stub of a candle corked in an empty wine bottle. Wallpaper did not cover the cracks in the plaster caused by bombing. It was midday, but the cloud-whipped skies made it seem darker. The phonograph's needle scratched out the worn recording of "Poor Butterfly," popular everywhere now.

His narrow bed was occupied by the lissome, long-limbed Aubrey. Only his threadbare blanket covered her nudity.

He dropped his towel. Even as his body responded to the desire stamped on her gamine features, he felt nevertheless an old-world reservation in coupling with her in her father's home. Still, it was she who had initiated that first act of passion.

Aubrey held up her slender arms to enfold him, and the bed creaked beneath his heavy weight. She sighed and buried her face in the hollow of his shoulder and neck. "Hmmm, you smell lemony, *mon amour.*"

He knew and understood her rather well by now. The tempo of her shallow breathing, the fact she had not offered her lips up to his, her long fingers slinking restlessly through the whorl of hair matting his chest… the uneasy silence.

A nagging, soul-sick voice at the back of his brain sometimes asked if she gave herself to him out of pity.

He raised himself on one forearm to look down at her. "What is it?"

She bit her lip, gazed up at him through dense, damp lashes. "Captain von Kroger, an Army Attaché in Madrid, has been reassigned here. I met him this morning at the Covered Market. He wants me to be his mistress."

"He said this to you?"

"*Tiens!* No. But I am a woman, Pierce. I know this is coming."

"Does your father know of this… the captain's interest?"

"Not yet. But it will be an excellent opportunity for me to spy, *n'est ce pas?*"

He searched her eyes, then looked away, scarcely noticing the wall's peeling plaster. What was he feeling? Not jealousy. He did not even know this von Kroger. How could he be jealous of him?

Was it possessiveness he was feeling? Aubrey had never been his to possess.

Surely not love. He was too young and inexperienced in that arena of warfare. He missed home. He missed American girls. And he missed flying. Espying German, French, and American planes dart and zip and fly in formation overhead… now surely that was what jealousy felt like.

And yet… he felt at times as if he and Aubrey were one, their jagged parts welded by the war into one unbroken whole. He could not bear to think of when they must part, when the goddamned war was over, when he must leave her. Maybe that was love.

War warped the way people acted, distorted the validity of thoughts, intensified feelings, and he was not sure he could trust these powerful feelings he had for her. The sheer lust for little intimacies about her, like her fresh, lavender scent and long, tapering fingers. The pleasure of talking with her about simplicities, such as the old woman in the apartment below them who always wore a ragged feather boa with her housedress. The desire to protect her against all hurt. But would all these things remain when the war was over and their lives returned to normal?

Beneath him, Aubrey's thin shoulders shrugged. *"C'est la guerre."* That was the reply to everything. "Such is war."

Learning that the French exotic dancer Mata Hari had recently been executed for being a double agent, the realization of the thin line that the Clermonts walked was brought home. No, intelligence work for either side, or both sides, as was Mata Hari's case, was not for the faint of heart.

But he could not—would not—let that happen to Aubrey. To sell her body like that, all for something called patriotism?

At that moment, a cacophony of sounds bombarded his ears almost simultaneously. "Poor Butterfly" had reached its end and, as the needle began its repetitious scratching, church bells began clanging wildly, while a shrill and asthmatic blast of a horn's bulb in the narrow street below demanded attention.

He crossed to the dormer window and peered through its panes dusted with ice crystals. Outside, a blizzard of white flakes swirled as if in a snow globe. Looking down, he was reminded of a line from the poem, *A Visit From St. Nicholas*—"When what to my wondering eyes did appear, but a miniature sleigh…."

Sleigh, the battered German motorcycle sidecar below was not… and neither was Preston Paladín, a German helmet tucked in the crook of his arm, St. Nicholas.

People were pouring from their homes to dance deliriously in the street. "The war must indeed be over!" Aubrey excitedly joined him from behind.

Joy that bordered on euphoria zephyred through Pierce, until the soft fingertips on his shoulder brought him back to reality and the choice he must make.

HANDS LIGHTLY CLASPED AT HIS back, in the familiar stance of the "at ease" military position, Preston stood beneath the high-arched nave of Metz's St. Etienne Cathedral. The cloying scent of frankincense and myrrh wafted from the thurible the altar boy swung.

Built in the 1200s, the enormous Gothic church claimed to have the world's largest expanse of stained-glass windows. They refracted the sunlight's rainbow prisms over the priest, Pierce, and Aubrey Clermont. As the couple made their wedding vows, Jules Clermont, standing next to Preston, served as the second witness.

The ceremony was hurried, as a line of couples eagerly awaited their turn to be married on that first day after the declaration of the war's end, but also because it was imperative Preston and Pierce rejoin their command outside Paris as soon as possible.

The solemn vows pronounced, Pierce's long hands framed his bride's face and brushed a hasty, feather-soft kiss across her lips. Aubrey and he turned to join her father and Preston. Stilted congratulations and best wishes were offered. After all, they all knew so very little about one another. Strangers they were, all four of them, Preston suspected, despite his twin's lengthy dwelling with the Clermonts.

Pierce, looking way too thin, flashed him a skitterish grin. "For a Best Man, you're the best of the best, brother."

"That's the sole reason I took my leave of Karlsruhe's prisoner-of-war camp—to be here today." His relief and joy at finding Pierce again were most likely as close as he would get to his soul's contentment. Certainly, he could not imagine a woman providing that sort of comfort. No, marriage was not for his maverick spirit.

Glowing, Aubrey bestowed him with a shy smile. *"Mon frère,* so happy I am to be a part of your family."

Her brother?

He had yet to think of her like a sister, but as he gave her emaciated body a quick hug, he realized that the familial term felt right. The sister he never had. Naturally, he liked her. The way she carried herself exuded charisma and class—and something else. A sort of nurturing aspect, although he couldn't identify exactly what alluded to this refining side of her.

Yet Pierce appeared strained. Which, given the circumstances, could be easily expected. Though as much as he and Pierce had been elated at being reunited, Preston sadly sensed with the acute instinct of a twin that Pierce's own elation did not extend to this finalization of his marriage. No, that wide mouth was creased in a smile that looked stretched thin.

If Preston knew anything, he unequivocally knew his twin.

THE BARONY, TEXAS
NOVEMBER 1918

Almost seventeen, Darcy Paladín was an excellent marksman with a rifle, but his mama and dad did not have to worry about his running off, as had Heath, to join the Army. Heath was heralded as an unparalleled flying ace, a brilliant tactician in the air credited with over fifty combat victories.

But killing was not in Darcy's blood. Killing was something for which he had not the slightest inclination.

Sure, he packed lead with him at all times. It was second nature to him. At The Barony, you never knew when you might chance across a diamondback or a wild boar or even a mountain lion. But the weapon was used for protection. Harming a living thing for the sport of it left a sour taste in his mouth and a churning in his gut.

When Teddy Roosevelt, on his second visit to The Barony, had hunted feral hogs with Darcy's father Drake and Uncle Kerry, Darcy, then seven years old, had trailed along.

Presented with the opportunity, he had tremulously shot at a huge hog, charging with its curving, razor-sharp tusks. However, he had only wounded the wild boar. It had screeched and bellowed and dragged its hind quarter through the chaparral, leaving a trail of blood.

Darcy's father had snatched the Winchester from his sweaty, trembling grip and quickly put the animal out of its misery.

He knew wild boars were extremely dangerous to both humans and other animals, destroying everything in sight with their rooting. Still, from that moment on, Darcy had decided to never again kill for sport. It had taken this hunt to showcase that he was not cut from the same material as his brothers Heath and Byron.

So, when the former president of the United States once more showed up at The Barony for a hunting expedition, Darcy declined to accompany them. From behind his Pince-nez, TR had eyed him curiously. The sixty-year-old was a passionate hunter, loving the thrill of tracking and chasing game.

Darcy had heard that TR had lost his son in aerial combat in the Great War. Perhaps that explained the remark the hero of the battle for San Juan Hill idly dropped that evening over dinner. The Rough Rider was commending Darcy's parents over Heath's service in the Great War.

"The men who evade military service are slackers. I believe antiwar people are un-American. That a mother who is not willing to raise her son to be a soldier is not to be a citizen. I applaud you, Missus Paladín."

Angel Paladín merely dabbed her linen napkin on lightly rouged lips that held a reproving smile. "It would seem to me, Mister President, that the business of being a soldier is to kill and be killed. That is not how I raised my sons."

Despite this comment, Darcy slunk deeper down in his chair. Evidently, he, his parents' middle child, was the underachiever among the many Paladín progeny.

He could outride and out rope the best of the *Paladíneños,* outshoot the rest of the Paladín clan, and was no slouch when it came to grades. His mother had homeschooled him and his brothers in the schoolhouse provided for The Barony and *Paladíneños'* offspring. She had him and his brothers reading Thoreau and Hardy and Wharton when other children were still struggling with their primers.

Nevertheless, he was no wunderkind like Byron, nor did he exude the dazzling pizazz Heath did. If anything, Darcy supposed he might be termed an idealist.

Over the rim of his wineglass, Drake eyed TR and said laconically. "And a war determines not who is right by who is left, wouldn't you agree?"

At that, TR's bushy mustache flapped with his laughter.

Of course, it was no laughing matter for his father, who made the two-hour roundtrip drive to the nearest post office daily to see if Heath's name was on the military's list of deceased posted that day.

The dinner conversation digressed into polite semantics, but Darcy knew during that conversation that his life had to have deeper meaning to it.

The era's fundamental zeitgeist of imperialism, of commitment to a world war because of wide opportunities for large profits, seemed outrageous. Military tribunals had tried conscientious objectors to the war, like Quakers, and had sentenced seventeen to death.

But how did one change something so fundamental, so widespread, so deeply ingrained in the psyche, as warfare?

The answer came to Darcy three weeks later by way of another dinner conversation—the traditional Thanksgiving celebration at The Barony, when the Paladín clan gathered from all over the state.

Of course, Heath, Pierce, and Preston were missing, as well as the older family members who had passed on.

Darcy's grandfather, the illustrious patriarch Alex Paladín, along with so many others sorely missed—Grandmother Therese, Uncle Wade and Aunt Sarita, who had, at last, been snatched from life by some female malady, Darcy never was sure just what. Then there was Aunt Tara. Family members said after Uncle Buck died during the Galveston hurricane of 1900, her un-wavering dedication to The Barony had dwindled, as had her health.

Time and the vagaries of aging had caught up with Aunt Catarina and not so much later, Uncle Kerry, as well. Without her, his own health seemed to accelerate in its deterioration.

With all the deaths of family loved ones who had passed their prime, Darcy was learning how fragile and fleeting happiness could be.

The topic of conversation that Thanksgiving was over the armistice that had been declared several days earlier. While the armistice only signaled the ceasefire on the Western Front, hostilities continued in other regions. No one knew when Heath, apparently the lone survivor of the Princes of Paladín, as newspapers had dubbed the Paladín males, would return home from the war.

Nicolás, Darcy's much older cousin by marriage, proposed a toast. "May our missing family members return home safely from the war."

Drake swallowed a sip. "President Wilson may not have kept us out of the war, as he had promised, but I can only hope he will finally keep our country at peace."

Darcy thought that same worried concern that rode his father's craggy face could be detected in the faces of the *Paladíneño* family members who had family serving in the war.

Giselle shook her head. "As long as we women are disenfranchised, Kaiser Wilson should know that America is not a democracy."

Darcy's forty-six-year-old cousin, Giselle, although more like an aunt be-cause of the age difference, had been a suffragist for decades. She still pos-sessed the cameo features of a much younger woman—and it was clear that Griffin loved her body and soul.

She began talking enthusiastically about a lecture she would be attending two days later in nearby San Antonio, which was more German than Hispanic. The lecture was to be given by the blind-deaf Helen Keller.

"Why, last month, Miss Keller told her audience," Giselle's knife attacked her portion of roasted turkey, "that Theodore Roosevelt never saw a war he didn't love—and that the Woman's Peace Party never saw a war it didn't hate." With both her sons Pierce and Preston presumed killed in the war, Giselle was devoting her energies to the Pacifist cause.

As duties called Griffin back to his Galveston architectural firm, he requested Darcy accompany Giselle to the San Antonio lecture.

San Antonio might be a bit more modern, but it still possessed frontier attitudes towards law and order. Indian raids, cattle rustling, and gunslingers had been replaced by bank robbers who used getaway cars. Organized crime abounded, as did narcotics, traffic accidents, and labor unrest.

The lecture was held in the Menger Hotel's grand ballroom, packed with followers of Helen Keller. Policemen were posted at every entry and, because of the recently passed Sedition Act in response to the Red Scare, speaking against American policies was a criminal act. Emma Goldman was already serving a two-year prison sentence for opposing the draft.

Nonetheless, Helen Keller boldly spoke out. Granted, her speech impediment often made it difficult to understand her, but her powerful presence and her valuable points resonated within him.

Then, filmdom's young English buffoon and friend of Helen Keller's, the comic genius and pacifist Charles Chaplin, stepped to the podium to thunderous applause. He wore his trademark bowler hat.

"In films, as in human experience," he told the rapt audience, "the most fundamental element of life is emotion. To truly laugh, you must be able to take your pain and play with it. We must laugh in the face of our helplessness—or go insane. But we must also do more. We must resist killing one another in the name of patriotism."

Darcy thought about that short speech and how the masterful pantomimist was able to move his audiences to both tears and laughter without a single word. Here was the answer for which Darcy was searching—how to change the warfare mindset.

Giselle had been invited backstage, and Darcy, to his delight, was introduced not only to Charlie Chaplin and Helen Keller but also, a few minutes later, to a young auburn-haired beauty from Uvalde, Texas. Estelle Bevins had to be a good three or four years older than he and eons ahead of him in maturity.

Hands on hips, the choice bit of calico gave him a once over, from his Tony Lamas to his Stetson, and settled on his rig riding low against his thigh. Heavily lashed eyes dancing with mischief, she smiled. "A pistol-packing pacifist. Now if that isn't a ripsnorter."

Dazed, he gulped in air and could think of no comeback.

Giselle chuckled, and the young woman went on to explain she was there to cover the lecture for the University of Texas newspaper, *The Daily Texan*.

Of course, this captured his cousin's interest at once. "Oh, I was a news reporter years ago for *The Austin Stateman.*"

The two got caught up in talking the perks and perils of reporting, and he, standing awkwardly by, hat in sweaty hand, learned Estelle Bevins was also a singer-songwriter and gave weather and crop reports via radio from an engineering lab on the UT campus.

When they took their leave of one another, hugging like life-long friends, he cupped Giselle's elbow, reluctantly prepared to escort his cousin away. He was affected by Estelle Bevins in a way he couldn't pinpoint. Never having had any romantic inclinations, he was prepared to pass this off. But then he overheard Estelle, as she turned away, softly whistling "I Gotta Go Back to Texas"—well, no doubt about it, by now he was smitten.

"Go on ahead," he told Giselle, "I'll catch up with you in just a minute."

His cousin smiled archly, as if she already knew that he had been struck by Cupid's arrow. "I'll wait for you at the coat check."

In five strides, he bridged the distance between him and Estelle and blurted, "Miss Bevins, I would like to call upon you."

She turned to fully face him and that close, his nostrils flared at her captivating scent of peaches. Though shorter than he by a good foot, at least,
her air of confidence and maturity made her appear taller and commanding. He would bet she was a ball of fire. And he was afire, lovesick for the
first time in his life.

Her gaze was coolly amused, but she scoffed. "Eternity will end before I
give you the time of day, cowboy."

"Doesn't matter. I'm gunning for you." Of all the stupid, grammar school
comebacks. The hot color of mortification crept up his neck, and he cringed
inwardly. But he knew this was the woman he had to have. He was ensnared
by the same spell by which love netted otherwise logical thinking, rugged
men. He winked, slouched his Stetson low on his head, and sauntered off,
whistling "You Belong to Me."

5

Was it worth it? Lieutenant Heath Paladín asked himself as he stared down—first, at the rack of medals pinned to his uniform and then, even lower, at the thousands who had gathered to wave unfurled American flags at the Hoboken dockside.

As General Pershing promised his troops, they would be in "Heaven, Hell, or Hoboken." The large number of troops awaiting transport after the war meant that most of the surviving soldiers would not get home until even later in 1919.

New Jersey's patriotic crowd was wildly welcoming the USN *Lake Daroga*. It transported not only returning soldiers from the Great War but also carried the first bodies of fallen American soldiers.

That was the price of the Great War—approximately fourteen million dead from battle, roughly seven million soldiers permanently disabled, and yet even more dead from illnesses, primarily the Spanish Influenza.

And for what?

The Doughboys had protected one another from danger, shared their beds and food. They had witnessed thousands of deaths. They had laughed and horse played in the quiet times and held their dying buddies in the awful times.

But now they had to start a new life—and the soldiers returning home were often unrecognizable from those who had left several years earlier. What would they do with their lives now?

For Heath, the answer to that question was a land mine he felt compelled to skirt for the time being.

It was enough of an ordeal that he and the other returning soldiers on the USN *Lake Daroga* were given a ticker-tape parade along First Street, replete with marching bands and speeches.

He shied from the grateful nation and its citizens, who felt they could not do enough for the returning soldiers. He was lauded as a flying ace, but it had been only his strategist skills that had kept him aloft, not a talent for acrobatic flying.

Preston, on the other hand, would have racked up a greater score of aircraft down, if for no other reason than his reckless do-or-die ways—except his early capture had ended his slew of victories.

Heath wished he had Preston's nerves of steel. Each morning, Heath had arisen, drinking acidic coffee that did nothing for his already burning stomach and frazzled nerves. The French saccharine tablets provided due to the sugar shortage had helped neither his stomach nor his nerves. Each morning, he had wondered if the missions scheduled for that day would be his last.

Well, he was alive... if this was what surviving looked like. And while a belt of brandy might help the nerves, it rusted his stomach just as badly.

The patriotic reveling continued at every train stop all that week. The only thing that kept Heath stable was knowing that he would be home at The Barony in time for Thanksgiving this year—and that Pierce and Preston were already there, having arrived via the USS *George Washington* in September.

At last, Heath arrived by way of a Missouri, Kansas, and Texas train in San Antonio's grand railway station, just completed at the corner of Flores and

Durango. His father, Drake, had been wise in retaining The Barony's railroad investments. Now that the war was over, the U.S. rail transportation system was booming.

He swung down from his coach onto the platform to the sound of hissing steam and wondered if anyone would show to meet him. Then, through the clearing haze, he saw the twins, striding toward him. His chest tightened. His throat choked.

He had made it home to Texas.

He gave red-headed Preston a huge, heartfelt bear hug. "Heard you broke out of your pen." He then turned his eyes to golden-haired Pierce, who was clapping him on the shoulder. "And that your body was finely penned by French intelligence."

"All but the right foot," Pierce quipped.

Heath could only nod. He didn't know what to say. Though Pierce was grinning, Heath sensed the deep anguish that lurked beneath the surface of his cousin's seeming bonhomie.

During the four-hour trip to The Barony, the three exchanged the lighter moments of their war stories. Preston, driving a yellow Jeffery touring car he had commandeered from the twins' father, Griffin, shared tales about the Godmother letters he received while in France—in particular, the sensitive yet sharp-witted ones, from a twelve-year-old French girl, no less.

Pierce told him about his new French wife, Aubrey, and how he met her. "She's brave and smart and beautiful."

"I do believe you've been bitten by the love bug, cuz."

Heath's attention was diverted more and more by the dearly familiar landscape unscrolling the nearer they drew to The Barony. He could feel his chest tightening once more with the overwhelming sense of homecoming. Yet, stretching his long frame in the backseat of the touring car, he could tell his muscles and tendons were easing a bit after so long a time of being maintained on high alert.

At the sight of the wrought-iron entrance gates with the name *THE BAR-*

ONY arched high over them, his tear-glazed eyes caught him by surprise. He swallowed the backwash of nostalgia and put on a game grin.

On The Barony's long, open veranda, Heath's mother stood on tiptoe, wrapped her arms around his neck, and wept hard, shuddering sobs that wracked her small frame. Over Angel's head, Heath looked at his father. The tall man's mouth tightened and a muscle in his jaw clenched. Nevertheless, his dark eyes glistened as he gave Heath a bearhug.

Some said he and his father were so much alike in their good looks—dark-eyed Devils each—but it was gangly Byron who shared both their father's inquisitive and inventive mind and raffish appearance, discounting the glasses.

Awkwardly, Heath shook Byron's hand, but his youngest brother looped an arm around Heath's shoulders and yanked him close. "Glad you're back!"

From the doorway, his cousin Hannah, stylish and stunning, flashed him a smile and blew him a kiss. What was she now—nineteen or twenty? Next to her, his cousin Claire and her husband David eagerly waited their turn to greet him.

And then Darcy was there, pounding him on the back. Darcy and he might not have seen eye-to-eye on the war, but they were family, and to the Paladíns, family was everything. Darcy gulped and blinked. "You can't keep a Paladín penned down for long."

Laughter broke out, and next other family members were pressing forward to welcome Heath back home.

His cousins, Griffin and Giselle—both brimming with joy now to have their twins back—hugged him fiercely.

Then there was his cousin Pearl and her husband Nicolás and... and Mariana, looking so studious and grown-up in her new eyeglasses. Behind those lenses, her eyes looked even more thickly fringed, probably due to the new French mascara females were using.

Those same eyes appeared to be watching him very closely, as if searching for something.

For what? Depression? Anxiety? He felt like a walking booby trap. True, she was easy to get along with, but she was hard to figure out. Which was probably why he enjoyed her piquing company.

Unsurprisingly, during Thanksgiving dinner the talk centered around the aftermath of the war. Giselle looked from one family member to the next, gathered around the table. "Why did we have to place so much emphasis on war? Was fighting more important than farming or teaching—" and at this she paused to look at her husband, "—or even legislating?"

Refusing to be drawn into the discussion, Heath focused on his food.

"Yes, Mama." Pierce's fork hovered over his plate, his eyes serious. "By fighting, we ensure that we can farm or teach—or legislate."

Watching the blinds close over his cousin's expression, Heath suspected Pierce was the most damaged by the war, and not just physically. True, injuries, shellshock, disease, stress, poor food and living conditions had taken their toll on everyone. Heath and his cousins had left as boys and returned as men… hardened, disillusioned, and lost.

"I might remind you, Mom," Preston started, taking up the argument, "that Dad fought in the Spanish-American War."

Griffin, who had grayed at the temples in the nearly three years Heath had been away, grinned. "Clearly, you twins should both take up legislating."

His relief at having his sons back was obvious, regardless of how affected by the war the twins had been—how changed everyone was. Giselle, Heath noted, teared up every time she saw Pierce limp. And both his parents exchanged concerned glances at how quickly Pierce and Preston shoved food into their mouths. With this, Heath could identify, because even he felt that irrational gut concern that this Thanksgiving dinner might be the last meal he received, a habit leftover from the war.

Giselle smiled a touch too brightly as she picked up a bowl of green beans. "Please, pass around another helping, you guys. We need to feed the hollows in those cheeks of yours."

Hannah's avid gaze swept from Heath to Pierce, then to Preston. "Did any of you three get to visit Paris while you were there?" She had just returned from a buying trip to New York for her parents' Dallas Emporium. Naturally, she would be interested in French fashion, which she would find had been reduced to threadbare from the little Heath had noticed.

"The closest I got," Preston cracked, "was a French croissant in the Rouge Croix food box at the German prison camp."

Pierce cleared his throat, and something in his intensity made the table pause and stare. "I'm bringing home a French bride, if that counts—from Metz, in the Alsace Lorraine region."

"What?" Giselle's napkin halted on the way to her lips. "All this time... and you haven't shared this with us?"

Pierce shrugged. "Preston and her father were our witnesses. Aubrey should be here within the next few weeks. I wanted to wait until she cleared immigration processing at Ellis Island before I said anything."

Preston stood and raised his wine glass. "I believe this announcement calls for an official toast. To the happily—"

The shrill ring of the telephone interrupted his speech. Heath caught his parents' wary glances at one another. Normally, the co-op telephone exchange was closed on Thanksgiving and Christmas.

Drake set down his stemmed glass. "Pardon me for just a moment."

"I can't imagine who would be calling," Angel glanced around the large table. "We're all here and accounted for."

Chitchat covered Drake's absence, along with the clatter of various dishes being passed along the table. Heath concentrated on the heavenly, mouth-watering taste of his mashed potatoes. Ordinary potatoes, who would have thought? When most of Metz had been starving, potatoes had been like rare gems. And these potatoes were creamed, with thick globs of butter and cream cheese and seasoned with dill.

He overheard Mariana modestly answering an inquiry by Claire's husband about her law studies. "Yes, if all goes well, Uncle David, I should be graduating early."

Heath thought if anyone in the family had reason to boast, it should be

Mariana. His childhood compadre had turned out accomplished, attractive, and charming. Since his return, he had felt her eyes on him, combing over every change in him.

Clearly unable to stymy her curiosity any longer, Giselle demanded to know more about her son's bride, but Pierce only shrugged. "She's a lot like you, Mom. She believes in giving her all for a cause."

That quieted the twins' mother for the moment.

Nicolás, his gaze raking in Heath, Preston, and Pierce, tried changing the subject. "Do you boys know what you want to do as far as work, now that the war is over?"

Boys? If anything, Heath felt like an old man—a very old man.

He figured that, for Pierce and Preston, anything but adventure would constitute a dreary job. For himself, he wanted exactly that—the isolation and peace he had known growing up on The Barony Ranch. Back to nature, back to stillness and quiet.

His mind had been splintered by the responsibility for the men in his squadron, a responsibility which he had carried on his shoulders around the clock during the war. The constant shelling and gunfire had shattered his once adventurous spirit. It wasn't the gunfire and bombs bursting that haunted him, it was where those bullets and bomb fragments proceed to bury themselves—in the bodies of comrades, young men, some a mere year or so out of boyhood, whose bodies never returned home.

These days, if anyone closed a door too loudly or a truck backfired, it was everything he could do to keep from diving for cover.

His father appeared in the entryway, his puzzled gaze roaming the table to settle on Heath.

"That was the Associated Press News. They roused the switchboard at San Patricio. Seems *Pathé News* out of Paris is distributing a newsreel in American motion picture theaters—covering your exploits in France, son. The news reporter claims you're a celebrity. That the newsreel subtitle is, 'Handsome Heath Fought for Peace.'"

He blinked, the wine in his glass sloshing. Then he scowled. "Impossible! That one-minute newsreel should have been buried in the French archives by now."

Darcy directed an apologetic look at Heath. "I was planning on telling you when we got a moment alone. Hollywood is jumping on the Peace for Prosperity bandwagon. When I told Charlie Chaplin the flying ace in the newsreel was my brother, he snapped it up for distribution."

GALVESTON, TEXAS
JANUARY 1920

After the great hurricane of 1900, Griffin had been kept busy as both mayor and architect rebuilding Galveston—mainly the Strand District and the East End.

There had also been his own home to build—and he had built this one to withstand not only future hurricanes but the apocalypse, if that were possible.

Typical of his style, he had combined simple geometric forms, but in bold massing, and used irregularly shaped stone, round Romanesque columns, and Tudor arches.

He had sourced out exotic materials, like the pair of Sienna marble columns flanking the entrance hall. The first-floor rooms had fifteen-feet high ceilings, coved and coffered. The mahogany staircase soared three stories and was banked by stained glass and lit by a large skylight, a perfect outlet for escape, should the need occur. The massive fireplace in the front parlor had been carved from imported Santo Domingo mahogany.

The lengthy family table, the same mahogany as the staircase, was bustling with conversation, people talking over one another, platters being passed around, glasses sluicing with wine refills and silverware clinking on plates. A celebration at Griffin's acclaimed chateauesque home on Broadway was in progress—the welcoming of Pierce's French bride, Aubrey.

Griffin's cousin Pearl and her husband Nicolás had made the short trip from Houston, where Nicolás had relocated his highly successful brokerage business after the hurricane—much like many wealthy individuals after the wave of destruction.

Griffin was committed to the task of rebuilding his city by winning the next election for mayor—which he had done for three consecutive terms years before—but right now, he had to rebuild his family. Underneath the hum of crisscrossing chitchat ran a thread of high tension that threatened to snap. Aubrey sat between the twins. She was doing her best to keep up with the rapid-fire quips between the two. Her classically sculpted face swung from golden-haired Pierce to fiery-haired Preston.

Over the rim of her wine glass, Pearl's gypsy-dark eyes twinkled at Aubrey. "I imagine our Texas wine is sadly lacking in comparison to your fabulous varieties back home. Although, the story goes that our Texas vines were used by the French to create root stock immune to an insect plague—and saved its wine industry."

Aubrey momentarily dimpled. "It would have been well had the insects shot—killed, I mean to say—our Pinard. Pierce calls the wine turpentine."

From beneath her lashes, Giselle regarded first the French girl, then their sons. Griffin knew his wife sensed the same disquiet, as if Aubrey seemed subdued. And Griffin also thought he detected a strain between his son and his French wife.

On the young woman's part, the uneasiness could be attributed to being in a strange country and having left her father behind. As for the twins, the world had changed enormously in their absence.

Women now had the right to vote, thanks in large part to demonstrations by strong, smart women like his wife. The stock market was booming. The pace of life was faster. Prohibition now banned alcoholic beverages, so, thanks to that, crime was on the rise.

But as far as Prohibition was concerned, by God, no one would tell Griffin what he couldn't do in his own home, election year or not.

Like so many soldiers returning from the war, his twins were at odds with what to do with themselves. Perhaps that accounted for their restlessness in the months since their return Stateside.

Griffin nodded his head ever so slightly at Nicolás.

A Mexican/French-American, he had literally fought his way up, or boxed as it happened to be, from Galveston's seamier side to its upper-crust affluence. "One of my agent stockbrokers is retiring," Nicolás mentioned casually, "and the position is open. Would either of you be interested in joining my brokerage?"

Silence from his nephews.

Then, thumb and forefinger toying with his wine glass stem, Preston shook his head. "Thank you, sir, but cooped up for months in a prison pretty much turned me off confined spaces like offices."

"What about you, Pierce?" Pearl, Nicolás's wife and Griffin's cousin, smiled encouragingly.

Pierce's squinted gaze flickered from her to Griffin and settled on Nicolás. "I don't think a throttle-jockey like myself would be desk material, sir."

It was all Griffin could do to keep from groaning. As an amputee, what in the hell did Pierce think he would be good for other than a desk job? His grandfather, Kerry, an amputee from the Civil War, had held the ultimate desk jobs—as both Texas governor and U.S. senator.

Griffin breathed deeply. His lips compressed into a forced smile. "Well, then, a draftsman or supervising architect would take you both out of the office often enough. I'll need someone to fill my place one day at the firm. What do you think?"

"I think," Pierce spoke dryly, "that both of us want to make our own place in the world, Dad."

"Well, for God's sake, then do something with your lives instead of just… just drifting!"

"It's only been a couple of months since they returned," Giselle intervened. "With time, they'll—"

The stem of Preston's wine glass snapped. All eyes darted toward the rapidly spreading stain of red wine on the white linen tablecloth.

"*Merde!*" Aubrey grabbed Preston's hand and bound her napkin around it. Blood, the color of the wine, stained the linen wrap she was knotting.

Preston's mouth crimped above her head, bent with attention over his hand. "Sorry about that, folks."

Preston was like that, Griffin knew—quick to temper, quick to subside. But Griffin caught the edgy look Pierce darted at first to his twin, then to Aubrey. Apparently, Preston wasn't the only one harboring an unexploded shell.

Pierce rose to his imposing height, drawing Aubrey to her feet beside him. "I think I have had enough of people wanting to arrange my life for me. We'll be on our way."

Preston stood as well. His napkin-wrapped hand draped the back of his chair. "I feel the same. Thanks for the dinner, Mom—and good-bye."

NEW YORK, NEW YORK
OCTOBER 1920

Hannah had visited New York once before to buy quality clothing for women not ordinarily available in Texas. Dallas Emporium's inventory had sold out immediately. Oil-wealthy Texans, flaunting their riches in classier fashion, besieged the store.

Eventually, she had persuaded her parents to base her out of New York. She loved its fast pace, cultural energy, and excitement. If anything new happened, it happened in New York first.

Her office was a tiny apartment with a Murphy bed in the fashionable Upper West End. While not as low-class as a tenement, her apartment was not on the scale of the upper-class either, like The Dakota with its tennis and croquet courts.

Nonetheless, one of The Dakota's tenants—the editor of *Vogue,* Gladys

Mae Winn—had found no problem in calling on Hannah at her apartment to interview her.

"Dallas Emporium wants to tap into a neglected segment of America." It was a comment Hannah had much rehearsed. She was only hoping her nervousness didn't show. "We want to introduce stylish apparel and lingerie for the younger female clientele."

"You've done just that." Gladys, who had taken the plunge and cut her hair, nodded in agreement as her bobbed hair swished beside her ears. "You've made Dallas Emporium a nationwide icon for *haute couture.*"

After that interview, Gladys, only a few years older, had taken Hannah under her wing. "You're lonely away from your family," she nudged an adorable Siamese kitten into her arms on one visit, "and you need a companion. Actually, you need more than that. You need a man. But the kitten will do for now."

Against Hannah's protests, Gladys introduced her to New York high society.

Hannah would rather have stayed home with Sam, as she had christened the Siamese, and analyzed her sales data and track inventory. So much depended on negotiating prices and her strong aptitude for math. Working with suppliers required confidence—something she was slowly gaining—and excellent communication skills.

But that particular evening, Gladys persuaded her she needed something more eventful—speakeasies. With the advent of Prohibition, they had spread all over America. They didn't need to be large to be in business. Little more was needed to establish a speakeasy than a bottle, a table, and two chairs.

However, the Bathhouse Club in New York had its own two specialties that made it unique. The first were musicians, who performed on a stage, along with scantily clad young women, who took turns dancing on a tabletops.

As this was Hannah Solomon's first visit to a speakeasy, she was both excited and apprehensive. It would never do for a graduate of Southern Methodist University to be hustled into a paddy wagon and booked at the police station.

She felt uneasy as she passed the bulldog-looking doorkeeper posted at the club's outer door. Leaning close, she whispered in Gladys's ear, "Has anyone ever been arrested at this club?"

"Never. The doorkeeper sends a warning to the bar that it's in danger, and the bar transforms into an ordinary establishment."

Hannah arched a doubtful brow. "Hmmm, I find that hard to believe."

"No need to be a bluenose, Hannah. As soon as a police raid begins, a system of levers is used to tip the bar shelves. The liquor bottles are swept through a chute and into the sewers."

The bar, according to Gladys, also included a secret wine cellar, which contained a door, concealed in a brick wall that opened into the basement of the building next to it.

The Bathhouse Club was more an escapade than an event. Nevertheless, Hannah was careful in her selection of clothing. She had a sophisticated image to uphold for Dallas Emporium.

That night, she wore a Chanel gown—an ecru-colored, sleeveless tunic of handmade Irish crochet lace. It flared out at her ankles, where its scalloped hem was decorated with a delicate ruffle of fine tulle.

Dropping off her stole at the coat check, Hannah felt somewhat fast and frivolous. Her skirt might be decorously long, but her arms were bared in the new flapper style.

Loud music, a ragtime-jazz combination, wrapped around Hannah and tugged her into the club's dim interior. A halo of a light lit up the piano player in a tux, his black fingers flashing like lightning across the white keyboard. Meanwhile, young people were laughing and talking in raised voices. For the first time, youth culture reigned over the older generations.

Gladys waved at a fabulously plumaged crowd of revelers in one corner and latched onto Hannah's elbow, leading her to their table. Introductions were made—two other women and four men. "She'll have a French 75," Gladys told the waiter, ordering for Hannah, "and I'll have a Zani Zasa, heavy on the gin."

Other than wine, Hannah had never tasted alcohol. "I think I had better stick to wine."

"Honey," a short, snappy-eyed male named Bumper rose to draw out her chair for her, "this joint isn't exactly a church."

"French 75?" joked a cherry-cheeked young woman. Her brightly rouged lips made a moue. "How can you go wrong with bubbles and gin?"

Everyone laughed except a man seated in the shadows of the corner table. Hannah could feel the force of his gaze, could feel her bare arms tingling. A woman sat next to him, but her energy paled in comparison to his.

Hannah felt the man studying her and felt uneasy. She was accustomed to being stared at. With her mother's rangy height, her father's dark good looks, and her hair cascading over one shoulder in long ringlets "a la Mary Pickford," she was striking.

But in school, her sharply-angled features and stork-like height had drawn painful gibes. Her innate shyness was passed off as cool and confident reserve.

"Just as there are not Atheists in a foxhole," the man's low accented voice came out as a rumble, "when religious wines are legal, there are no Atheists in Prohibition. Give her the wine—the Grand Vin De Bordeaux."

Her eyes were adjusting to the dimness now. The man—Michael Kraft, as she soon learned after a brief mention of his name—had brown eyes so light they seemed gold and contrasted starkly with his wealth of dark brown hair.

She nodded and mouthed, "Thank you."

The prestigious wine he had ordered for her was heavenly. She relaxed a little as the others wisecracked back and forth. Every so often, she would steal a glance at the couple in the shadows. Always, she encountered the man's gaze dueling with hers.

She refocused her attention on Bumper, who was flirting outrageously with her. With his speech slurred, he was practically ossified. He wanted her to come home with him, but she simply shrugged. "You'll be lucky if you can find your way home."

In one piece, she mentally added. When he was distracted, she discreetly dumped half the contents of his glass in the potted palm next to their table—

only to glance up guiltily and find Michael Kraft watching her again. The challenging curl of his lips seared a path between her breasts all the way past her navel. He was obviously sure of himself, lacking no confidence in his skills in the barroom or the bedroom.

Then, midway through the evening, it came—the doorkeeper's warning shout. Like magic, the bottles vanished from behind the bar, as did the dancers through a side door. In economic, efficient swoops among the tables, waiters grabbed and dumped glasses into containers and then disappeared with only seconds to spare.

The piano player launched into a discreet and classical rendition of Al Jolson's "Swanee." The club appeared a harmless place of entertainment.

At that point, half a dozen blue-uniformed policemen with their truncheons and sidearms came storming through the inner door. Patrons looked up innocently at the raid in progress. Profuse apologies should have been issued, and the police should have retreated from the premises at their obvious error in judgement.

However, one policeman, wearing the high domed blue helmets labeled New York Police, paused before Hannah. When he thrust a gloved hand to lift the linen tablecloth, she inhaled sharply—when he produced the opened bottle of Grand Vin de Bordeaux, her mouth dropped open.

A blur of lights and shouts and flashing images ensued around her. After it was over, she realized she had been handcuffed. Dumbfounded, she accompanied the arresting policeman. All the while, Gladys was screaming invectives at the police.

Hannah had time to consider the scenario while incarcerated in the Ludlow Street Jail. Meant for civil rather than criminal cases, the county jail had housed the beauty, Victoria Woodhull, the first female candidate for president and a free-love advocate, who had been accused of sending obscene material in the mail. And it was her initials, VW, Hannah found scratched onto the wall of her own cell.

How Aunt Giselle, writing for such divergent publications as *Collier's*

Magazine, Harper's Bazaar, and *The New Yorker,* would have made the most of this with the news media.

Hannah was only trying to make the best of it. She wanted no notoriety to mar the refined image of the Dallas Emporium. That could be ruinous. She was terrified of her arrest getting out but even more terrified of having to call her parents.

But, how had the wine bottle ended up below the table in front of her chair… unless it had occurred during the hullabaloo of the Bathhouse Club's rapid transformation from illegal to legal.

Still, why was she the only one arrested in a club that had never had a patron arrested? Another thought flitted through her frustrated mind—it had been Michael Kraft who had ordered the wine for her. More bewildering, it was Michael Kraft who showed up the next day on the other side of the bars of her ten-foot-square cell.

She raised a winged brow. "Did you come to rescue me or torture me?"

6

"Chaplin shoots all the exterior scenes outdoors, including the dust storm," Darcy explained patiently. "He won't be satisfied with the fake scenery of a studio storm."

"How did I let you talk me into this?" Heath muttered, tugging on his flat-crown, wide-brimmed hat. Other than the spurred riding boots, he wore uneasily the gaucho pants and red sash belting in his white, full-sleeve shirt that was unlaced at the neck. "Duds of a dandy," he had scornfully designated the costume.

Darcy couldn't help but grin at this brother. "I believe it was because you said you were fed up with your wastrel life. And, if I recall correctly, you said that being second in command to Dad at The Barony wasn't your—"

"I know what I said. But being painted like a harlot to prance around the set might just be worse than being a wastrel."

Heath, Darcy, and a stuntman waited on the studio's backlot of desert scrub while a giant electrical fan was wheeled into place behind an equally giant sandbox. "Look," Darcy smiled, "just pretend you're riding the range at The Barony. Do what comes naturally."

For Darcy, the trick-riding, two-gun drawing, and risk-taking stunt work came naturally. So did camerawork, to his surprise. He had finally found his niche in the world.

Charlie Chaplin was a neurotic stickler for perfection. It was nothing for him to do a score of takes for a scene. He had cofounded United Artists so that he could maintain complete control of his motion pictures. To ensure that control, he wrote, directed, acted, and did the camerawork.

While Chaplin was acting in a scene, Darcy filled in behind the camera, filming under Chaplin's barking instructions. "Darcy, move in! Get that face!" Cinematography was key when, with no sound and no dialogue, a film depended on lighting, acting, and set.

"Positions!" Chaplin shouted. Grabbing the reins of one of four horses, the short Englishman took his place, his back to the sandbox and fan, which presented less risk of the blown sand irritating the actors' eyes.

Heath groaned but strode from beneath the tent toward the second horse, a palomino. Mounted on a chestnut was Douglas Fairbanks, and astride the horse next to his was the ingénue, none other than Estelle Bevins. While waiting for the director's "Action!" she was softly whistling to herself.

Darcy could have suggested to Chaplin that Estelle was ridiculously miscast. Helpless, simpering female she was not. With her robust Texas drawl mixed with her Welsh-Irish brogue, she had bombed on the radio as a weather and crop reporter at the University of Texas.

Nevertheless, Chaplin had locked her up in a contract with his United Artist studio the same evening after Darcy had met both him and her backstage at the Helen Keller lecture. Fascinated with Estelle Bevins, Chaplin intended *The Four Centaurs of Armageddon* to be a star-making vehicle for her.

After this film was released, Darcy strongly suspected her days as an ingénue in Hollywood would be numbered. On the other hand, while loading the film reel, one glance at his older brother's charismatic features assured

Darcy that the public would not be able to get enough of the darkly handsome Heath Paladín.

The problem was, Darcy could not get enough of Estelle, try as he might. Starlets on the studio payroll were invariably casting an eye at the young lanky cowboy with the butternut locks, but she brushed him off like a pesky horsefly. "Don't come callin', cowboy, because I won't play the role of your girlfriend, wife, or mother of your children. Got it?"

He gave her an amiable, one-sided grin that belied his nervousness. "Now that just make me want to dig in my boot heels all the more."

"Until you lose that peach fuzz, I'd be much obliged if you'd drop off the face of the Earth."

Her smile was syrupy sweet. She wasn't about to let him forget he was too young for her to bother with. He would have thought that she, like all other females, would have eyes for Heath, but she was as indifferent to him as she was to Darcy. So, he suspected, it had to be another male who held her heartstrings.

Still, he had meant what he told her. He wasn't the kind to give up.

COOGAN'S BLUFF, NEW YORK
OCTOBER 1921

Bootleggers and bookmakers mixed with governors and glamor girls to consume champagne and caviar while watching game eight of the World Series from the upper-deck luxury suite of the Polo Grounds. Rockefeller and Hearst jostled drinks with Pickford and Valentino.

Red, white, and blue bunting draped over the upper deck of common bleacher seats below, where thirty-eight thousand other baseball fans cheered on either the New York Yankees or the New York Giants.

The Series had drawn fans from across the continent, from Mexico and Canada to as far south as Cuba. Hotels were booked up, and both the New

York Central and Pennsylvania Railroads had made plans to add cars and run their trains in sections if necessary, to handle the extra traffic expected.

One and all, the fans had come to watch Babe Ruth's prowess with the bat. That year he had connected for an unbelievable fifty-nine homeruns. But it was the bottom of the third, and he had yet to play due to a wrenched knee and an infected arm.

Although the elite of the fans may have filled the cigar smoke-hazed luxury suite, Hannah did not count herself among its VIPs, not when she had made the trip to the stadium via the Subway. Not when her mug shot was archived somewhere within the New York Police Department.

"You're worrying for nothing," Gladys reassured her after she had been released the year before. "Your arrest was a mistake. A bad one, I grant you."

The stranger, the man at the Bathhouse Club, claimed otherwise. He had become her surety, paying her bond, which had been set at an unheard of $825, far above the $11.75 usually charged for giving a bond. His only response was a vague, "You have enemies in high places, Miss Solomon."

And then he was gone, as if he had never existed. When she had prodded Gladys about him, Gladys's features expressed equal bafflement.

Who was he, this Michael Kraft who had the power to derail her focus on her career? After a year, she would still wake up some nights with his distinctive voice, lingering like smoke in the back of her mind. Something nagged at her—something just out of reach.

Later that afternoon, Gladys was just as reassuring as she had been a year ago. "The suite won't be raided, I guarantee you. Who do you think supplies the champagne? Friends—bootleggers—of the Mayor, that's who. And the gent power guzzling with him is Scott Fitzgerald. You are safe here, my child." She wandered off to join the crowd gathered around the young, successful New York novelist whose wife, Zelda, was at home, due to give birth at any moment.

Safe? An entire year had passed since that nightmarish night spent in jail, and yet Hannah didn't feel safe. She felt as if eyes were always following her.

As if she were being stalked. She never told her parents about the incident, knowing her father would instantly recall her to Dallas.

Nor did she tell them about the small, inexplicable incidences that continued to arise. Back in February, her cat had gone missing, and a tenant neighbor had found it dead in a trashcan… a couple of months ago, she had been turned away from a prestigious trade show without any explanation… and just last week, she had received a notecard embossed with only three initials—KKK.

Her critical and analytical thinking skills vitally necessary for making purchasing decisions were rapidly dissipating.

Even with the feeling of being watched, even in the company of 38,000 people that afternoon, she felt a loneliness, a sadness that siphoned all energy, all joy, from her. Perhaps she did need to get back to her roots. Perhaps she did need to see the spectacular Texas sunrises and sunsets once again—to smell the crisp, clean air where nothing putrefied and to be enfolded in the familial comfort of Thanksgiving at The Barony.

Yes, that was what she would do. Go home for Thanksgiving.

A rich, deep voice rumbled like a train out of a tunnel just behind her. "I see you are once again putting yourself in danger."

She whirled to find Michael Kraft frowning down at her. She still wasn't certain if he was one of the good guys or not. Maybe the black fedora in one swarthy hand was a clue. Whichever side he was on here, her pulse had definitely picked up its pace. "That is why you are here."

A dark brow raked up that high, intelligent forehead. "I beg your pardon?"

He was more handsome than she had remembered. His wavy hair was deeply parted and sleeked back in the Brilliantine style of the day. He wore a three-piece banker's striped black suit. Her practiced eye noted its classic, sophisticated cut. "You know, the Chinese say that if you save someone's life, you are responsible for them forever." She took a steadying sip of champagne, wondering if he had, indeed, saved her life or had been responsible for imperiling it.

Tugging first on one of his sleeve cuff links, then the other, he responded mildly, "The Chinese also say crowded elevators smell different to midgets."

At that, laughter burst from her, and she spewed champagne. "Oh my God! I am so terribly sorry!" Before he could respond, she whipped the red silk handkerchief from his coat pocket and began dabbing furiously at his double-breasted jacket.

He caught her wrist. "You've ruined my suit."

Mortified, she looked up into those pale brown eyes and gulped.

"The least you can do at this point is attend the trotting-horse trial with me this weekend." His insouciant smile eased the bluntness of his stipulation.

———————

THE HARLEM RIVER SPEEDWAY IN upper Manhattan was used primarily by harness enthusiasts for trotting-horse trials, but it attracted leisure lovers to watch both the harness and boats racing up and down the Harlem. That far past 151st Street, pleasure cars were not allowed on the dirt track.

Wealthy sportsmen often paid exorbitant prices for a fast Standardbred trotter. The sulky Michael owned fairly flew past the timers' tower as fast as any Roman chariot, closing the one mile in just under two minutes, according to his Cartier wristwatch.

As the trotting mare Rose Scott breezed past the white fence, Hannah shouted with as much jubilation as if she had been gaming and won. She clapped her hands. "Oh, she is majestic!" The nippy air pinked her cheeks— that, and the excitement of the race... and the palpitating nearness of Michael. She supposed the sense of danger had that effect on one.

He canted his head, his eyes narrowed—squinting at her as if examining her under a microscope—then glanced away. "She has a heart that knows no limits."

She stared back, trying to discern the man behind that haughtily hewn profile. Not entirely certain of his motives, she had been reticent that afternoon until the actual race. Then the thrill of it released her reserve. Fond memories of The Barony's rodeos resurfaced.

He excused himself to talk to the sulky's driver, and she watched him walk over to the cart. His carriage was aristocratic, arrogant even. She took the advantage to edge closer and stroke the muzzle of the lathered horse. She could hear him telling the driver, "Try the blinkers next time and see if that helps Rose Scott's focus."

When he turned back to her, she smiled. "You sound like my Uncle Drake. Actually, my great uncle."

"I don't know if that's bad or good. I certainly don't want to be an uncle figure to you."

What did he want? "It's good. Drake Paladín knows his horseflesh."

"All The Barony's heirs do."

Her fingers locked on the mare's halter. "I never mentioned The Barony."

He took her elbow and guided her down toward the riverbank. Rowboats and fishing boats plied the silted water. "No, you haven't. I had you investigated last year before I paid your bond."

Her stomach did somersaults. Caution urged her to swing away, but curiosity compelled her to walk at his side. She moved stiffly, her long, angry strides matching his easy ones. "Why?"

"Why? Isn't that obvious?"

"Nothing about you is obvious. I don't even know who you are. Really. You appear and disappear, and then reappear after a year. All too conveniently."

He released her elbow to tuck his hands into his suit pants. His gaze was fixed somewhere in the distance. "As the Vice President of the General Electric Corporation of Germany, I only make quarterly business trips to the States."

She looked down at the sparse grass, because to look at him meant to lose her concentration, he had that much of a disconcerting effect on her. "Then you were last here three months ago."

"Yes. And, yes, I checked on your... well-being... each time."

Her inhalation rasped the back of her throat. Suspicion raised its viper's head—had the encounter at the Polo Grounds been preplanned—and before that the raid at the speakeasy, as well? "Again, why?"

He stopped and turned to face her. "Because you're smart, passionate, fun-loving, and resilient. And because I won't tolerate persecution of any kind, including religious."

"So, you know I am a Jewess?"

"Yes. For the record, I am merely a cultural Jew. I enjoy its humor, its Lower East side cuisine, and find the Yiddish language enormously expressive. Circumcision is the closest I have come and will ever come to a Jewish ritual." He grinned. "And atheism is the closest I come to religion."

His dry humor was disarming. Could she believe any of what he said? She raised a skeptical brow. "Exactly who is persecuting me and exactly what do you plan to do about it?"

"Someone with potentially more power than even the President of the United States is persecuting you—a Supreme Court Justice. And what I plan to do about it is to marry you."

His high-handedness was definitely not at all disarming. "And if I am not so inclined?"

Before she realized his intent, he lowered his head to skim the softest kiss over her lips. His mouth, warming hers against the chilly air, squeezed off her lungs' breath from reaching her throat. Her bones liquefied, and she would have sagged, had his arm not lapped her waist, pulling her against his hardness.

"When I want something, I can be very persuasive, or so I am told. I want you, Hannah Solomon. I have for a long time."

———————

FOR HANNAH'S SAKE, MICHAEL ARRANGED for them to be married the following month in a little Jewish synagogue in New York's lower east end. Her friend Gladys and his jeweler Benny served as the requisite witnesses. Benny Stiegel was one of Michael's few American associates with whom he kept in contact. Benny knew everyone who was anyone in New York.

And in these dangerous days, that was important. Michael had Hannah to protect. He had to hustle her out of the country, far from her family's foe.

The four of them stood beneath the chuppah's canopy and obligatorily half-listened to the spry old rabbi's monotonous delivery of the wedding ceremony. Or, at least, Michael only half-listened. How could his attention not be riveted on the object of his desire? She was the only thing he had in this world that meant anything to him.

His patience, waiting for Hannah to trust him enough to permit him to come around, was like a hot flame. For as long as he could remember, he had been determined not to lose his heart to someone incapable of giving him hers.

But this young woman was different. And so, he had patiently wooed Hannah. He knew everything about her, recognizing the determined set of her chin, the shift of her slender frame, the tension in her fragile neck. He knew how to massage her body where she most wanted it. And where he most enjoyed giving his attention. His need for her was sensual and volatile. Jesus, she was all of his wet dreams.

He realized the rabbi and Hannah and Gladys and Benny were looking at him expectantly. He swallowed over the thickness in his throat. "I do."

SAN ANTONIO, TEXAS
CHRISTMAS 1921

Until the 60,000 upper-and middle-class Mexican immigrants fleeing Pancho Villa's carnage flooded San Antonio between 1914 and 1920, the frontier town had consisted of predominately German-speaking denizens. Their idyllic neighborhood of large, impressive houses bordering on a portion of the San Antonio River became known as Sauerkraut Bend.

Undoubtedly, Roger Clarendon's three-story Italianate home was the most fashionable. Its lush landscaped grounds included a chair lift, a wash house, servants' quarters, and a carriage house converted into a garage.

Clarendon was the highest paid and most successful attorney in the Southwest. His auto accident four years earlier seemed only to impassion his courtroom arguments that much more, so that he won virtually every case. The fact that he presented his arguments from the throne of his wheelchair most likely garnered the jurists' sympathetic attention as well.

His father was not that sympathetic that December. Not that the house gave any evidence it was Christmas. No tree, no manger scene, no decorations at all. The old man cut his honeyed ham slice with crisp, precise motions. "I'm backing off the Solomon woman, Roger. She's been seen in the company of Michael Kraft. Word is they might be married. His word carries some weight in the D.C. circles. I will not risk investigation."

Roger smiled at him over the rim of his wineglass. Nevertheless, one eyelid steadily blinked a half-beat behind the other, and Brighton knew uncontainable rage boiled his son's blood. "I'm not necessarily asking you to strike the Paladíns dead, Father. Just make them suffer. Greatly. For a long, long while. Then let the Devil claim his own."

He was Brighton's only child and all he had left. His wife of forty-three years had died three years before. Both he and she had hoped for grandchildren, but the accident that had crippled Roger's body had apparently also crippled his capacity for genuine companionship, so that his marrying was as nearly impossible as his having children. All his compassion and passion were transmuted into venom.

His son had taken to wearing a shoulder holster, as if its revolver sheathed beneath his armpit added to his manhood what the accident had taken away. Foolish, because if speed were required, the rig made it difficult to clear leather.

"I'm telling you that anger is unproductive behavior. It's like tennis—losing your temper is going to lose us the match!"

Roger's one lid beat like a hummingbird's wing. His smile curled lips corrupted by too much wine and too much rage. "But I can't play tennis anymore, can I?" He grimaced in hatred and disgust for his own appearance. "Then take the heat off the Solomon woman for now, Father, and put it on another Paladín. Sooner or later, I shall have them all roasting in hell."

7

EL PASO, TEXAS
MAY 1922

With or without his right foot, Pierce figured he could do only two things well—ride a horse and fly an airplane. Airplanes were a thing of the future. And yet in the past, his great-uncle Wade had utilized the horse in a way that Pierce figured he could utilize the plane in the future—and that was to deliver mail.

A regularly scheduled airmail route had already been inaugurated between Washington, D.C. and New York City, with an intermediate stop in Philadelphia. Pierce planned do that one better. As a southerly route, El Paso, or Sin City, was ideally located midway between New Orleans and Los Angeles. That kind of long haul was unheard of. However, with intermediate stopovers proposed in Houston and Tucson or Phoenix, he figured he could make it work.

He merely had to do two things—land the contract with the Post Office Department and finance the venture. The Post Office Department was desperate to create a transcontinental service and was taking on all comers without inquiry, so that part should be easy.

Financing the venture had required more than his meager deferred military pay. It had required he assume the managerial position of Lone Star Smelter, his aunt Angel's legacy from her late father, Rod Obregon, for additional income. The Smelter's heirs—the Princes of Paladín—were indifferent to their legacy.

Hollywood had rolled out the red carpet for Heath, though Pierce knew it was not something his cousin really wanted for his life. But the film career had come about easily, without any effort on Heath's part. And, without effort, he was challenging Rudolph Valentino for Box Office dominance.

Darcy was giving D. W. Griffith a run for his money as Hollywood's most innovative director. And, while attending a small military college in Roswell—not that far from El Paso's Texas border—Byron's brilliant brain had enabled him to set up from scratch his own research lab in the emptiness and, thus, relative secrecy of New Mexico's high desert.

So much for the other Princes of Paladín. As for himself, Pierce was struggling. He could have appealed to his father for financial assistance, but, like Preston, he was hell bent on making it on his own without interference or control from the old man.

Long hours spent learning the smelter business required Pierce to be absent from home far too often, so he had encouraged Aubrey to do volunteer work at the Hotel Dieu Sisters of Charity Hospital, named after the famous hospital in Paris. It was only five trolley stops away from their home in Chihuahuita, where most of El Paso's middle-class Spanish-speaking residents lived.

El Paso was known for its sunny, arid climate, and the Hotel Dieu served both the many people coming from all over to find a cure for consumption and a local population rampantly infested with smallpox and influenza.

As busy as Aubrey stayed, he could tell his young wife pined for the Old World charm of her native country and her father, with whom she periodically corresponded. Though she tried to conceal it with her funny wide grin and sparkling banter, she was not able to veil completely the melancholy trapped in her delicate patrician features.

As the daughter of a Dutch baroness, she was a cosmopolitan and blue-blood. How could she not be appalled by the isolation imposed by the desert fringes of El Paso, the Six-Shooter capital of the world? The brown Rio Grande River, often compared to the Nile, which looped around the base of the desolate Franklin Mountains fell far short of the pristine beauty of Metz's confluent Moselle and Seille Rivers.

Their home was a respectably comfortable four-room adobe, replete with a claw-footed bathtub in which she washed their clothes, although plenty of laundries existed. Here in Chihuahuita also lived about three hundred Chinese who had built the railroads through El Paso. Their laundries and restaurants, with their gracefully lettered signs, abounded.

To ease Aubrey's ennui, he both gifted her with a Yorkshire Terrier, which almost diminished his spending money, and endured the presence of the new friend she had made at Hotel Dieu, Veronica Lampier.

At thirty-one, older than Aubrey by ten years, Veronica worked on the hospital's second floor business office. A Marseilles war bride, her El Pasoan husband was one of the casualties of the influenza.

Veronica's floozy flair was as different from Aubrey's understated elegance as El Paso was from Paris. Veronica was coarse, with frizzy blonde bobbed hair, cheeks and lips slashed with scarlet, and a body bordering on corpulence. Loud and opinionated, she nevertheless offered some source of consolation to Aubrey, though he was at a loss as to determine just what beyond their mutual native language.

So, with great reluctance, he invited Veronica to join them for the twenty-first birthday dinner he had planned for Aubrey at Mesa Garden Restaurant, when he would much have preferred it be just he and Aubrey.

Mesa Gardens Restaurant nestled atop Franklin Mountains just above the fashionable Sunset Heights—a wealthy district composed of prominent Anglo-Americans and Mexicans who fled their native country because of political revolution. A renovated Greek Revival mansion, the restaurant faced the west and overlooked 3,000 feet below both El Paso and Ciudad Juarez.

Before Prohibition, El Paso had been famous for its sporting element. Other towns also had it, of course, but none excelled El Paso. With irrigation from the Rio Grande, El Paso del Norte's large number of vineyards produced wine and brandy that had ranked with the best in the realm.

After prohibition, El Paso's major source of livelihood, consisting of ninety-six saloons catering not only to drinkers but to 600 professional gamblers, plus prostitutes and saloon keepers, had shifted across the border to Juarez.

The seedy Mexican border town across the river glittered magically by night. By day, Juarez was a visible hotbed of illegal activity. Its significant criminal vices, namely booze and opium controlled by the Chinese immigrant population, now flourished like poppies under a benevolent sun.

"To the double-header I missed!" Veronica spoke a little too loudly, hoisting her glass of what appeared to be iced tea. She and Aubrey had just returned from the Ladies Room.

"What?" Pierce asked blankly. They sat at one of the candle-lit tables gracing the patio. It was banked on both sides by lush gardens, with city lights winking below and heavenly lights above.

"*Eh bien*, the public double hanging at the City Jail, *bien sur.*" Her accent increased with each liberal douse to her glass from the flask tucked away in her purse.

Aubrey giggled, then abashed, she toyed with the harlequin-patterned scarf knotted at her throat with her long elegant fingers. She seemed lighter of heart, and this eased his preoccupation about her wilting spirits.

It didn't ease his preoccupation with their other problems, however. His problem, he supposed. Those questions he could not bring himself to ask. Was her passion during their lovemaking feigned? Did the sight of his stump repulse her? And, most importantly, was she complicit in a possibly needless amputation of his foot?

Her answers might just well mean the end to the fairy tale he had scripted to justify his own choices, foremost facing up to his inadequacies. Paladíns didn't have inadequacies, did they?

And then there was his choice to bring her home as his bride. That had not been necessary. He could have weaseled out of it easily. But how did he justify his choice not to?

Her captivating grin waned as she reached into her handbag and dug out the envelope. "This came for you today, *mon amour*. I thought it was my citizenship papers."

He fished the single folded sheet from the slitted envelope with the return address of the U.S. Post Office Department. Rapidly, he scanned the single paragraph. His application for the airmail route had been rejected without explanation.

He almost asked Veronica for a guzzle straight from her flask. When he got home later that night to answer a call from the smelter's night watchman, he wished he had asked to drink her flask's entire contents.

The Lone Star Smelter was ablaze. He couldn't work for the post office, and the only livelihood left for him was up in flames. A legacy from his mother, the smelter was in ruins. He plowed a shaky hand through his hair.

Aubrey's comforting arm stole over his shoulder. *"Mon amour,* I am so sorry."

With a half-sigh, half chuckle, he caught her forearm and pulled her down into his lap. "Rome wasn't built in a day. Neither was The Barony. And just so for Paladín Aviation."

HOUSTON, TEXAS
AUGUST 1922

The yellow Stutz-Bearcat coupe rolled into Ridley's Filling Station. The convertible's horn tooted impatiently. Preston wiped his hands on the oil rag, flung it onto the toolbox, and abandoned the engine he was rebuilding to stroll from the service shed out to the pump—an improvement over the buckets and funnels of old.

It was his second week on the job while studying business and economy at Rice University. The months spent under the hood of his French SPAD, overhauling its engine, had paid off in transitioning to automobiles.

He had walked off from his last job, that of a rivet driver, because of the shoddy work the bridge inspector was approving. Some hapless drivers were going to end up in Buffalo Bayou when the bridge collapsed.

He emitted a low whistle as his eye scanned the pure-bred race car. Its interior forwent luxury and amenities in favor of lightweight construction. A pert young blonde wearing a pink head scarf sat behind the convertible's wheel. "Hey, handsome. I haven't got all day."

He plucked the long cigarette holder dangling from the fingers of her left hand and ground it out on the pavement with his boot. "You haven't got even a day left if you keep this up."

Her eyes flared, and her lips sputtered. "Why... why you rude...."

"Son-of-a-bitch?" His gaze dropped to her short skirt, which revealed shapely knees. Contrasted with the pale-skinned, long-haired and full-bodied women he preferred, she had that boyish look—flat chested, short permed hair, and tanned skin.

She blinked. "I could get you fired. My daddy owns this station."

He could have told her that his father was the Mayor of Galveston and that his Uncle Drake could buy and sell her damned daddy ten times over, but it wasn't worth his effort.

Besides, her old man was eccentric. Sharp on most things, a goofus on some things—like using clothes pins rather than suspenders to hold up his trousers. A wildcatter, he had just happened to strike it lucky on one well that was already dropping in barrel production per a day.

"Go for it. After he fires me, he can put his Reo's engine back together by himself."

Through narrowed lids, she watched him refuel her speedster. The weather was steaming hot and sultry. As he cleaned the Bearcat's windshield, sweat beads rolled down his jaw to plop onto the glass. "Hey, you're spotting my windshield."

He reached around the windshield and jerked her scarf from her head. "This should clean those spots just spiffy."

Her mouth opened and closed like that of a landed fish. Her gaze slammed into his. "Obviously you're not worried about supporting your family!"

"Nope." He flashed a smart-aleck grin through the windshield and finished cleaning the rest of it. "Don't have none and don't want none."

"You against relationships or something?"

"Just bad relationships." He dropped her now grimy scarf into her lap. "Glad to be of service."

"Why you...."

"Son of a bitch?" he supplied again, this time grinning at the spoiled brat.

"You just wait until I tell my daddy!"

Hands on hips, he watched the Bearcat roar away and figured he was watching his job roar away with it. Mentally, he tallied what cash he had stashed away between his deferred military pay and what he had earned from his various odd jobs he had held over the last three years.

His father had wanted him to design buildings. Balking at what he felt was his father's mayoral way of manipulation, Preston had created unbridgeable ill will between them. And he hated that. But living up to his father's ideal standards was impossible for him.

In fact, he had angrily remonstrated with his father, reminding him how he had faced up to his own father's not wanting him to be an architect and instead, follow in the family business.

"So why the hell can't you understand, Dad, this goddamn terrible wanting to find your own path?"

"Because I got lucky, son, and I love you too much to see you rely on luck."

Luck or not, Preston aspired to do something larger than design buildings. He aspired to acquire them. Eventually, four-star hotels, restaurants, railroads—as long as it was Texas real estate.

If the Great War and imprisonment in Germany had taught him anything, it was that he didn't ever want to leave Texas again.

Of course, he knew he had to start at the bottom. So why not force the tomato's daddy out of business? Yep. Paladín's Filling Station had a nice ring to it.

———————————

THE BARONY, TEXAS
THANKSGIVING 1922

Mariana dipped her spoon in the duck soup, only half listening to the banter between Byron and his father. "It took you longer to bag that duck," her uncle Drake teased, "than it did for your mom to pluck and gut it."

"Dad," her cousin protested with an embarrassed grin, "you're just bumping gums."

She knew he was feeling exhilaration with his new life. This once-sickly child now had free reign to live and do whatever he pleased, on his own means in the isolated and health restorative high desert of eastern New Mexico. She could only admire Byron for striking out on his own. But then, hadn't all the Paladín offspring, including herself?

Beer and wine were flowing, as was the crisscross of conversation. "The last time I ate underground roasted pig," Aunt Claire was telling Mariana's mother, "was when the *Paladíneños* prepared it to celebrate yours and Nicolás's engagement."

Her mother smiled wanly, and Mariana knew that this Thanksgiving season her mother terribly missed Becky, who had died three months before. Mariana suspected her death was caused by the grief of Dan's execution.

And Mariana was keenly aware that Griffin and Giselle's engaging smiles did not mask the pain of a parent's grief. Yet another year had passed, and neither of their twins had not come to the traditional Thanksgiving gathering of the clan.

Then there was Mariana's father, Nicolás, still striking at fifty, though not as handsome as Heath. No one was as handsome as Heath. A multitude of frenzied female fans could not be wrong. Surreptitiously, her eyes peered through her glasses down the length of the table, where he and Darcy sat on either side of their mother, the three talking.

Aunt Angel showered her sons with affection, but, she, like Mariana and everyone at the table's tableau, were attentive to the blushingly beautiful Hannah. The bride and her new husband, Michael, talked quietly with her father. Both men shared the Jewish faith, as did Hannah, although none of the three were practicing Jews.

Michael Kraft had a strong Roman nose and an aggressive masculine appeal that reminded Mariana much of her own father. She wondered if the almost imperceptible strain in Hannah's smile indicated Michael could be just as dominating as Nicolás Cordova.

Hannah had missed last Thanksgiving's family gathering when Michael had both married her and moved her all in one week to the *haute couture* world of Paris, from where she now ran the buying operations of the Dallas Emporium.

"Michael and I are trying to alternate our time between Paris and his business in Berlin. The charm of Europe would have beguiled me, even if Michael hadn't."

Arm looped casually over the back of her chair, he smiled easily. "I was the one who was beguiled."

At that moment, Mariana felt acutely alone. Glancing around the table, she acknowledged that her family loved her, but did they understand her? Did they have the slightest idea of the frustration that roared through her like a subterranean river?

She had gotten her law degree, but hanging out her shingle in Houston was proving difficult. She had known the odds were heavily against her—that Mexican part of her heritage combined with her gender and inexperience. She had discipline and talent and skill, but she needed the knowledge that only experience as a criminal defense attorney could bring.

Her father had offered her an office in his brokerage building, but, like her cousins, she preferred to make it on her own. "You're living up to your childhood reputation as stubborn and rebellious," he had chastised her.

Her bird-like college friend, Betty Chan, had offered her mere pennies rent at her late mother's vacant seamstress shop on the second floor of a 1910s-era building. The seamstress shop resided in the declining Second Ward area of Houston, which had been settled largely by Germans, followed by Italians and Anglos, then Mexicans.

Its first floor was devoted to a bail bonds outfit. Outside, bootleggers and prostitutes plied their trade until a slowly cruising patrol car would scatter them like billiard balls at the break. Granted, Mariana would have a ready clientele—but a clientele without ready cash.

But it was a start, and Mariana decided she would take up Betty's offer when she got back to Houston the next day.

She was merely toying with her food, pushing it around the plate, so she excused herself early to retreat to her favorite place when at The Barony—its gazebo. Her great-grandfather had built it of cedar from the nearby Nueces River. The place had hosted picnics, weddings, dances, intrigues, and, yes, trysts.

Hitching the hem of her satin chemise, she perched on one railing and wrapped an arm around its supporting post. A full moon, as orange as the pumpkins in the garden patch in the back of the rambling white stucco *hacienda,* filled the midnight-blue horizon. Frost hung on her wistful sigh. She should have grabbed a sweater or jacket.

"When I was a kid," came a voice from behind her, "I used to pretend the gazebo was my pirate's ship. Where you're sitting now was my crow's nest."

Of course, she recognized Heath's voice. As he entered the gazebo, the scuffed boards creaked beneath his boots. "I'm sure you made a wonderful swashbuckler back then." She hoped her voice did not sound as breathless as she felt. The heat of his nearness thawed the evening's chill. "And an even better one these days, much to Douglas Fairbanks disgruntlement, I would imagine."

He hunkered one hip on the post's other side and, folding his arms, braced his shoulder against the post, where the paint had blistered. "I suppose the adage is true—be careful what you ask for. I would much prefer being a common rancher than a celluloid swashbuckler."

"Common, you will never be."

She heard his chuckle and inclined her head past the post so that she could see better his handsome features. "Then, why don't you?" She could think of nothing she would love more. To have him nearer to her, to feast upon his features here at The Barony rather than on a movie theater screen. Though, damn't, she knew he never thought of her in the romantic way she thought of him. "Why don't you come home, to The Barony?"

Funny that idea, when she lived in Houston, but The Barony would always be home to all the Paladín clan.

"Commitments. People depend on me for their livelihood." He squinted those gypsy's dark eyes at her, and his lips curled in that *bandolero's* grin that made females everywhere want to abandon their husbands for him. "Besides, The Barony is my father's empire. I need my own." He smiled and sat down beside her. "Now you know why I escaped out here to the gazebo. Why did you?"

How did she explain that just being around him reinforced her sense of loneliness? That just as he had come to the gazebo as a child to pretend to be the pirate, she had come to pretend to be the pirate's romantic interest. She compromised, keeping as closely to the truth as possible.

"Honestly, I sometimes feel that no matter where I go, I feel as if it is time to leave, as if I have overstayed my welcome immediately upon arrival—or, more appropriately, I would imagine, as if I am supposed to be somewhere else. I just don't know where in this gigantic universe I belong."

"Yes, that sense of misplacement." He was studying her, so she turned her eyes toward the moon once more. "But why," he continued, "would you ever feel misplaced? A stunning, luminescent creature like yourself?"

Her mouth gaped. "Me?"

Then he was looming before her. "Yes, you. You hide those bottle-green eyes behind these peepers," he eased her glasses off her nose, as if he were easing her chemise off her body. "But your intelligence, your wit, your vitality—those you can't hide, cuz. One day, some guy is going to get lucky enough to grab you before you split and run."

His affectionate grin told her that he certainly didn't consider himself that guy, that he considered himself nothing more than a caring cousin. While her body and soul were clamoring that he was her everything.

Damn it all to hell!

8

PARIS, FRANCE

JULY 1923

"Homosexuals?" Coco Chanel arched a perfect drawn brow. "Those queers want to kill their competition. They want to be women—but they make appalling women."

Hannah choked down the champagne she had just sipped. She was a guest in Mme. Chanel's *maison de couture* at 31 Rue de Cambon, the most fashionable district of Paris. Gladys had arranged Hannah's *entré* into Paris *couture* society by a note of introduction to the editor of *Vogue* Magazine's French edition.

The richly appointed boutique was crowded with France's *crème de la crème* who had been invited to the exclusive showing of Coco Chanel's collection. Exclusive or not, the crowd was constrictive, the perfume was smothering, and Chanel's opinions were sickening.

It was to Maisie Fellowes, the Franco-American editor of *Harper's Bazaar,* that Hannah turned towards. "Get me out of here, please."

The sparrow-like heiress to the Singer Sewing Machine fortune, who subsisted on croissants and cocaine, was described by Gladys as, "rapacious, salacious, and a voracious man-eater." But the unabashed Maisie was, if nothing else, egalitarian. "Yes, I do believe the perfume is beginning to stink in here."

On her way out, rather than set her flute on the tray provided, Hannah balanced the crystal atop a nearby white-beaded fringe lampshade.

Within minutes, a tiny taxi was speeding them through Paris's noisy, serpentine streets to the apartment of another French couturier, Elsa Schiaparelli, who had just moved back from New York.

"Schiap was the *cocotte,* the kept woman, of the exiled Grand Duke Dimitri Pavlovich until Coco stole him away." Maisie tilted her head and eyed Hannah. "Perhaps you would be the perfect siren to steal Dimitri from Coco."

At that, Hannah threw back her head and gave a throaty laugh.

"Why do you find that so absurd? You are a tall, long-legged beauty who could do more justice to Coco's little black dress than all the British and French aristocracy combined."

"Because I am already a kept woman, by my husband."

"Bah! He leaves you to the prey of men like the Sergei Diaghilev."

"Yes, the man appears determined to cuckold as many husbands as possible, but my Michael will not be one of them."

The Russian art critic and ballet impresario had managed to corner Hannah at practically every event she attended. This concerned her because she knew how both protective and possessive Michael could be.

True, Michael had whisked her across an ocean from the lethal tentacles of Justice Clarendon and his son Roger, but Michael could also be controlling when other men tried to poach on what he considered his.

Due to both of their job constraints, he divided his time between her garret in Paris and his apartment in Berlin. She feared the few disagreements they had, over her reluctance to move to Berlin, could one day turn into serious arguments.

But neither could she give him up. Even after two years, when with him, it was as exhilarating a feeling as drinking absinthe for the first time. And the time they spent together in Berlin was thrilling, decadent, with life lived on the edge.

"We need to find you some good egg listed in Burke's Peerage."

"We need to find me a place where I can take off these high heels."

At Elsa Schiaparelli's small *atelier* on Rue de la Paix, the young woman was draping a shocking pink jersey material on a waif of a girl. "So, you have come slumming," the *Bohème Sauvage* mumbled, a pin clenched between her lips.

While not as famous as Coco Chanel, she had designed the notable Speakeasy dress, with its hidden pockets for flasks.

Maisie made the introductions. Schiap, dressed in a flowing brightly patterned skirt and peasant blouse, removed the pin and grinned. "Dallas Emporium, you say? I am getting ready to launch my new collection of knitwear. I would be delighted if you would attend the showing."

"I'd be keen on the idea."

When Schiap was finished, she shooed the girl off to change, then vanished and reappeared with a tray of pastries and a tea service. Settled on a settee and chairs in the atelier's alcove, Hannah and Schiap discussed places and people they had in common in New York.

Peeling off her satin gloves, Maisie shared Coco's caustic comment about homosexuals. "I was afraid Hannah would tell off our hard-boiled hostess. We had to scram immediately."

Schiap looked pointedly at Hannah. "I won't mince words, Hannah. As a Jew, you must be careful of the enemies you make in France. True, scads of Jews have fled their eastern ghettos to live here. They have even coined the expression 'happy as God in France.' Nevertheless, there is an element here—the social elite—who dislike Jews, who feel they are a Bolshevik threat to Europe, and that includes top level British officials and even the Royal Family. Tread carefully, my beautiful friend."

THE BARONY, TEXAS
THANKSGIVING 1923

The Model T rattled across the Chihuahua Desert beneath a frieze of frigid stars. The Spanish had deemed it *El Desierto de los Muertos,* the desert of the Dead.

Its crossing would have been made much faster if Edna Goodman, the secretary at Byron's small research lab, would have agreed to board the Tin Goose, as his cousin Pierce facetiously christened his four-passenger, all-metal test plane.

Edna snuggled closer to Byron beneath the blankets. He reveled in the way her spaghetti-thin body trembled in his arms and turned him ramrod hard. Damn, she was unstoppable, and it was her brisk, positive energy that he had found most appealing from the beginning.

Wearing skunk pelt fur coats, they rode in the converted rumble seat of the jalopy, while Pierce and his wife sat in front. Sat but did not snuggle. Something was wrong between them, but Byron could only speculate.

So many pressures. For Pierce, it might be the pressure of a homecoming at The Barony after several years' absence. For the extraordinarily luminous Aubrey, it might be the pressure of still trying to adjust to such an atypical culture. Or it could be the contents of her flask, stowed in the Model T's glove box.

Still, despite the strain between the two, the way she painted Pierce's face with her eyes was surely indicative of her soul's love for him. Something ineffably sad and tender resided in both hers and Pierce's expressions.

For Byron, his soul was most at home in Southwest Texas, where, after his bout with tuberculosis, his health was also at its best. These days, arid New Mexico and Edna's cooking also helped pack twenty pounds of muscle onto his six-foot-three once spindly frame.

With his tool company financing his aerodynamic experiments, he had set up a lab outside Roswell because it had a similar climate and isolation as The Barony but also had the appealing feature of a nearby prominent college, the New Mexico Military Institute, which he attended—and at which he could doubtlessly have taught.

The locals valued personal privacy, and when the curious asked where his facility was located, they would likely be misdirected.

It was Edna who had convinced him to make plans to take out time during the holiday week at The Barony to pay a call at Kelly Air Field in nearby San Antonio. The Army largely failed to grasp the military application of large rockets and liquid fuel engines. They said there was no money for new experimental weapons.

"But that hasn't stopped your mail from being opened," she persisted. "Even some of the reports I mailed you have gone missing."

He suspected Germany's Abwehrof pilfering his mail in hope of stealing his scientific work but couldn't prove it. His pace of research was slower than the Germans' because he did not have the resources the German military intelligence did.

Edna, who physically reminded him of the comic strip Olive Oyl, was a godsend. Measuring a perfect 57... 19-19-19, he teased her about her lack of the perfect hourglass figure, 36-24-36, and she cared not one whit. She coddled him. She was enthusiastic about his rocketry work, completely trustworthy, and aided him in his experiments and paperwork.

Best of all, she had an easy-going nature. She was indifferent to his inclination to forego wearing socks. They enjoyed going to the movies in Roswell. Taking advantage of New Mexico's salubrious climate, he painted its spectacular scenery, sometimes along with the local young artist Peter Hurd. Meanwhile, she played bridge.

If only he could convince the independent-minded Miss Goodwin to marry him because, as reluctant as he was to admit that he was as susceptible as other mortal men to the biochemistry that generated attraction, he was hopelessly lost in love with her.

At sunrise that Thanksgiving, a nippy but refreshing morning, he hoisted Edna astride one of The Barony's thoroughbreds, a first for her, and gave her a five-cent tour of the ranch. "I didn't realize the enormity of your place," She looked around with wide eyes as she sat uneasily in the saddle.

"You have no idea." They were returning from a ride to the *Paladíneños pueblo*, Baroncita, and passing through the scrub brush that unscrolled between it and The Barony's red-tile roofed *hacienda*. "As the saying goes, 'the sun will rise and the sun will set, and you will still be on The Barony yet.'"

Abruptly, he reined his chestnut in front of her mount. "If you don't accept my marriage proposal this time, Edna, I swear I'll abandon your scrawny ass to the buzzards here and now."

Beneath the absurd Tom Mix ten-gallon Stetson that almost swallowed her, her lips screwed up in a smirk. "That isn't much of a choice. Marriage or buzzard bait. Of course, there's always a third option—I could secure the patents to your work in my name instead. That should make me richer than you and the rest of your Paladíns."

"You believe in my patent that strongly?"

"I believe in you, Byron." Her screwed-up smirk shifted to a lopsided smile.

That evening, the Paladín cousins were arranged around the long table, spread with an assortment of mouth-watering cuisine. Sage, pumpkin, cinnamon, and rosemary tantalized the nostrils. Only Preston and Hannah, along with her husband, still in Europe, were missing from the Thanksgiving gathering.

Somehow, amidst the cousins' outstanding achievements, he had managed to carve a niche for himself—or perhaps Edna's dedication to him and his dream-scheme had been his rocket fuel.

With the clinking of glass, clanging of silverware, and hum of conversation reverberating in the dining room, he stood to make his announcement. Of course, monumental transitional announcements seemed to be obligatory at the Paladín Thanksgiving dinners.

Wine glass lifted, he looked around the room, finally settling his gaze on Edna's. "After pointing out the error in her ways, the perspicacious Miss Edna Goodwin has, at last, corrected a small oversight and consented to join me in the yoke of marriage."

The expected oohs and ahhs and cheers erupted around the table. Edna thrust out her hand to display the simple gold band. "I'm officially hand-cuffed and open to suggestions for marital bliss."

His aunt Angel came to her full five-foot height and flashed his uncle Drake a saucy, sassy grin. "Here's to the three C's—communication, compromise, and commitment—only on the part of the husband, of course."

Rising somewhat nervously, Aubrey raised her own glass. "The fourth C—*confiance.*" She shrugged her thin shoulders. "In English, it is called, I think, trust." She glanced down at Pierce, her melancholy gaze tempered the scowl made by her thick brows. "Cardinal rule number one—is that not so, *mon amour?*"

WITH GISELLE BURROWED IN THE alcove of one arm, Griffin took a slow sip from the steaming Mexican hot chocolate. Over the *jarrita's* rim, he studied their son by the moon's chilly light.

Pierce hunkered one hip on the veranda cedar railing, his artificial foot tucked behind one calf. For balance or concealment? The sight of it still wrenched Griffin's heart.

He and Giselle sat in the swing. They were catching up on lost time with Pierce. He possessed his mother's old-gold hair color. Griffin would attribute that stubbornness of Pierce's also to his mother. Politicians were supposed to be gifted with eloquence, but Griffin's attempt at conciliatory letter writing over those past four years had received but negligible responses from Pierce that avoided addressing their issues.

And nothing from Preston in Houston.

Griffin granted that he, too, had been headstrong in his youth, determined to go his own way. He had wanted to be an architect. Nevertheless, when the Panic of 1893 meant he had to take control of The Barony Enterprises, he had put his own career desires on the back burner. His forebears had taught that sacrifice for the sake of a larger issue was the right thing to do and, ultimately, was worthy of a reward.

Apparently, it had taken Aubrey's diplomatic nudging to convince Pierce to come with Byron for Thanksgiving this year. Then, saying she was tired and retiring early, she had conveniently excused herself this evening after dinner so that the three of them could be alone on the veranda.

What troubled Griffin was what had not been said. Had his daughter-in-law been implying something more with that provocative statement about trust before she had excused herself from the dinner table?

Frowning, Pierce swirled the cinnamon remnants in his own *jarrita*. "Despite how many times I refined and resubmitted my application with the Post Office Department, I was rejected. So, this year, Mom… Dad, I struck out on my own. Paladín Aviation. With the little Aubrey and I save from the Smelter's pay, I am buying parts and building my own fleet in an abandoned warehouse, one plane at a time."

"Son, we're bucking—all of us Paladíns—Roger Clarendon and his father, which means just about the entire Supreme Court of the United States."

"And if that isn't enough firing power, word is Roger is packing heat in a shoulder holster," Giselle added, completely the mother. "So, don't even think of crossing him face to face. He's sneaky and would have no honor when it comes to any Code Duello."

Griffin was determined, by hook or crook, as Grandfather Alex used to say, to stop the Clarendons before it came to that. "Where would Paladín Aviation fly?"

"With Roger Clarendon and his old man on my back, I'd stay in Texas to avoid Federal regulation."

From a pocket in his old leather flight jacket, he removed a pen and drew a triangle on his outstretched palm. "El Paso, San Antonio, Dallas." He tapped the three points with his pen tip. "Given a few years, a hangar space in each city, I think I can swing this route. Problem is, right now, too much of my time is consumed with the Smelter. It caught fire a while back, and recovery has slowed down production."

Griffin opened his mouth to ask about the fire, just a hunch he had, but

Giselle, never one to back off from a problem, asked something else. "Pierce, are you giving enough time to Aubrey?"

He tucked the pen away in his pocket. "It's just taking time for her to adjust to life here in the States, Mom."

"Is it time that is the issue… or the trust she mentioned?"

His mouth went from grim to obdurate. "There's another C-word, Mom. Confidential."

9

Due to Hollywood's inexpensive real estate and sunny climate, the rapidly growing colony greatly appealed to new, up-and-coming film directors. However, 1924 was not a good year for either the studio or theatre owners. The growing popularity of radio was exacting its tolls on the box-office takings—although Charlie Chaplin's *The Gold Rush* had drawn large crowds.

Heath was not certain if he and Darcy had made the right decision, forming their own production company, Double Take. Even with their indivisible brotherly bond, their commercial venture was an uneasy alliance. Darcy's strongly pacifist's leanings were counterpoint to Heath's more intensely dramatic inclinations. Money and distribution problems haunted their studio. Despite Heath's rapidly rising stardom, the Double Take's loans and investment requests were repeatedly rejected.

Double Take was at the low end of the studios. Foremost were the Big Five, studios like Warner Brothers and Metro Golden Mayer. Built on a grand scale, the Big Five had sky-light buildings with laboratories, costume and research departments, acres of outdoor sets, and gated entrances with security guards.

Next came the Little Three—Universal Studios, United Artists, and Columbia Pictures. Bringing up tail end were those on Poverty Row—Disney Studios, Republic Pictures, and 20th Century Pictures, with Double Take Studios finishing dead last. Both the Little Three and Poverty Row's studios lacked the most essential ingredient for success, owning their own theatres.

Heath had little time off from acting. As romantic lead in their studio's film, *East of Morocco,* he had solidified his position in the polls of Hollywood's leading men. Relentlessly, Darcy publicized him—leading parades, cutting ribbons, making speeches, and squiring a bevy of stardom's beauties to glittering functions.

That evening, he and Darcy were among a mass of guests invited to Pickfair—the twenty-five-room mansion owned by Hollywood's reigning couple, Mary Pickford and Douglas Fairbanks.

Darcy was angling for a chat with one of the guests, noted pacifist and Nobel Prize winner in Physics, Albert Einstein. Heath knew their brother Byron would be salivating for the opportunity to talk to Einstein, if only for five minutes.

Heath ambled his way to the Old West style saloon-room where a dozen or so guests were mixing and bellied up to the ornate burnished mahogany bar to order. Considered Hollywood royalty, people instinctively stood up when Mary and Douglas entered a room, so when Mary entered a few minutes later, the guests all rose to greet her. Heath, his long legs balancing one haunch on a tall stool, remained where he was.

Noting this, Mary made her way to the bar and perched her tiny frame on a stool next to his. "I've been wanting to meet you for a long time now, Mister Paladín."

"Heath, please."

"Doug has worked with you before and has only the best to say about you and your work."

"I can only aspire to what your husband has accomplished in the film industry. And yourself, for that matter, Miss Pickford."

"Mary, please." Her smile was genuine, as was her interest, and he was content simply to sit and talk movie business. At least she had no designs on him specifically.

The adulation of hounding females, who really knew nothing about him, was utterly boring and was becoming unbearable. He couldn't even go to a barber shop without hordes of females, young and old, clustering outside to peer at him through the plate glass, then later to beg for clips of his shorn locks.

Mary was an astute businesswoman, producing her own films, so the conversation was a respite. Or would have been, until he excused himself to go to the men's room.

No sooner had he unzipped than the linen closet door burst open, and a teenage girl popped out, autograph book in hand. "Mister Paladín, I was so hoping it would be you! Could I have your autograph?"

Astonishment gave way to heated exasperation. "But, of course," he said, re-zipping. "Do you prefer penis or ink?"

Her mouth dropped open. He seized her pen, scrawled his name on a vacant page, and stalked from the men's room.

Searching out Darcy, he found him in the gaming room playing billiards with a couple of other guests. He inclined his head near his brother's. "I'm leaving."

Startled, Darcy glanced up. Heath did not bother with even a perfunctory smile for the other two men who might be inclined to eavesdrop. His expression must have alarmed Darcy. His brother laid his napkin to the left of his plate. "I'll have the Buick brought around."

"No, I mean, I'm leaving. Leaving Hollywood. Leaving the management of Double Take to you."

HOUSTON, TEXAS
SEPTEMBER 1924

ONE-STOP SERVICE STATION

The large sign above the corrugated canopy that ran the length of the two existing buildings acknowledged that Preston had taken the first step toward achieving his goals.

"It's impressive." Darla Ridley smiled, linking her arm through his.

He shifted his gaze from the sign to her face. A pretty face, perky, with an upturned nose and the barest sprinkle of freckles. Her eyes and finger-waved hair were the same color, a golden brown. He probably would have done better by driving her father out of business altogether.

Initially, after Glen Ridley had fired him, he had set out to do just that by buying up the dilapidated hardware store going out of business next door. From there, all he would have had to do was contract with a refiner and install a curbside pump. With his mechanical knowledge of automobiles, he could have put old man Ridley out of business by New Year's Day.

A bizarre conversation had changed Preston's intent. He had been hunkered before bins, plowing through the hardware store's leftover dusty inventory, mostly nickel and dime stuff, when the door's bell tinkled— apparently an intruder, as the store was weeks away from being ready for re-opening as a gas station.

Glen Ridley, over fifty, overweight, and overwrought, stormed down the aisle littered with buggy whips, bicycle chains, spark plugs, and headlight lenses. "What the hell do you think you're doing?"

He sighed, dropping the bolt into a cardboard box and looking up at the blustering man. "What do you want, Ridley?" He hoped to get this over with quickly, because he knew all too well how short his own fuse was.

Bulging gray eyes blinked rapidly. His only child's pretty looks didn't come by way of him, for sure. "I want…." His thick fingers twitched on his pants' clothes pins. "… I want you out of here. Out of the area."

"Well, that's not going to happen. I own the store." *And what I want is to kick you in your blimpy balls.*

Veins in Ridley's temples, the same purple color of those in his bulbous nose, throbbed. "Then close it. Close your store."

"That's not going to happen, either." Preston pushed himself to his six-foot-four, braced his weight on his back leg, and hitched his thumbs in his Levi's pockets. "Of course, if you want me to buy you out…." It was an impossibility, since every cent he had was now tied up in the hardware store, but it pleasured him to turn the screw on the old man.

"I can't. The paperwork… if the Bureau of Investigation finds out who I really am, they would have me killed."

"What?" Was the old man a member of organized crime—a boss of some gang like Al Capone's?

Ridley glanced around, as if someone in the cavernous building might overhear, and lowered his voice. "Jesus."

"Jesus?"

"Yes. I am Jesus, Son of God."

He groaned.

"Sshhh." Ridley looked around again, quite serious.

It was all he could do to keep from laughing, except it was so blood chilling. He didn't have to worry about driving Ridley out of business. The old man would be locked in the looney bin and his daughter Darla out peddling flowers—or her body—before the year was out.

Three hours later, when Preston was on his back, repairing a display case's warped bottom, his undershirt grungy and sweaty, Darla came to stand over him. His gaze ran up the length of her shapely legs, past her knees… and the blood surged to his balls. The wrench he had been wielding dropped from his sweaty hand. His breath was a heated rusk. "Damn."

She hunched down to peer over at him. "Uhhh, Preston?"

"Yeah?" He swallowed back the lust rising from his crotch and groped for his wrench.

"I know my father stopped by to pay a visit."

He went still, waiting.

"And, umm, I just wanted to say he's not always like this... you know... this raving like a madman. His mind... well, he has syphilis. And it's getting worse, you see."

Preston's lust plummeted like a thermostat in winter. "I see."

When he made no further reply, she too waited, then rose, rubbing her palms together. "Well, I just wanted to let you know."

"Thanks, Darla. I'll keep that in mind."

After she left, he did what some folks called soul searching—though he wasn't certain if he even had a soul—and revised his game plan.

He contacted his cousin Mariana. She was as down and out on funds as he was and had been delighted with the Benjamin he was able to send her way in exchange for filing all the legal papers to set up him and Ridley in a joint venture.

By combining the hardware and filling station into a one-stop service for customers, their alliance was proving to be unbelievably profitable. People were willing to spend money. Cash registers were cha-jinging. Business was booming. Newspapers proclaimed the new economy as the Roaring Twenties.

The One-Stop Station was an innovation, and there was no stopping sales—at least, until the time would come when Ridley's syphilis totally corrupted his brain. Meanwhile, his daughter kept an eye on her father.

And kept an eye on Preston.

He could have told her he was a lone wolf, that he had never found love nor wanted it, but that wouldn't have thwarted her efforts. She already had him in her bed. Their joint venture in gratifying their lust was proving to be just as profitable in its own way.

But she wanted that other form of alliance, the merger of more than just their companies and their bodies but of her name with his. Her old man might be crazy, but she wasn't. She had been spoiled by him, and she intended to get what she wanted.

Preston felt sorry for her, because either way, she would lose.

PARIS, FRANCE
NOVEMBER 1924

Another Thanksgiving at The Barony Ranch with her family Hannah had failed to make.

She missed those gatherings terribly. But, The Barony was far away—an ocean away. At times, its raw, barren beauty seemed more a product of her imagination.

Michael was her family now. That evening, she met him at the Gare de L'Est train station on the Paris-Berlin quay and was at once swept up in his whirlwind energy. While steam hissed around them and commuters threw them ogling glances, he dropped his briefcase and caught her up against him, her feet dangling.

His kiss breathed life into her. All her worries about such things as the Dallas Emporium's spring inventory or getting complimentary tickets to the upcoming Paris Exhibit of Art Deco for customers vanished. Every cell in her sang with his life force.

"This once a month rendezvous is playing havoc with my nights."

She could feel him hard against her and laughed exultantly. "I shall take care of that later, my love. Let's get something to eat. We need to sustain ourselves through the long night ahead."

They caught the Metro and exited up the Trocadero stop's ornate cast-iron balustrade, directly across the river from the massive Eiffel Tower. Flurries of snowflakes mutated the city into a dazzling snow globe. The view of Paris from the plaza of the Palais Chaillot was spectacular.

In preparation for the 1925 Art Deco Exhibition, the city was a blaze of light by night—its monumental gates, bridges, and fountains. The Eiffel Tower, emblazoned now with the Citroën logo, was the most majestic.

At a small café on the plaza, they dined on choucroute garnie, held hands, and, over wine, fell in love all over again—as they did each month, the time for which her entire body waited, as if in incubation for birth, like a butterfly emerging at last from its cocoon. Paris was the center of the artistic universe, but Michael was her center.

"Move to Berlin," he urged, as he did nearly every month. "General Electric's shares have tripled in value. You wouldn't even have to work."

"But I like what I do."

"Then you could operate from Berlin just as easily as Paris. It's the third largest city in the world now and the most creative and innovative."

"And the most dangerous."

True, libertine and cosmopolitan Berlin for the first time reigned as one of the world's cultural centers. The city was obsessed with the arts, pioneering in filmmaking, and caught up in science, technology, séances, striptease acts, and transvestite balls. Thrill-seekers came to the city in search of adventure and booksellers sold guidebooks to Berlin's erotic night entertainment venues.

But Germany, ravaged by defeat in the Great War, was also mired in financial and political problems. Systematic layoffs of Jewish factory workers were taking place, and Hannah had seen newspaper photos of lines of people waiting to purchase whatever items they could with worthless marks. Berlin was the hub of prostitution, drug dealing, and the black market.

Michael squeezed her hand "If you live in fear, Hannah, then you are not living at all."

She squeezed back, too happy to debate the issue. "You are right, of course," she teased, skirting the issue of the move.

"I'm always right." He reached around to help her with her coat. "Now, let's enjoy some nightlife—and then enjoy the night itself later."

She was tempted to tell him to forget the nightlife, to come back with her to her garret that was more an attic with a skylight. With her European success establishing Dallas Emporium as a renowned American luxury, specialty department store, she could well afford a mansion in St. Cloud but preferred her view of Paris's smokestacks and rooftops.

In the lightly falling snow, they descended a long series of steps to the Seine. Beneath one of the gorgeous bridges, he backed her up against its stone arch. His lips made a foray from her ear lobe to her collar bone. "Are you cold?"

Enveloped by the sheer force of his exuberance and effervescence, his *joie de vivre,* she was deliriously happy. She felt she could never be either cold or fearful.

EL PASO, TEXAS
DECEMBER 1924

Whoever claimed El Paso had a wonderfully warm and sunny climate had never braced against an artic wind barreling down off the Franklins. It swept, unobstructed, across the harsh expanse of Chihuahua Desert, the largest in North America.

Shoulders hunched in his flight jacket, Pierce climbed down from his prototype single engine airplane. In the gathering dusk, tumbleweed hurtled ahead of him to collide with creosote, mesquite, agave, and ocotillo bordering the dirt airstrip. Leaning into the freeze-burn wind, he loped as fast as his artificial limb permitted to the small hangar. Numb fingers shoved up the wide, metal roll-up hangar door.

He should be pleased. He had flown roundtrip to Roswell, New Mexico, to meet with Byron. Coordinating with Byron's Paladín Tool Company, highly profitable due to the continuing oil boom, they had negotiated a contract with the government to build a liquid-fueled rocket. The fact that the negotiations were top-secret meant that, for the time being at least, he and Byron could elude the seemingly inexorable vengeance of the Clarendon's.

He crossed the hangar to the cell-like office alcoved at its rear and flipped over the calendar sheet to the day's date and his scribbled notation—Ysleta Mission Restaurant, six thirty p.m.

The popular restaurant resided next door to the Ysleta Mission, still run by the Indians who had settled there under a Spanish land grant, centuries before. A cluster of galleries and artists' workshops were located around the mission—an attraction he thought might awaken Aubrey's flagging spirits.

He glanced down at his wristwatch. Shit! Ten after five. Just enough time to hustle home and get ready for the dinner, a Christmas present for Aubrey.

Except, Aubrey wasn't home. Brandy, the Yorkshire terrier he had given her, yapped stridently, its tiny teeth tugging at Pierce's trouser cuff. He glanced down at the doggy bowls. Both empty. Had Brandy been fed and watered today? Wandering through the rooms, he saw that their small home had not been picked up of clutter.

Rubbing his forehead, he tried to remember if this was the day she volunteered at the hospital. No, it wasn't, and he was getting worried. Gut knotting, he telephoned the one friend she had, Veronica Lampier.

"No, Pierce, I have no idea where Aubrey is," the French floosy purred. *"Eh bien,* the last I saw her was this morning, when she asked me to give her a lift to the laundry. She was going to walk from it to the hospital."

Aubrey washed most of their laundry in the tub, but occasionally she took their dirty clothes to the Chinese hand laundry Veronica had suggested. He attributed it to her fastidiousness. Except lately, her personal habits had not been so fastidious. Occasionally, her clothes were rumpled, her hair a rat's nest, and her breath smelled... quite pleasant and vaguely flower-like.

He knew his suspicions could be far off target. Nevertheless, he aggressively cranked the lever at the front of the Model T and floored its foot pedal. The jalopy rattled down St. Louis Street toward Hop Sang's Laundry.

A vermillion placard with spidery black figures advertised in two languages that shirts were washed for one dollar and ladies' dresses for fifty cents. Inside, the shop reeked of steam and starch and the faint odor of sandalwood incense... along with something else.

Impatiently, he watched as a little man in flowing black robes and coarse black slippers shuffled through a curtained doorway to the counter. The Chinaman's parchment lips creased in a solicitous smile. "I can help you?"

"My wife—Aubrey Paladín—she was here this morning?"

The Chinaman shook his head, as if puzzled. "I do her lawnly?"

"You do our laundry."

The slanted lids slid almost closed over black lacquered eyes. "I not know Missy Paladín."

At a loss, trying to piece together the puzzle, Pierce tapped his knuckles twice on the counter, then swung away only to halt abruptly. He rotated back to the counter. In a cotton twill laundry bag beside the curtained doorway was a load of dirty clothing. Spilling from its opening, he spotted a portion of a harlequin-patterned scarf.

Fury and fear roared through him. He pushed past the protesting Chinaman and strode through the curtained doorway. He plowed past wash tubs, scrub boards, and drying racks. At an oblong table, another Chinaman, with a long queue and wearing a black coolie hat, wearily wielded a heavy charcoal-heated hand iron.

Beyond him was a second door. Pierce jerked it open. It led down a set of steps, lit by a bare lightbulb. Descent of the steep, wooden stairs was awkward for his footing and slowed him down. At the bottom was another doorway, this one more heavily curtained

He shoved it aside. Aghast, he stared through the chamber's wisps of redolent smoke at the figure's recumbent on opium beds. Within easy reach of each platform was a supply of paraphernalia—long bamboo-stemmed pipes and filigree oil lamps necessary to heat the opium until it vaporized.

Like El Paso's many brothels, gambling houses, and saloons, with the advent of Prohibition, El Paso's opium dens had gone underground, literally. A labyrinth of opium dens snaked beneath El Paso. Chinese dealers known as the Tongs supplied the opium and prepared it for the visiting non-Chinese smokers.

One smoker, holding his pipe's clay bowl, was inhaling the narcotic vapors. The other three males, sprawled in drowsy abandon on their platforms, drifted in and out.

And then, yet another figure, lazed with her legs folded to one side, her back against the adobe-brick wall. Her long-lashed lids drooped, and the pipe lay lax in her palm.

Pierce's skin tightened and crawled along his bones. He crossed to Aubrey and lifted her frail body, cradling it in his arms. Carefully negotiating the stairs, he found the two Chinamen watching nervously from the storefront room. Silently, they parted for him to stride past with the burden he carried.

Aubrey did not stir as he sped the Model T back to their little adobe. Upon arrival, he laid her on their bed and began removing her clothing—after the shoes, a herculean feat in itself. First, her suede velour coat, then her loose-fitting dress, her constraining sidelacer that released her small breasts, her pastel stockings, her garter belt, her knickers, and lastly, her step-in chemise.

Why had he not noticed her lack of nourishment? How could he have not noticed how her ribs and pelvic bones protruded? Right then, her ravaged body needed sustenance, something light, like soup. But first, he intended to give her a sweat bath and begin the purging of the opium.

He ran the tub's hot water until steam filled the little bathroom, then he easily carried her inert, nude body from the bedroom and slipped her into the bathtub. As the steamy heat enveloped them, he hovered over her.

He was disturbed by everything about her—the rich shadings of her auburn hair were absent, its strands fuzzy at their ends. The peach-lustered glow of her skin was now a waxy surface and the shape of her body so little resembled its earlier piquant femininity.

God help him, how he loved her.

With a washcloth, he sponged off the perspiration that beaded her skin, and for the first time she made a noise—a half-moan, half-whimper. Her lids fluttered open.

"Why?"

Her parched lips made a little moue. "The pleasant poppy dreams… are they any worse than the burning alcohol?"

"Who introduced you to the opium?" But he already knew the answer— and knew that he would first deal with Veronica Lampier and then the man for whom he suspected she must work.

Death was said to be painful in the throes of the poppy, but when he was finished with Roger Clarendon and his father, the two would welcome the opportunity to die addicted to it.

Aubrey's raspy, elegantly accented voice reached out to him through the steamy mist. "Why do you not just ask me, *mon amour,* if we cut off your foot on purpose?"

Because he was afraid to know the truth.

10

Dropping from a stagecoach between a team of run-away horses… crashing through glass windows on horseback… taking horse falls in a somersault… leapfrogging over a horse's rump into the saddle—this was all in a day's work for Darcy's whipcord strength and tensile prowess.

He was so successful that he had made a name as a devil may care and affable personality in the film world. So, between his stunt work and his camerawork, he also earned extra cash through endorsements like Purina Dog Chow.

All this allowed him to capitalize on his business plan—to own his own fleet of theaters across the United States. Well, only three so far, with their grand openings scheduled for the Fourth of July.

But these three theaters were installed with something unique, something that only New York's Rivoli Theatre possessed—a climate-controlled system that Carrier Engineering had perfected. Its air conditioning would transform the sweaty summer months from a financial disaster for the movie industry to its most profitable season of the year.

For a while, Heath's departure from the film industry had cut drastically into Double Take's profits, but with the economy surging, so was film attendance, bolstering Double Take's bottom line.

This latest little fiasco of an accident had also set Double Take back somewhat. Who would have thought that, after all the dangerous risks Darcy had taken, he would break his nose tripping over a set's electrical cable? His first picture in which he both starred and directed, *The Vaquero,* was delayed now.

With the greatest reluctance, he waited to be wheeled into the operating room so the plastic surgeon could perform his own magic. At least, that was what Darcy was hoping for. "I've got three grand openings to make, Doc."

"Well, this is only a small opening I am making," the silver-haired surgeon reassured him with a practiced professional smile. "There is no need to worry."

"Yeah, but I've noticed your office full of portraits by Picasso."

At that, the doctor lost his dignity and laughed. That was the last thing Darcy heard before the local anesthesia put him under.

The next thing he heard was a female's whistle. "In my humble opinion, Darcy Paladín, you make a better mummy than a leading man."

Peering groggily past his bandages, he made out Estelle Bevin, standing just inside the doorway. He thought how often her whistling techniques, from melodic to mocking, annoyed him. "I'd like to make you my leading lady," he mumbled. "In real life, not films."

"I'd settle for films, cowboy."

His gaze swept over her, from head to foot. He was not so groggy that he didn't notice her appearance—her scuffed shoes, the frayed cuffs of her blouse, a shabby cloche hat. Apparently, she was finding herself on the wrong side of the studios' gates.

"I'd settle for however I can get you, Estelle. I'm making *Red River Rider.* Its above-the-line expenses could include your salary." He figured he could produce thrilling western films on a bare-bones budget and snare a hefty profit by running Double Take as if he were ramrodding The Barony.

"It's a deal."

Doubtlessly, when the anesthesia wore off, he would regret his impulsiveness. Not good business practice, his father would say. "But you have to play it my way."

She stiffened. Her fingertips clenched her purse. "Meaning what exactly?"

"Come here." His hand lying on the hospital bed beckoned her.

Warily, she stepped into the room. One footstep at a time, she approached to stand beside the bed.

He took her hand. He delighted in the firmness, the grit, in her grip. "This isn't a casting couch offer. You want to succeed in the business. So do I. Your features are too strong to play the role of a simpering maiden." In fact, they nearly overwhelmed her petite stature. "And you'd be miscast as a siren. Everything about you shouts that you are too open, too frank, too solid for the role of a *femme fatale.*"

She arched an artfully plucked brow. "What role did you have in mind then—Rin-tin-tin?"

He grinned. "A cowgirl."

Abruptly, she released his hand, spun around, and headed for the door.

"It pays $125 a week," he called to her back.

She stopped, pivoted like a sergeant-at-arms. "When does shooting start?"

"As soon as this muzzle heals. And, by the way, I'd like to change your name, too."

"Deal's off, cowboy," she began to pivot toward the door again.

"No, not in marriage. Estelle Bevins doesn't fit you."

She halted and slowly rotated back to face him. "Okay, what then?"

His faculties weren't exactly at optimal speed. He really wanted to doze off. "We need to give you a semblance of glamor."

"Indeed?"

He could almost hear the gnashing of her teeth. "Belle. Belle Bevins, it is. And you're going to be singing. A singing cowgirl."

"You been eating loco weed?"

"Nope. Heard that Warners is investing half a million buckaroos with

Western Electric in the Vitaphone sound system for a talking picture next year. Risky, but I think we should give it a try, too. Now give me a goodbye kiss, so I can get some shuteye, Belle."

She crossed to him and leaned over to plant a kiss on his forehead. "All too often, I want to curse you for simply breathing. You make my teeth clench at the same time you make me want to smile. But, all in all, you aren't so bad for a saddle-bum."

"What you got against cowboys?"

"They're not good for much."

At the door, she paused, looked over her shoulder, vamped a sultry expression, and blew him a kiss.

He grinned. There was still hope.

BERLIN, GERMAN
OCTOBER 1925

"Willkommen," purred the vigorously fit blonde hostess, dressed in a shockingly abbreviated black tuxedo and bowtie.

Michael's hand, resting lightly at the small of Hannah's back, guided her in, following the hostess to their table near the chic Europahaus's stage. At his urging, this would be her first exploratory visit to the wild and wicked Weimer Germany.

She and Michael could have joined his friends and coworkers that evening, but they both wanted only to be with one another. He painted life with broad strokes. She came most alive when with him... and this worried her. She could lose herself in him, in his sweeping personality.

The cabaret dancer, Anita Berber, shimmied forth from parted blue velvet curtains. She was wearing only a sable coat and holding her pet monkey. As she and the monkey launched into their erotic performance, Hannah and Michael caught up on their divergent lives over the past two months since last being together. With her work requiring her to live in Paris, and his in Berlin, those times they found to be together were intense and visceral.

His gaze roamed over her face with direct intent, as if the way she looked, despite four years of marriage, was still new to him, as if he were comparing her eyes, her lips, her collarbones, to his memory of each.

She told him about the green-fairy parties in Paris. "Every variety of absinthe is offered, Michael. And would you believe the writer Colette carries a flask containing cocaine capsules?"

He capped her hand with his larger one and inclined his head next to hers so he could be heard over the accordion music. She could feel the heat and power emanating from him. "You take risks, living there with that fast crowd."

"And you don't? I worry for your safety, my love. Last week, I read about the violent brawl staged here by the National Socialist German Workers Party."

He laughed. "Beer glasses, chairs, and tables were flying everywhere. I know. I was there."

Fear tightened her throat. "You joke, but the article said Hitler's thugs beat about two hundred Communists. You could have been among them."

He squeezed her hand. "I am not a Communist. I am not a Nationalist." He leaned in to brush her bejeweled ear with his lips and whispered, "I am a man in love. I need you always. I need you in all ways. I need you at my side. I need you beneath me."

She flushed, feeling herself go warm and damp below. She turned her face so that her lips brushed his jaw and teased softly, "Now? Here?"

He emitted a lust-soaked groan. "My body aches almost as much as my soul does for you. And I will move heaven and earth if I have to, Hannah, to find a way for us to live together."

She sighed. "But since General Electric doesn't have a Paris office and Dallas Emporium—"

"Hannah, my days at G.E. are numbered."

Her head canted, her brows furrowed. "What do you mean?"

"Its directors are advocating support of Hitler. I have told them in no uncertain terms that I won't tolerate that kind of philosophy, this suppression of German democracy."

She almost smiled. Michael and his high-handedness. "I love it when you whip out that word 'tolerate.'"

He was watching her carefully. "Siemens, an international company, has asked me to come on as a vice president of financial operations."

"Are you seriously considering it? Do they have a Paris office?" Hope linked with excitement bubbled up in her.

"They have an opening in their Luxembourg office, which is half the distance that Berlin is. That's one step closer to you."

She took a deep breath and slowly expelled it. "What if living together becomes hum-drum? Living together could be deadly in a relationship based on glorious fantasies."

"Whose fantasies, yours or mine, Hannah? Because the only fantasies my imagination entertains is growing old with you."

"You do not think you would eventually find me boring?"

"So, that is what is worrying you? It would take a lifetime to plummet your depths. You are introspective, with so much going on in that intelligent mind of yours, mine is too dazzled to catch up." He squeezed her hand. "You anchor me, and I love you, Hannah Kraft."

The ear shattering *rat-a-tat-tat* ripped like fireworks through the darkened cabaret. The monkey squealed and scampered beneath the sable coat lying on the stage. Anita Berber fled through the blue velvet curtains. Patrons screamed and scurried to the exit.

My God, this was what Berlin was?

Everything seemed to be moving both in slow motion and a rapid blur of noise and action. Michael jumped toward her, as if to use his shoulder as a shield. And in the next instant, she felt his solid body slump against hers. She sobbed out his name, even as she saw the stain on the white damask tablecloth spread slowly into what looked like a scarlet Rorschach inkblot.

THE BARONY, TEXAS
DECEMBER 1925

Bit by bit, Don Alejandro de la Torre y Stuart, Baron of Paladín, had created his empire from a 1767 Spanish land grant and made sure it stayed in the family.

The land grant unfolded from the coastal plains of the Wild Horse Desert in a sea of tall, waving grass and thorny brush, with mottes of trees to break the monotony. First Kerry, then Griffin, Tara, and Drake Paladín, each succeeding their father, had improved upon the original land grant, so that by the time of Alex Paladín's death in 1906, at a still active age of ninety-six, The Barony was one of the largest ranches in the world.

What in the beginning had seemed a fool's escapade into a desert wasteland had evolved into the patina of myth, the aura of legend. "Buy land and never sell," had admonished Heath's grandfather.

Until now, Heath had never fully appreciated his heritage. It had taken an almost year-and-a-half quarantine from Hollywood for him to ease back into the creaking saddle.

Before daybreak, when the temperature had dropped to its coldest, he and his father Drake trotted their mounts out of The Barony's stables with the intent of bringing down a buck, duck, or turkey for the New Year's celebration two days away.

The 35,000 square-foot white stucco and redbrick trimmed *hacienda,* with seventeen bedrooms, nineteen baths, and open patios, faded into the darkened line of mesquites and pecan trees behind him and his father. Ahead, beyond the Nueces River, stretched pasture and brush and the limitless expanse of desert.

The breath eased from Heath's lungs in a long, gentle, almost inaudible sigh. His bunched muscles gradually relaxed against his lengthy bones. He had needed to get as far from Hollywood and its contamination as possible. Short of the Antarctic, West Texas came awfully close.

Twenty-seven barren miles stretched between The Barony's gates and its main house. Not the most ardent fan would brave both that desert distance and the guards posted from the loyal *familias* of *Paladíneños*. Only Darcy's occasional phone calls kept Heath posted on Double Take's bottom line—and it, thank God, was in the black.

He and his father rode through a couple of sections of back acreage, and Heath noted here and there the cow patties. Not good.

"Overgrazing," Drake muttered, catching the targets of his son's gaze. "I'll have to get with Diego, formulate some kind of plan."

They tied off their horses on a huisache tree downwind from a tank. In the spring, the huisache's delicate yellow blossoms cascaded in an eye-dazzlingly fountain of color, but that crisp morning, its limbs were nearly denuded.

Stealthily, he and his father crept up to the south bank of the tank, bellied up through the yellowed, dry grass to lie side by side on the tank's berm, levering their rifles into position to await the dawn and the deer.

While they waited for sunrise, he and his father spoke in hushed voices. "Your mom and I had hoped Hannah might make it for Thanksgiving or Christmas this year."

He peered through his gunsight. "Yeah, the assassination headlines made for gruesome reading." He loved the cool, crisp, clean smell of a Southwest Texas autumn. "Byron told me the FBI is pointing fingers at the directors of General Electric of Germany."

Against the rosy sky, Drake's jaw, already shadowed by a morning without benefit of razor, tightened. "I got other ideas."

"Yeah? Like what?" The intense cold was numbing his fingers and toes, and his nose was beginning to run. Not the stuff movie heroes were made of.

"Like the Clarendon's." His father's breath frosted with each word. "The old man retired from the Supreme Court but was just recently appointed Secretary of State by President Coolidge."

Tales of the Clarendons' far-reaching, extracting vengeance were folklore in the annals of Paladín history. Tantamount to that of Heath's grandfather's archenemy, Liam Obregon. But his grandfather had bested the Obregons by absorbing their offspring via marriage, Heath's mother being one of them. He felt the Paladíns could, with time, quite ably neutralize whatever threat the Clarendons presented.

"Worse," his father muttered, "Roger Clarendon is the most sought-after attorney in America." He spat a wad of tobacco juice into the frost-glistening grass. "Worshipped like some goddamn idol. When he's so pussyfootin', he has to wear a concealed gun."

A rustle, almost indistinct, warned Heath. He knew deer were cautious about approaching a water hole and that it could take nearly thirty minutes or more for them to close that last thirty yards.

Gently, he eased back the Winchester's cock. "I never did feel that Michael Kraft was the right man for Cousin Hannah. Too possessive. And she is too free-spirited."

"She was. Don't know what she's like now. Not after losing him. I know David is doing everything he can to persuade his daughter to come home, short of firing her." His father laid his stubbled cheek alongside the stock. "Claire is threatening to set sail for France."

Cautiously, five graceful doe and two fawn crept from the shredded umbrella of nearly bare mesquites and cottonwoods and edged closer to the waterline. He held his fire. The doe and fawns were merely decoys, sent ahead by the buck.

Soon a spike came into view. Still, Heath held his fire. Then, the magnificent buck appeared, all quintessential male.

In the fitful morning light, Heath lowered his gaze from its giant rack and sighted in on its chest. For some reason, he hated bringing down the stag. He identified with it—had at one time felt himself dead in the sights of every female.

11

The rhythmic dip and splash of Pierce's oar soothed the soul… or so he hoped.

The banks of the Rio Grande in spring were an explosion of color. Chinese tamarisk, catclaw, and manzanita blossomed forth in a profusion of pinks, purples, and whites. Flooding, due to mountain snowmelt, was often a problem, and where Pierce put in the canoe, the water ran fast.

Drawing in his paddle, he stepped amidst giant cane and tugged his canoe onto the muddy bank. From her stern seat, Aubrey smiled drowsily up at him. The slender fingers of one hand swished lazily in the rushing current. "So, it is torture time, *eh bien?*"

He scooped her frail body up in his arms. It had always been slight, but her occasional indulgences in opium were reducing her to a delicate wraith of humanity. "Hey, the wealthy pay big bucks for such a luxurious spa."

"Bah." Her thin arms draped submissively over his shoulders.

It had been a little over a year since he first discovered her in the opium den, and since then the fear she still might die, as corrosive as battery acid, ate at him constantly. The weaning process was taking longer than he anticipated.

Veronica Lampier did eventually die, though not by his own hand. When the Tong realized she had become a liability, they killed her. Her leech-covered body had been discovered floating amid cattails in Rio Grande backwater, a wreath of fingerprint-sized hemorrhages encircling her neck.

Two more awaited Judgement Day, and he would take care of the Clarendons just as efficiently when the right time presented itself. No one hurt him or what was his.

Nudging aside the cane stalks, he hobbled along a rutted path leading to the hot springs, twenty-five yards beyond the wall of cane. For a millennium, the Folsom Man, the *conquistadores,* the Apache and Comanche had been using the thermal hot springs for therapeutic baths. Four sandy basins, with water ranging from hot to cold, stair stepped in rocky ledges. Gingerly, he placed her on one that overlooked a steaming pool.

She sighed and settled back onto her forearms, tilting her face up to the warming sunlight. "If I swear this was the last time…."

"Then what happens?" He had discovered she was getting morphine from the hospital. He shucked his khaki pants and stripped out of his work shirt and undershirt. Lastly, off came his socks and shoes. He left the metal prosthesis on. Nude, he knelt alongside her.

She did not move but peered languidly at him from beneath the weight of her thick lashes. "Then you will talk to me." She tapped her fingers on her chest. "From here, *mon amour.*"

The sandstone heated his flesh, now chilled. He began removing her clothing. "All right, from my heart. You already know my passion is flying."

"Mai oui," she murmured, almost petulantly.

He drew her slender torso against his in order to slip the broderie anglais blouse off her. "I talked with the commanding officer at Biggs Field." She lifted her hips for him to slide down her black jersey skirt. She made no resistance when he drew off the sidelacer that flattened her already small breasts.

He rocked back on his good heel, talking quietly while he covertly perused her stylishly boyish beauty. Their desire for one another bonded them, if nothing else. Despite his disfigurement, she appeared to revel in their lovemaking.

Yet, she wanted children and he…. How could they bring a child into a marriage that had so little else going for it? His refusal was always couched with flippancy.

"I think I may be able to get clearance to use the Biggs Field hangar for maintenance and refueling once I get Paladín Airways registered with the State." He continued with the emotional cover of small talk.

Small talk, maybe, but important to him nonetheless. Not only was Fort Bliss home to the largest horse cavalry force in the nation, but its Biggs Airfield possessed a well-known landmark—an enormous airship hangar. People motored out just to watch a Zepplin land.

"I'll need more space than my tiny hangar can provide—at least until I can afford to expand operations."

She reached out, her fingers tracing the line of hair arrowing down the washboard of his stomach. Its muscles jerked in response. "What you need now is to remove your brace before we go into the pool, yes?"

He eyed her steadily. "Yes."

"Let me do it for you."

"No."

"Why not, Pierce? I was there when they cut off your foot. The time has come. Why not tell me now what you think happened? If we cannot share our truth, then…." She made one of those Gallic gestures that clearly imparted whatever was needed—which is just what she had always seemed skilled at doing.

"Why not?" He managed to smile. "I'll tell you why not. Because I am willing to listen to more lies than cross ties on a railroad. Because it doesn't matter if you did know that my foot would be cut off needlessly. You could cut away at me, piece by piece, and it wouldn't matter because you already have my heart."

At that, she buried her face in her hands and wept silent, shoulder-shaking sobs.

And he could only wonder, could their love for one another be that dark?

———————————

ROSWELL, NEW MEXICO
JUNE 1926

"My mom brought home from the San Patricio Public Library a copy of War of the Worlds," Byron told his and Edna's dinner guest, Robert Goddard. "After I read that, I was fixated on space."

Following dinner, they had retired to the parlor to discuss theories about rocket fuel mixtures, high-pressure piston pumps, and fuel-curtain cooling, with Edna caught up in the concepts of physics, energy, and space.

Although Byron was reticent to discuss his ideas, he felt completely at ease sharing his dreams with those who shared the same interest and those whom he could trust. Professor Goddard was one of those he immediately trusted.

A small, thin man with fly-away hair, Goddard had a direct gaze that gave no quarter. On one of Byron's first encounters with Goddard, the man had directed that gaze at Byron's sockless feet, shod in Chuck Taylor All Stars Converse shoes. "Jesus Christ Almighty, can't you afford a pair of socks, son?"

With his chair at Clark University, the very college that had turned down Byron, Goddard had been facing harsh criticism from media and other scientists.

"To suggest that a rocket could be made powerful enough to escape Earth and travel into space is, indeed, the height of either fiction or lunacy," claimed an article in Popular Science. The New York Times scoffed, with the front-page headline "Believes Rocket Could Reach Moon."

"I want to scale up the experiments, but both Clark and the government's funding won't back me." Goddard shook his head. "And the Smithsonian, the

Aero Club of America, and the National Geographic have turned down my solicitations, as well. Worse, I am finding it increasingly difficult to conduct my research without unwanted distractions. If I moved my operations to Roswell, would you be willing to let me work with you?"

"I don't know how safe your work would be here," Edna interjected in a quiet voice. She didn't look at Goddard but devoted inordinate attention to stroking the grizzled fur of the German shepherd stretched beside her rocking chair.

Like a bird, Goddard tilted his head and eyed her. "Why?"

She glanced at Byron.

He cleared his throat. "I have been working on a way to stabilize a rocket by using gyroscopes to control motion. Just last week, I set off a fuel-injected rocket that rose forty-one feet."

"Why... why, that's astounding!" Goddard sputtered.

"And then it did a nosedive. The cone was a twisted piece of metal, but the fuel tank was intact—at least enough to detect sand in it. There have been other such incidences."

"You suspect sabotage?"

Byron nodded at the German shepherd. "That's why I brought Fritz here home. Old Hector Velasquez, our nearest neighbor, has a ranch a couple of miles out on Lee Highway. But as far out of town as we live... well, what happens if sabotage of machinery turns to sabotage of human life?"

He made the statement matter-of-factly, but he was worried sick, even nauseous at times, mostly about Edna's safety, for those times his tests took him out onto the range and away from her.

Edna grinned, showing the gap between her front teeth. "At that point, I trot out my double-barreled shotgun."

God, how he loved that skinny-minny!

———————

THE BARONY, TEXAS
JULY 1926

Frederick Woodward Bonaventure and his young wife had returned. Their first visit had been more than a year ago, just before New Year's, to discuss horse breeding.

Heath had been wanting to breed a thoroughbred, a major stakes winner. Granted, it was an insane idea. The horses foaled at The Barony were bred for cow country. They were primarily quarter horses known for their lightning speed at short distances. The vast majority of major stakes-winners were bred and foaled in Kentucky.

But, if anyone could pull off a futurity winner from cattle country, the snowy-haired Bonaventure could. The first effort at breeding last spring had failed. So, the Bonaventures were back again.

The retired *Los Angeles Clarion* newspaper mogul was also famed as a breeder of quarter horses and had three racing stables throughout the southwest.

He was a gentleman of old-world charm, a still vibrant man of an era that was rapidly passing—and his much younger wife, Emelda, bridged both the old and new world.

Petite, she had the wiry stamina of a jockey and was renowned in her own right as a horse trainer. Her delicate features were those of a Caravaggio Madonna—brown eyes so deep one could drown in them, with a mind just as deep. Her waist-length, rich chocolate-brown hair was thick and lustrous with a life of its own. She possessed full lips untempered by restraint of duty or discipline.

After Hollywood, if he could do nothing else, he could feel a woman's interest. He had sensed her interest last year, and that made him uneasy. But he wanted a stakes-winning foal and figured over a couple of days, little could go wrong.

Throngs of women had besieged him. Many had made it into his bed, but none had made him feel they had any interest in him other than his image. Photoplay had written, "Heath Paladín's expressive smile is the conduit of his charismatic film presence. It communicates to audiences at once warm ami-ability and, more subtly, imperious self-assurance.”

Strange, his mother could peg a piker a mile away, but she seemed obliv-ious to the signals the twenty-three-year-old Emelda was emitting. Though Emelda barely directed her attention at him, he could feel her eyes on him, smell her heat when, passing him, she touched his arm in a seemingly care-less manner.

Hell, he wanted her, as well. While learning to take over The Barony’s reins from his father the past two years, he had been living the life of a monk at The Barony. Well, not entirely. Sure, there had been a few liaisons over that time. Women who thought they were in love with him, when they didn’t even have a clue about what made him tick.

One had been an influential interior decorator his Uncle Griffin had rec-ommended to his mother. In three months, the interior decorator had trans-formed the dark wood, heavily masculine *hacienda* into light, intimate spaces featuring a fiesta of Mexican colors. Apparently, he had transformed this in-dependent and bright interior decorator into a slavish stalker. Not good.

Another had been the sister of The Barony’s veterinarian. The age of Heath’s mother and a divorcee, she had found reason to accompany her brother on his professional visits and had made herself available to Heath. They were both lonely in their own way and had found quick comfort in each other’s arms until she had given into her ex-husband’s unrelenting pleas to reunite.

Emelda knew what made him tick. She possessed the unerring instincts of a rutting animal and surely sensed he was attracted to her heat. However, he was not foolish enough to bed a married woman.

They both leaned on the stall gate. She was wearing a riding outfit that accentuated her petite curves. Manure and musty hay that Manny the stable boy had been earlier cleaning out of a stall tanged their nostrils.

A horse fly buzzed around them, and Heath flicked it away absently. “The new mare is out of Sierra Sage, and the father on the top side is Gold Strike.”

Emelda nodded. "When she's lifting her tail and winking her vulva, about the third day, it'll be the best time to put her and the stallion together."

Her reference to the mating process would have been a completely natural matter-of-fact statement for a horse breeder, except he detected in her sidewise glance a gleam that was an overt provocation. Silently, he groaned. Another bullet to dodge.

"Mister Frederick prefers the natural breeding rather than hand breeding," she continued. "It works better for us... and, of course, better for the horses."

In the shadowed stable, he peered down at her. "Why do you address him—your husband—as Mister Frederick?"

Without turning her head, she peered up at him from the corner of her eyes. "I address him as such out of respect for him. But as for being my husband... we've never consummated our marriage. Unlike our stallion, Mister Frederick is too old for mounting behavior."

He stared hard at her. He couldn't be wrong. His instincts about women were just as sharp as hers about men. She was no virgin. He'd bet his film royalties on it.

As if she had read his mind, she gave him a grim smile. "At twelve, I was selling my body on the streets of Juarez. Mister Frederick spotted me and... well, fell in love with me at first sight."

Fleeting compassion diluted the strong warning signals assailing him. "And you fell in love with his money?" He didn't bother to hide his contempt. It helped dampen his desire for her.

She flicked away long strands of hair caressing her neck. "Life breaks every one of us, and some of us are stronger at the cracked spots, Heath." She turned and, standing on tiptoe, slid her arms up over his shoulders, her small hands cupping his neck. "And your soul is as cracked as mine."

"It may be cracked, but it's not shattered." He reached up to unlock her clasped fingers and froze at the sound from the stable doorway a few yards away, catty-corner from the stall.

What happened next seemed but a blur. At one moment, a man's shadow stood in the blinding shaft of sunlight. In the next moment, Bonaventure grabbed for Manny's pitchfork, propped next to the flung-wide stable doors. He charged forward and sunlight glinted off steel prongs that had Heath as their target.

12

The top floor of the stately, six-story Nueces County courthouse had two death cells in its jail, but the gallows had never been used. Three years before, Texas ordered executions to be carried out by means of the electric chair.

Apparently, Heath Paladín was to be its next victim. Or scapegoat, as Mariana Cordova preferred to designate it. Naturally, the judge was not allowing bail on the second-degree murder charge.

Ironically, the courthouse, symbol of law and justice in that wild and woolly coastal town, towered over the very spot where pirates once bivouacked.

How farfetched it was once again to be sitting across a table, this one an aluminum one bolted to the floor, from a prisoner for whom she held such deep affection. First Dan and now Heath.

Except what she felt for her cousin Heath also entailed, and had always entailed, something else, something far greater—greater even than the urgency of desire. It was a soul-deep tether that ping-ponged through every cell of her body. The daring curve of his smile made her tremble in her skin. It felt as if her unrequited love for him was incinerating her insides, and so she had always buried herself in her work.

At that moment, a frisson of fear for Heath rippled up her spine. From behind rimless eyeglasses, she focused what she hoped was an even-keeled gaze. She had badgered him to let her represent him even though she was inexperienced.

They both knew he didn't stand a chance in the courtroom, so, of course, he would concede to her importuning to represent him as his counsel.

Roger Clarendon, of course, had the county prosecutor in his pocket. Clarendon was the guiding force behind Herbert Godley. A clean-cut, urbane man with Charles Lindbergh's good looks, Godley represented all that was noble and honorable about the democratic legal process.

She represented a mere female of Mexican-American lineage—and her Banker's Special Colt was no match for their semi-automatics. True, she thought, she could bring out all her guns, but her experience in no way matched that of the trial's prosecutor's.

What she did have going for her was that Texas had voted in a general election the nation's first female governor—Ma Ferguson. If Ma could stand off against a barrage of male candidates, surely, she could find a way to stand off against the fusillades of Roger and Brighton Clarendon. But the odds didn't look promising.

"In good conscience, I should advise you, Heath, to opt for the plea bargain." Fidgeting, she nudged her slipping glasses back upon the bridge of her sweat-slicked nose. She focused her gaze past his face, on one of the brown flying cockroaches climbing the concrete wall. "The State is offering life imprisonment. The offer is better than hanging if you're found guilty."

"But I'm not guilty!" He ran his hands through slightly wavy black hair that had grown past his nape since his incarceration. This was the first time she had been allowed to see him. As his criminal defense attorney, this two-week delay in allowing her visitation with her client was technically illegal. But then, nothing was legal in the frontier town of Corpus Christi.

"Bonaventure was blind with fury," Heath told her, although she had already heard the gist of the mud from Uncle Drake. "There was no reasoning with him. I was wrestling with him for the pitchfork, when Emelda stepped between us. I turned to fling her out of the way, and…" —his jaw muscles visibly tensed— "… Bonaventure gutted her."

"It's his word against yours," she reminded him gently. "And you are the one charged with the murder. Yours are the bloody fingerprints, not Bonaventure's."

Bonaventure was claiming he had tried to grapple the pitchfork away from an enraged Heath after his virtuous wife had rejected the hot-blooded lover's advances.

"That's because I was the one who yanked the pitchfork out of her."

So far, Mariana and Betty Chan, who, thank God, had stepped in to help with the legwork, had scoured up nothing in the way of damaging information regarding Bonaventure. He was squeaky clean.

Mariana's mouth twisted. "Remember, he's one of the nation's biggest philanthropists—and he owns the *Los Angeles Clarion*. And, I must tell you, newspapers across America are having a hay day with the 'Legendary Lover's Peccadillo.' That's only one of the multitude of headlines covering this fiasco."

A groan of exasperation escaped him. "I never bedded her, Mariana. You have to believe me."

Bittersweet was the powerful attraction she experienced when with Heath. Being able to see him, to touch him, and still being off limits as her cousin.

She reached across and squeezed his cuffed hands, feeling the electrical current that jolted clear through to her heart. She pressed into his palm a harmonica.

His mobile lips that buckled her knees and conveyed so much on screen to adoring female fans fought for a grin. "Gee whiz, thanks a lot, Mariana."

"It may not be a file or a chisel, but I will get you out." Or die trying.

JUAREZ, MEXICO
DECEMBER 1926

"After midnight, even the rats desert Juarez," Aubrey told Mariana.

Aubrey and Pierce sat opposite her at the popular and exclusive restaurant, nightclub, and casino. Known as Hideaway Hacienda, it was the mansion of a former governor of the State of Chihuahua.

Riotous music, spicy cuisine, and high-proof cocktails were served up like *hors d'oeuvres* at the Hideaway. It was jammed with a large number of Americans who crossed the border from El Paso to circumvent prohibition, dance the Charleston, and gamble. An ample portion of Juarez's tourist trade also came from soldiers at Fort Bliss—that trade mostly plied at the numerous bordellos.

Because of the complicity of corrupt police, government officials, and local elites, El Paso's twin city had become unsafe after the bewitching hour. But that was precisely when the jockey-cum-hooch runner had agreed to meet with the three.

"Do you truly think this Ramirez will have anything on Bonaventure?"

Pierce looked Mariana in the eye. "If there is anything to be had, yes." It was Pierce who had tracked down and arranged the meeting with the jockey. The Paladíns might have their familial skirmishes, but they united against aggression by the outside world. "Persuading Ramirez to part with any information he might have could be more difficult. If he is caught turning stoolie, he'll end up spilling his guts in more ways than one."

At seventeen minutes after midnight, Florio Ramirez appeared at their table. He was small and wiry with large, intelligent brown eyes and a magnificent mustache. Pierce made the introductions.

"Con mucho gusto," he told Aubrey and Mariana, sweeping off his black fedora with a gallant flourish but slid into the vacant seat next to Mariana.

Mariana felt as if she were sitting in a council of the League of Nations with a neutral country's flag hoisted on their table. Tension flushed the Mexican's narrow face and waxed those of her good-looking cousin and his beautiful French wife. But Mariana didn't have the patience for the time-consuming deliberations that accompanied international mediations and deliberations. Not with Heath facing a potential death sentence.

"I hear you race both horses and cars, *Señor* Ramirez." Having grown up with a multi-lingual father, she navigated the language only slightly better than Pierce, who had picked up the lingo from The Barony's *Paladíneños*.

If Florio was impressed by her knowledge of Spanish, he gave no indication. "My Model T can out race even the best of thoroughbreds, especially on the long stretch of desert between here and San Antonio," he replied in impressive English. "When I run out of gasoline, a mason jar of 190 proof hooch will get her engine purring again."

Florio was a likeable guy in bowtie and tails but shod in spectator shoes. She found herself smiling. "I'm more interested in the horses than the hooch, Florio. I understand you race Mister Bonaventure's horses at the Juarez Race Track."

Pierce had briefed her about Florio. He had a large family to support. Due to the lover's-triangle murder scandal, his jockey's income had fallen off because Bonaventure was laying low—probably following a dictate of Roger Clarendon's to do so until the trial was concluded.

Uncle Drake and Aunt Angel were offering a very generous donation that would greatly enhance the lifestyle of Florio Ramirez and his family in exchange for concrete information he could provide.

The short man shrugged narrow shoulders and replied affably. *"Claro, que si."*

"And you knew Missus Bonaventure, as well," Pierce prodded. "Emelda Bonaventure."

His brown eyes shuttered over like horse blinders. *"Si."*

Time was wasting with the pleasantries. Grateful for the loud music, she leaned closer to him, her voice pitched even lower. "Are you aware of any incidences of Missus Bonaventure's... indiscretions?"

Florio's eyes slowly swept the dining room before returning to focus on her. *"Si,* with certain others. Even with myself, she tried this... this come-on. But I knew better. My job—*tal vez*, my life—would be in...." His small brown hands groped for the right word in English.

"In jeopardy?" she supplied.

He nodded twice. Perspiration now beaded his forehead.

"Have there ever been lives taken?" Aubrey asked quietly of the slight man.

From the little Pierce had shared with Mariana about Aubrey's role as a courier and spy for French intelligence during the Great War, the slender, fragile-looking Frenchwoman was not to be underestimated.

Florio hesitated. "Not by *el patron*. Not directly. You understand, in this part of Tejas—so far from the rest of the world—deaths can be arranged. No questions asked. Not like The Barony—with the country's, the world's eyes even, always on it. Arranging things like... a body disappearing... might be *un poco* difficult for The Barony, *sí?* Not so out here."

Mariana glanced at Pierce. They were both thinking the same thing. Knowing Uncle Drake, that possibility—the disappearance of both of the Bonaventures—had undoubtedly been a viable option that fatal afternoon four months ago.

The Barony, with its lawless remoteness was an empire unto itself. And, knowing Heath like she did, Mariana had a good idea that he had probably been the one to insist calling the authorities. He wouldn't cower before the Devil or God.

"The offer we discussed" —Pierce nodded at Florio— "stands if you can deliver proof of the Bonaventures'... crimes. Such as murder."

There. The word was out in the open.

Florio nodded again. "Give me three days, *señor.*"

But, on the second day following the midnight meeting at Hideaway Hacienda, the El Paso Post reported a grisly find—a severed human head jammed on the spire of the finish-line pole at the Juarez Racetrack.

EL PASO, TEXAS
JUNE 1927

The commercial flight was a first for Paladín Aviation. The trimotor plane was made of duralumin, light as aluminum but twice as strong. It had twelve seats, a cabin high enough for a passenger to walk down the aisle without stooping, and room for a nurse, or stewardess, to administer to ill passengers.

But Mariana was its first and only passenger on Paladín Aviation's history, making flight between Houston and El Paso. She sat in the cockpit next to Pierce in the pilot's seat. His striking profile evidenced his excitement of finally fulfilling his dream.

"Aubrey was a Nervous Nelly about my making this first flight," he told Mariana. All the while his gaze swept back and forth across a panel of confusing gauges. "And there was no way I could convince her to fill the co-pilot's seat."

Mariana was nervous herself. Thermals jounced and bounced the aircraft over a terrain that looked like wadded up parchment paper. "Well," she managed to say calmly, "I figured if you made it from El Paso to Houston, then I was safe enough on the return flight."

Time was of the essence. Heath's trial was set for November first, the Day of the Dead. Her status as defense attorney would be just as dead, considering her investigative work had found little.

Eagle-eyed Betty had run a reporting request through R. G. Dunn & Company, and it gave Frederick Woodward Bonaventure's financial status high ratings. Nothing suspicious there.

His politics were of the extreme right. Even though he had recently retired as editor-in-chief, his *Los Angeles Clarion* continued to carry sensationalist articles and caricatures for overt Nazi propaganda purposes and hailed the charismatic firebrand Adolph Hitler as a rescuer of Germany's downtrodden.

So, it was back to El Paso she was headed for further investigative purposes. More specifically, back to Juarez—to visit the widow of Florio Ramirez. Pierce insisted on accompanying her.

The Ramirez home, in a nicer section of Juarez, had been torched soon after Florio's decapitated head had been found. Rosa Ramirez and her three children had been away at Mass. Then, they too had vanished. Mariana feared she and Pierce had reached a dead-end.

Neighbors' lips were stitched closed about the incident. They pretended to misunderstand Mariana's Spanish or pretended ignorance as to where the family had fled.

On the third day of door-to-door canvassing, Mariana and Pierce found a lead. A playmate of one of the Ramirez's children unwittingly divulged the widow and her children had decamped to Juarez's notorious *barrio*.

The *barrio* was bad enough by daylight. Mariana could only imagine what it was like after dark. Houses—constructed haphazardly of tin, cardboard, and dilapidated adobe bricks—were propped against each other for support. Sewage spilled from open pipes onto the dirt streets. Rats almost as big as cats scurried through the debris of trash littering grassless yards.

Ramirez's widow and children had taken refuge in a single-room hovel with a dirt floor. Looking far older than her thirty-two years, the widow stood in the doorway. A flimsy pine tabletop serving as its door was hinged only to the top of the doorframe. She cradled a wailing infant in one arm. Two drooling, dirty, and nearly naked toddlers, no more than a couple of years apart, clung to her long, patterned skirt.

At Mariana's appeal for information, the woman shook her head, and her long braids flopped against her bony chest. "I do not know anything about my husband's death." Fear etched deep lines in her swarthy face.

She tried to shut the door, but Pierce forestalled her by quickly thrusting out five hundred-dollar bills. She stared open-mouthed at the proffered money.

"It will help buy a new life for you and your children," Mariana told her. It was virtually the same assurance Mariana had given Florio Ramirez—and look where that had gotten him. A huge lump of guilt backed up in her throat.

For a long moment, Rosa Ramirez stared hungrily at the money. Then she shifted her agonized gaze up to that of Mariana's. "All the money in the world," she said in terror-laced Spanish, "cannot protect us!"

She shoved the door closed and would not respond again despite all Mariana's offers and reassurances of safety—and, giving up at last, Mariana could not blame her.

Leaving the *barrio,* she had the feeling of hostile eyes watching from hidden places. The fine hair at her nape prickled. Both she and a dejected Pierce, limping beside her, offered easy targets. Tucked under her arm was her calf-skin clutch purse, but she doubted she would be able to whip out her Banker's Special in time.

"Well, that was my last resort," Pierce grumbled. "I haven't been able to turn up anything else. But, by God, I'll keep trying."

"You have to, or else Heath will swing."

And, impacted by the actual realization—that she had failed as a defense lawyer, that she had failed Heath, that she might never see him on God's green earth, might never experience his kiss or his embrace—she whirled toward a startled Pierce and the shelter of his broad chest to weep copious, snotty tears.

EL PASO
DECEMBER 1927

As the Nueces County jail allowed a prisoner only one visitor at a time, Preston left Mariana babysitting the gum-popping Darla outside the Visitation Room and took a seat at the aluminum table across from his cousin Heath.

If his cousin had returned from the war with hollow cheeks, everything about him looked hollow now. His cheeks, his eyes, his hopes. Mariana had wrangled a postponement of the trial, but even on the trip up from Houston, she had admitted that the prospects of winning Heath's case were about as good as coming up all horseshoes at one of Galveston's underground slot machines, which the Mafia made sure rarely happened.

But, of course, hope springs eternal, and that was what Preston was doing there that frigid Christmas Day—offering hope, though it be false hope, to his cousin.

Cuffed hands knotted together atop the table, Heath smiled grimly. "Well, well, Preston, you aren't known exactly for a gadabout, so your visit is a surprise. A pleasant and most welcome surprise."

He detected the slightest ease in the tension knotting the set of Heath's wide shoulders. "Every occasionally, I pop out of my hole like a prairie dog." Keeping his tone light, he forced a grin. "I figure if I managed to break out of the Karlsruhe prison, I could break you out of here, and we could make a run for the Mexican border."

Heath's returning grin was more of a grimace. "I know you too well, cuz. What has it been—a decade since the war's end? And since then, the few times we have slugged back drinks together, you have sworn straight-out never to leave the states. Now relieve me of my boredom. Tell me what you're doing. And about this girl in your life. Darla, I think Mariana said was her name."

He shrugged. "Things are still status quo. The garage business is making me money. And Darla is keeping me company."

Heath raised a brow. "Do you love her? Do you plan on marrying her?"

"No, to both questions. Absolutely not. She's a friend I hold dear, but that's all." Regrettably, he knew she felt something stronger for him. "Now, my turn. Do you love Mariana? Because she loves you."

Heath groaned, and his back slumped. "Good God, Preston." He eyed him directly now. "I'm already facing execution for a murder charge. Do I want to face charges for having sex with my cousin, as well?"

Interesting, Preston thought. Heath had not denied that he might love Mariana. In fact, his reply indicated he might also have lustful fantasies centered around her during all those hours he must spend doing nothing but waiting in his jail cell. "Well, whether you love her or lust after her or both, she's waiting below to see you next."

Heath's elated expression confirmed Preston's suspicion.

13

If ever there was an era for a self-made man to realize the American Dream, it was this one. Anything was possible if one had the passion and drive to fulfill his vision for the future.

And Houston was the place for an entrepreneur to do it. These days, Houston was growing by leaps and bounds due to its construction and oil boom, and with its railroads and port, it had become a major transportation hub. Wooden derricks filled the prairies around Houston, refineries were springing up along the Houston Ship Channel to feed the nation's insatiable appetite for gasoline and oil, and fortunes were made and lost in real estate speculation.

Bellying up to oil tycoon Pappy McBride's gambling table in the suite he kept at his plush and prestigious Cattleman's Hotel, Preston figured he was closing in on the next step to his own dream—the acquisition of a prime piece of Texas real estate. The ultra-swank Cattleman's Hotel itself was his target.

The Italian renaissance style edifice featured brass and beveled glass front doors and a marbled lobby with a sweeping staircase flowing to the exquisite mezzanine above. Best of all, the hotel was located across the street from the huge 25,000-seat Sam Houston Hall being planned for the Democratic 1928 convention, the first nominating convention held in a Southern city since 1860.

Once he had the hotel in his coffers and got his affairs in order, he meant to pay Heath another visit. If top-dollar real estate could be won or lost in a game of poker with good ol' boys, then surely a human being's life could be plucked from the jaws of death… somehow, some way. Preston reckoned he had been doing a piss-poor job of keeping in contact with the family, but then, some distance assured some privacy and independence.

"Okay, boys, the Red Cross drive is running a little behind." Pappy, the heavyset, congenial oilman, hosted a weekly high-stakes poker game in suite 8F, and usually the first hand went to some charity. He popped into his mouth a handful of pecans gathered from the tree below on Bagby Street, then garbled, "All the money we bet here on the first hand goes to the Red Cross, and it costs $5,000 to get in."

Recalling the Rouge Croix food boxes that had filled his concave belly at the German prison camp, Preston figured he owed the organization that much and forked over the five grand in a check, along with the other five players.

Besides Pappy, he knew two others—Benny Friedman, a dapper man with a pencil-thin mustache who owned a popular restaurant and Jesse Jones, a tall, strapping man who possessed a chain of lumberyards and was expanding into the newspaper business.

Capitalizing on creative credit, Preston planned on expanding as well. Tonight would be his foray into hotel acquisitions.

Glenfiddich was poured. Havanas were lit. The first hand went quickly, with jokes circulating around the table. Benny took the first round, with none of the players begrudging their loss to the charity.

Then the players settled into deep concentration. The first couple of rotations, Preston studied his opponents. Jessie took an inordinate amount of time, eyeing each of the other players, and Preston made it a point to steer well clear of him.

If the Paladín cousins didn't know anything else, they knew cows and poker. They had learned from the *Paladíneños'* gambling games like Cut-Throat Poker, Mexican Sweat, and the shill game, Three Card Monte. Seven-card stud had to be a breeze.

Also, from the *Paladíneños,* he had learned how to bluff—the latter of which he hoped to do exceedingly well tonight.

He won a few hands and lost a few, permitting his loot taken little by little to surpass those of the other four as the pots grew larger and the drinking grew heavier. Only Pappy's stack of chips was higher.

When smoke wreathed the suite and Glenfiddich had refilled the tumblers several times over, despite prohibition, four had dropped out of the hand. Preston eyed his cards—a pair of fours and a random six, five, and three. He raised the stakes. "My three One-Stop Stations and fifty grand," he told Pappy, "against your Cattleman Hotel."

The cigar clamped between Pappy's teeth bobbled with the mirth that also shook his ample belly. "You meant fifty million, didn't you, Slim?"

"Nope." If he had to pay up, it meant not paying his rent, among other things. That was life in oil-rich Texas—wealthy one day, busted the next, then back in the saddle again.

Pappy took the cigar from his mouth. "Slim, this half-ass raise of yours," he drawled, "your piddling service stations and fifty grand against my hotel—well, I'd be down-right embarrassed if I were you."

"Are you a gambler, or aren't you?"

"Tell you what. I'll pit my Lone Star Savings and Loan against your raise." Pappy jammed the cigar back in his mouth.

Preston shrugged fearlessly. "I'm in, Pappy."

But it would be his hide if he lost Darla's half interest in the One-Stops. She would sure as shit shoot him. He ought to shoot her. Too often, he had caught her hand in the till, as it were, withdrawing funds from One-Stop Stations' account that far exceeded her fifty-percent share. Of course, she hadn't been the same since her old man committed suicide, blowing out his brains over a shower curtain. He felt badly for the old man. He had liked Ridley when he was in his saner moments.

He really wanted the Cattleman Hotel, but the bank, located in the declining Second Ward where Mariana practiced law, was better than nothing—if he could pull off this bluff. If not, then it was back to pumping gas. Win or lose, the sky-high adrenaline surging through him was what life was all about. He might be a risk taker, but his was an all-or-nothing gamble and he made sure he drank little that night. A clear head, steady hand, and impassive expression was what he was striving for.

The last card was dealt face down. Preston's abrupt raise had set Pappy thinking. Preston sweated that Pappy would make the call. Preston nudged him a little. "For a mere hundred dollar chip, you can choose either one of my hole cards, and I'll show it to you."

The hefty man considered it for a little longer, then tossed Preston the $100 chip and chose a card.

Preston flipped over the three.

After another long pause, Pappy eventually deduced that Preston would only make such an offer if both his hole-cards were treys, therefore giving him a full house, treys over fours. He reluctantly folded.

Sweaty relief seeped, it seemed, from every pore in Preston. He had scored big time. Some of the players began slapping Preston on the back. Others were commiserating with Pappy. The old man stuck out a beefy palm to shake Preston's hand. "You got pluck, son. Good luck."

Preston knew he would need it. He now found himself owning a second-rate savings and loan and facing the unpleasant task of telling Darla Ridley *adios*.

———————

GALVESTON, TEXAS
FEBRUARY 1928

If anyone could chew gum and smoke at the same time, it would be Darla. Her Mary Jane bobbing on one foot to the western swing fiddle music wildly popular in honky-tonks, she perched on a stool at the bar of The Grotto, a speakeasy owned by the rum-running gangster, Dutch Quinn. Her embroidered silk stockings snaked around her ankles and up her gams to her bare, powdered knees. A spangled headband adorned her platinum blond hair.

The Republic of Galveston Island, a whimsical moniker, had spawned a tourist industry dealing in illegal businesses to offset Galveston's decline as a commercial and shipping center following the devastating hurricane of 1900.

The island called itself the "free State" because it considered itself above prohibition and other repressive mores and laws of the rest of the country. Only a little more than an hour's drive from Houston, it had emerged as a popular resort town, attracting celebrities to dance to Guy Lombardo's Royal Canadians band.

However, gambling, illegal liquor, prostitution, and other vices were a major part of its tourism. A rum row of booze-laden ships from Cuba, Jamaica, and the Bahamas anchored thirty-five miles beyond the coastline, where smaller boats like Dutch's transferred the goods and freighted them to shore.

Preston slid onto the stool next to Darla. "I'll have a South Side." It was five in the afternoon and few patrons graced the dive. He turned to Darla. "We have to talk."

She purred a smoky exhalation. "How did you find me?"

"Your dance tickets, your bar bills." He took a sip of the gin. "I want to sell out my portion of the One-Stops."

He would need all the money he could get for his step up into Houstonian high society—to begin with, restoring the Lone Star Savings and Loan to its former dignity. His father's architectural firm would have a list of statewide, suitable construction crews. But working with his father was a step of last resort.

Instantly, Darla's gum-smacking and foot-bobbing ceased. She leaned close to him. "Preston," her vodka-husky voice whispered, "there's no way I could buy you out. I'm dangerously close enough as it is to trading in my Mary Janes for cement shoes."

So, she was up to her pretty chin in debts to Galveston's mobsters. "Who's got your IOU's?"

She glanced around the nearly empty, smoke-hazed bar. Her eyes wore the haunted look of the condemned. "The Albertellis."

Dangerous, indeed. The Albertellis family had been involved in a wide range of criminal activities, including loansharking, gambling, prostitution, extortion, political corruption, and murder. They dominated the bloody gang wars for distribution of illegal alcohol and had eventually come to control Galveston's underworld.

He and Darla had shared their business and shared their beds over the past few years. He wouldn't exactly term their relationship as that of lovers, but it certainly wasn't a sibling relationship either. Perhaps, it was merely one of convenience, as she never pressed for a commitment. Still....

He drained his glass and stood up. What he was about to do went against the grain of his fiercely independent spirit. "Well, I'm going to see the man who controls Galveston's upper world."

At that hour of the day, his family was just settling down for dinner. With a nod and a flash of his complexly disarming grin, Preston strolled past the startled housemaid and on into the ornate dining room. His father had done well for himself.

His mother was the first to react. Her soup spoon dropped, sloshing gazpacho on her chemise dress of ivory silk. Bursting into tears, she jumped to her feet and flung herself into his arms. "My baby, my baby."

Taken aback, he awkwardly patted her heaving, slender shoulders like he was a kid again, making mud pies. He recalled his responses to her many letters that had found their way to him—curt and noncommittal—and the same to her telephone calls that occasionally tracked him to any of the three

One-Stop Stations. Shame smote him. He had skirted his family, so afraid had he been of surrendering to the curtailing of his independence by his all-powerful father.

Griffin Paladín was, if nothing else, a powerful figure in Galveston. After the hurricane, the young and distinguished architect had come up with a means to save the completely demolished city. As its multi-term mayor, to help expedite recovery, he had developed what was nationally known for such subsequent catastrophes as the "Galveston Plan."

And he was the Prodigal Son.

Preston gave his father an awkward over and under the arm hug. After all, he had left home at seventeen and had faced death hundreds of times over by the time he was nineteen. This was probably the first time he had faced his father as a man since the showdown on his return immediately after the war.

"Seems I have been derelict in my familial duties, Dad. Got an extra bowl of gazpacho for me?"

He detected the emotion welling up in his old man's eyes that was quickly followed by the glint of suspicion as to why his son was showing up after all this time. And rightly so.

Still, Preston knew he could not have become the man he was had he stayed rooted by family expectations. Maybe he was wrong, but he knew early on he had to spread his wings and leave the nest. He had stayed away longer than the rest of his mama's chicks, but it had taken that long for him to learn how to fly.

He only wished his parents could have witnessed all the worry and work and self-doubt that he had put in over the years into making him the man he had wanted to be. And yet, he knew he had so much further to go, so much more to make of his sadly deficient self.

Over dinner and, later, cognac in the parlor, they caught up on the past—personal history was recounted, and questions flew.

"Have you kept in touch with Pierce?" his mother asked, biting her lip with maternal concern. She leaned forward, the balloon-shaped snifter cradled between her hands. "We only get occasional letters, and I worry about him and Aubrey, cut off so far from the outside world."

"Do you ever get a chance to drop by and see Mariana?" His father stood behind Giselle's chair, gently swirling his glass of cognac.

Preston felt as if he were looking at his mirror image, although his father's flaming red hair now sported a touch of silver at the temples and a few pounds had been packed on around the middle. "No," he hedged, "her work on Heath's damn murder case keeps her running."

"Yeah, your mom and I have gotten in a couple of jail visits but have been turned away even more times. Drake has been keeping me abreast of her work for Heath."

"I just spent an evening with Pappy McBride, Dad. As you know, he'll bet on anything, including the color of cash. He might know something about the Bonaventure horse racing. Let me see what I can find out."

"Your brother is planning on flying your Uncle Drake down into Mexico—seeing if they can dredge up anything suspicious around the Bonaventure ranch in Durango. Pierce would more than welcome you if you would want to go along with them."

"Give them my regrets, but I have no plans to leave the great state of Texas ever again. I'll do my footwork here."

He patiently answered a few more of their questions and then shot back with a few innocuous ones of his own. "When was the last time you two visited The Barony?"

Thanksgiving, naturally.

"How is Hannah faring in Paris? Do you think Uncle David and Aunt Claire will force her to return stateside?"

They doubted anyone could force Hannah to do anything against her inclination.

"Did you know Byron is working on some top-secret government project?"

This one surprised them.

"Have you thought about taking a tour of Darcy's Hollywood studio?"

No, but they had seen two of his talkies.

And then the question Preston most dreaded posing, the question that would put him in debt to his father. "I have a friend who is in trouble with the Albertellis here in Galveston. Gambling losses. Can you protect her?"

For a moment, his father stared down into his amber-colored liqueur. When he looked up, his fair features were saturnine. "Salvatore Albertelli and his sons emigrated from Palermo, Sicily, shortly after the Great War. He is the boss of organized crime on the island."

He nodded his knowledge of the gangster.

"Well, when I requested a state committee look into the mobster activities at the Albertelli's nightclub, I was told by the local sheriff that he had not raided it because it was a 'private club' and he, the sheriff, was not a member."

Preston choked back his warmed cognac to keep from laughing at the ludicrous, albeit alarming conversation.

"I have the strong suspicion that someone high-up in Texan politics is protecting the Albertellis—much better than I could protect your friend—but I'll do what I can, son."

———————————

AT SUNSET THE NEXT DAY, hands jammed in his pockets, his cuffs rolled to his knees, Preston wandered barefoot along Galveston beach. Its sand was the color of his cognac from the night before. Like a snifter of cognac, his nameless feelings swirled inchoately.

His shoulders were hunched against the bitterly cold wind driven off the Gulf. The last of the dazzling red sunlight blazed against the sky and water, much like the brief but fiery bomb shelling during the Great War. Many of his comrades-in-arms had died just as quickly as those blinding flashes of light, leaving nothing for him to grasp but the reminiscence of having fleetingly shared something fragile and elusive with them, something impossible to convey.

Strange how the term "bombshell" was now being used to describe an incredibly attractive female. The only female bombshell he had known, Darla Ridley, had been found dead an hour ago—her body washed up on the beach, wearing her Mary Janes but with ankles and wrists duct taped.

That was the reason he was currently making a trail along the shore, as he was the only one left in Darla's life who could be called upon to confirm the identity of the body.

———————

AUBREY REALIZED SHE HAD EXPERIENCED a chaotic childhood, and living through the Great War had only magnified that chaos. The constant, debilitating fear. The brutal conditions. The strain of subterfuge. The perilous risk-taking. The starvation…. At one point, she had weighed only eighty pounds.

And then golden-haired Pierce Paladín had appeared. Her Prince Charming, straight out of a dark novel like *The Picture of Dorian Gray,* had swept her up onto his charger and taken her away from all that chaos. He had rescued her, saved her, time after time.

Dark. That was a good term for the strange relationship she and Pierce shared. An obsession with one another. Soft and sweet at times and hard and extremely erotic at others. She should end the marriage, walk away. But she couldn't, because she was insanely caught up in the loving torment of their relationship. She may have been addicted to opium, but its control over her was nothing compared with the maddening effects of her addiction to Pierce.

His powerful nude body was arranged in a casual pose on their rumpled bed, his head braced on one upraised hand. He was still partially hard after their recent torrid lovemaking, the evidence laying against one muscled thigh. As she crossed to the bathroom, her cast-off gown clutched modestly to her chest, his intense metallic eyes were watching her

There, hidden from his smoky, wolfish gaze, she wetted a towel and began to cleanse his ejaculated spray from her stomach and breasts. In the mirror, she saw his bronzed body fill the doorway. He had strapped on his prosthesis, and as he strode with that slight unevenness toward her, his heavy genitals swayed. His hands cupped her shoulders and he bent over her, his teeth nipping her ear lobe.

Merde, that slow, scintillating smile. Now she understood why she loved him. One of the many reasons she loved him. After all this time, he still heated her blood, made her weak behind her knees, and ache deep below her navel.

"I need you to do something for me."

There was nothing she wouldn't do for him. She would suffer any punishment if he could but admit he loved her, too. And despite all his mistrust, she felt he did. Could she be wrong? She knew he had to come to this knowledge all on his own, with no prompting or explanation from her. *"Oui?"* Her voice was the rasp of a nail file between jaws clenched with anxiousness. What now?

"I need you to do some investigation. Sort of like the intelligence work you did during the war. Will you help me?" His hand slid down her chest, between her breasts, to press her naked spine against the hard length of his renewed arousal. The delicate hairs along her skin rose. His touch fractured all her thoughts until nothing remained but him.

Her hand clasped his lightly haired wrist. Her breathlessness betrayed her feigned indifference. *"Mais bien sûr, mon amour."*

14

CORPUS CHRISTI, TEXAS

APRIL 1928

"Do you know the difference between a female lawyer and a pit bull?" Heath quipped. He was doing all he could to make the jail visits easier on Mariana. His tight-knit family had managed to get in visits throughout this ordeal, but she was his strength.

Mariana rolled her eyes. "No, what?"

"Lipstick."

She smirked. "That's the best you can do, Paladín?"

His response was part gravel pit, part leopard's purr. "I could do a hell of a lot more if I were out of the Big House."

She emitted a sigh that could have been either sympathetic or exasperated, and he wondered if his double entendre had missed her usually keen perception.

He also wondered what she looked like without her glasses. When the androgynous females were exposing knees and elbows, her lovely olive skin was revealed only in her face and elegant hands. When the boyish look was the rage, her ample breasts tantalized his imagination. When the females were waving their bobbed hair around their faces, her thick, lengthy midnight tresses were wreathed at her nape by a bandeau of rose-colored ribbon.

The flapper was characterized as a carefree, spirited young woman, but Mariana was a most serious game player—a disciplined strategist, both analytical and creative. He had learned that early on as a child during the chess games they had waged at The Barony during holiday and birthday gatherings. She was a paradox—a singular woman with an *avant-garde* mentality and old-fashioned sense of dignity and charm.

Dwelling on how her hair would look fanned out on his pillow told him that he had been too long without a woman—over a year-and-a-half due to her repeated appeals for trial postponement while she sleuthed.

But it was more than that. He realized that all this time he had entertained the same notions as she, though neither of them had been completely aware of the other's feelings. They both had been desperate in their attempts to act casual and cool around each other. Perhaps this was partly the reason that, though thousands of women threw themselves at him, he could find flaws with each and every one. They were not Mariana.

"This is the most sensational case in years," she was saying, "and you can bet plenty are the envious males in the camp of those demanding your still-beating heart be cut from your chest."

He grunted in annoyance. Outside the Corpus Christi courthouse and jail, even after a year-and-a-half, hundreds of swooning, shoving female fans kept watch for a glimpse of his face in the barred window.

"Well, that's a great comfort going into a courtroom where my eternal destiny is settled before a judge and jury who know everything about me, at least according to the newspapers, radios, and magazine—and the jury, of course, will be all male. Totally reassuring when the verdict is already in and the penalty is death. Unless I have the only defense attorney in all the universe who can save me. And that would be you, my dearest Mariana."

Her gaze dropped to their clasped hands, hers darker now than his sun-starved ones. *Starved.* He had not realized how truly starved for human touch he was.

"I have researched Frederick Woodward Bonaventure with an anthropologist's excavation brush. Whatever less than sterling acts he may have committed, his Judgment Day Book appears blemish-free. I can find no one to come forward to testify against him."

"I'm hoping you'll tell me this is April Fool's Day."

"Look, we've still got three weeks left before the next trial date, unless I can win another postponement."

Which, he thought, was most unlikely. "That doesn't give us much time."

"Your mom has been placing ads in newspapers across the country, offering a reward for any substantial leads."

"Yeah, she told me on her last visit. But I'd wager she's getting an unwarranted and bothersome amount of responses from bloodsuckers eager to capitalize on a worried family's funds."

Head tilted, Mariana ignored him to refasten a tiny pearl stud in one small earlobe. "Betty and Aubrey are canvassing the neighborhood around Sunland Downs for leads. Byron let me know he has managed to procure El Paso telephone operators' tickets and is sifting through them for information. No telling how he acquired them. Another one of his secret projects. Darcy is putting out feelers in Los Angeles, home base of Bonaventure's Clarion. And Pierce flew your father down to Durango to do a little snooping."

She paused, out of breath, and he knew she was trying to reassure him. "And I'm filing petitions, briefs, affidavits, appeals for continuance, scouring federal district court opinions…. I promise you, the game is afoot, Sherlock. We're doing—"

"There is something else you could be doing."

Her head jerked up. Her winged brows knitted. "What?"

Maybe he was cabin crazy, given his enforced isolation, but he had known many females and, despite all their wiles, despite the fact that this one invincible spirit across from him was his cousin, she was the one he wanted at his side. "Reassure me that marrying a cousin doesn't go against your legal code of honor—that is, if you get my miserable hide off the hook."

He was somewhat shocked that the statement actually came out of his mouth. After all these years of stuffing down his strong—and legally prohibited—feelings for her.

He worried that she would be disgusted by his statement, since they were cousins, but her expression of sheer joy said everything. Her next words, however, hedged. Just like her to do that. And that was why he loved her.

She shot him a smirk. "Which cousin?"

HOLLYWOOD, CALIFORNIA
MAY 1928

Darcy had become fast friends with Douglas Fairbanks since doing some stunt work for him on *The Gaucho,* released the year before. Since then, Darcy had competed regularly at Fairbank's private gym located on the Pickford-Fairbanks lot.

Darcy figured he must be a masochistic to keep returning. Especially today, when he had wrapped up a scene with Belle at four that morning. Although there were plenty of female gate crashers who would love nothing more than to indulge in an erotic interlude with him, Belle continued to give him the brush off.

After a round of fencing with the swashbuckler, followed by a turn at the punching bag and mechanical horse, he underwent the Turkish bath's steam. He then took a plunge in cold water and shifted to the sauna's dry heat. What he really wanted was to relax his beat-to-shit muscles under the powerful kneading of Fairbanks's masseur-in-residence, a former wrestler.

Alas, Darcy had more pressing matters to attend to—that of Heath's fate.

Next, joining Fairbanks in the steam room, he sat nude on one of the cedar benches, their backs against the wood-lined wall. For a while, they talked shop—production teams, companies of actors, studio wiring for talkies, cable rigs for stunt work.

"I hear Grauman's Chinese Theatre is wanting to place your hand and footprints in its wet cement," Fairbanks drawled. He got up to pour water on the wire basket of stones. The water hissed and sizzled. A thick cloud of steam momentarily obscured his sleek albeit short figure.

The tight muscles of Darcy's lanky frame eased with the instantly shrouding mist of beneficial heat. "Hell, Doug, I'm more pleased that the Texas governor is naming me an honorary Texas Ranger. My Uncle Buck was actually one a lifetime ago."

Eyeing him all the while, Fairbanks sauntered back to the bench. "You know, Darcy, when an actor is stripped of his costumes, he's merely a bare-ass naked man open to assessment by others for his true worth. Your worth, in my estimation, has gone up."

Darcy had to grin at the double-edged compliment. He took advantage of the moment and slid in his request. "I hope the value of our friendship extends to helping me get the goods on Bonaventure or his wife."

Hands clasped between his knees, Fairbanks shook his head in sad disbelief. "Um-um-umm. What a debacle your brother has on his hands. Mary and I wined and dined the Bonaventures at Pickfair, and I have gone sailing with him before he and Emelda retired to Mexico. Even granted a fair number of interviews to his Clarion over the years. But never heard of any underhandedness on his part."

"And on Emelda's?"

A short silence. "She came on to me several times."

He strove to keep the excitement out of his deep and resonant Southwestern drawl that made him a natural for the talkies. "Would you testify to that in court?"

"Hell, no, Darcy. I don't need a scandal in my own backyard. No need for the world to know that Hollywood is a sinkhole of depravity."

He suspected Fairbanks had bedded Emelda, but it would be useless to pursue that direction of questioning. He could argue that the notoriety from his brother's case hadn't tarnished Double Take Production's squeaky-clean reputation. If anything, its earnings were shooting up like that of the stock market's.

He grunted, another dead end. He had questioned actors, actresses, set people, deliverymen, florists, and caterers—all leading nowhere.

Fairbanks lowered his voice, although there was obviously no one else in the sauna. "Why don't the Paladíns just buy off the prosecution? Your family fortune is as solid as Fort Knox."

"Because Roger and Brighton Clarendon want their pound of flesh."

"Jeepers creepers, your family could have been a little more selective in picking its enemies."

Darcy thought about that after he left the Pickford-Fairbanks lot. As he pulled up in front of the small and modest Spanish-style bungalow tucked away in west Hollywood, he suspected he was about to make another enemy.

Over the course of the five singing westerns Belle and he had filmed together, she had made huge strides as an actress. Not only had she learned to project a delicate nuance of gesture and facial expressions, but she had demonstrated in her investments, none of them with Wall Street, that she was an astute businesswoman.

He hadn't done badly for himself in the acting department either. Variety had noted that "Paladín has developed into an actor capable of subtlety and restraint while playing the stock character of the heroic cowboy. A disenchanted country, weary of sex and crime, have turned their adulation to self-effacing idols like Charles Lindbergh and Darcy Paladín."

Well, he would need all his acting skills to convince Belle that it was now or never with him, as far as he was concerned. The chaste kisses they exchanged on screen told him she could be most susceptible to deep passions, despite her pretense at indifference to him.

She met him at the door but without her usual Mona Lisa's secret smile. Her eyes were teary, her nose red, and her auburn hair a snarled ball of yarn. She wore rumpled, pink gingham pajamas. "Oh, I thought it was the milk man."

He strode past her without an invitation. A box of Kleenex set on the small dining table. "Why are you crying?"

"I'm not. I've got a cold."

"Like hell you do." He picked up a letter lying next to its torn-open envelope and a couple of wadded up tissues. It was signed simply. "Dad."

Dear Estelle, we received the check. The checks keep food on the table and Timmy clothed. He asks about you often, wanting to know when his sister will come to visit, but....

"Put that letter down!" Belle screeched, coming up behind him.

He held it out of reach of her frantically grasping hand and finished reading it. "...I tell him how busy you are. What else do you tell a ten-year-old? That he's a bastard and his mother is winning her roles on the casting couch?"

There was more, but what he read was enough. Astonished, he half turned to look down at her furious face.

She circled by him to swipe the letter away.

He let her have it. "Timmy is your child?"

"Get out."

He caught her shoulders and propelled her backwards until her calves came up against the sofa and she plopped down onto its floral-pattered cushions.

"No, I won't. No more secrets, Belle." He stood over her, his fists on hips, his elaborately stitched boots planted apart. "What is this" —he nodded at the letter in her hand—"—*that*—all about?"

She glared at him. Her malleable lips compressed, determined to utter nary a word.

"So, this Timmy is your son? Out of wedlock?"

Stubborn silence. But the rapid rise and fall of her breasts told him she was perilously close to falling apart. He dropped down alongside her on the sofa, stretched out his legs, and draped his arm around her, pulling her into the cradle of his chest and shoulder. The letter fluttered onto the hardwood floor. "By deduction, my fair Belle, I would wager that the father has to be one of those saddle bums you so loathe."

At that, she broke into eerily quiet weeping that wracked her small body. He held her close and waited. It seemed like an hour passed, but it was probably more like ten minutes, before her spasms of grief subsided. She sniffed several times. Her head bobbed. "A rodeo circuit rider."

He inclined his head better to see her face and gently wiped away the tears. "My God. And all these years you've punished yourself, cowboys, and me, especially."

She hiccoughed. "Here today, gone tomorrow."

He smiled. "Well, I have been here for nigh on seven years. That should be good for something, Belle."

Her head bobbed in assent once more. Her chin pointed at the tear-stained paper on the floor. "It's always like this… twice a year, a letter. Just to remind me… what a fallen woman I am. I wanted what I thought was best for my unborn child." She hiccoughed again. "And my parents were worried what the neighbors would think. Passing him off as my mother's late-in-life child… it seemed the solution."

"Guess the only way we can remedy this is to marry and adopt Timmy."

She started crying again, and his fingers captured her chin, tilting it up. Was he wrong in thinking she might feel more for him than she demonstrated? His gut knotted, but he took the risk. "Am I all that skunk-stinkin' ghastly to you?'

More sniffles, then her lips crimped into a small, tremulous smile. "I'm crying happy tears, Darcy."

THE BARONY, TEXAS
NOVEMBER 1928

The entire Paladín clan was gathered around the long mahogany table, with its turkey-theme runner painstakingly and devotedly embroidered by the ranch's *Paladíneños* women. The notable exception was Heath, though there was also the notable inclusion of Darcy's bride, Belle, and her nine-year-old Timmy, who looked like one of the rascals from *Our Gang*.

And there was one more new face—Stoney Jackson.

Of middle height and compact build, the twenty-one-year-old sported flashing, albeit uneven, white teeth beneath a brown handlebar mustache and gray eyes that laughed. Drake had temporarily lured the veterinary medicine student away from Texas A&M to fill in Heath's place at helping Drake run the ranch's cattle and horse operations—at least until the trial was over.

The trial, finally set for January, crouched at the back of everyone's mind. But just for the day, all tacitly agreed to put the frightening aspect of Heath's fate on the backburner. Amidst the passing of platters and bowls and refilling of glasses, all were focused on catching up with one another.

"Listened to the broadcast of your performance at the Grand Ole Opry," Hannah's father, David, told Belle and Darcy.

"Belle wasn't just whistling Dixie."

She blushed and glanced at Darcy. Hannah couldn't help but envy the loving look the two exchanged. Forever gone for Hannah was that precious pleasure—something she had never taken for granted when in Michael's stimulating presence.

"That whistling was Darcy's idea. I'm trying to teach Timmy."

The boy, sitting between the two, ducked his head, and Darcy reached out to ruffle his cowlick. The kid grinned, displaying a missing lower front tooth, and went back to pushing his cream peas around his plate with his spoon.

"We have a calf, born just this morning," Stoney smiled. "Maybe Timmy would like to see it after dinner?"

Timmy's head perked up and Byron jumped in to say, "Speaking of newborns, there'll be another Paladín kid soon to teach ropin' and ridin'."

From behind her glasses, Aunt Angel's eyes lit up, green like a traffic signal, and swiveled to her youngest son. "Am I finding out I am a grandmother twice-over in one day?" Her smile encompassed Timmy as well.

Edna's shoulders hunched up almost to her ears, and she gave her gap-toothed grin. "Next May."

"Oh, how wonderful, you two!" Aunt Giselle dabbed gently at her eyes.

Wine glass in hand, Uncle Drake unwound his lengthy legs and rose to his door-frame lofty height. "Then it's that time during our Thanksgiving dinners when we rejoice in our latest blessings. To the next Paladín family member!"

Cheers were exchanged, but Hannah didn't miss the longing look that fleeted across Aubrey's classical features, followed by a surreptitious glance from beneath incredibly thick lashes at Pierce. His handsome face betrayed nothing but general good will. Preston's gambler's gaze, of course, never betrayed anything anyway.

Aunt Pearl sniffed happily. "Many more additions to our tribe, and we'll come close to creating our own nation."

Uncle Nicolás hoisted his glass. He was still darkly good looking and a dapper dresser, despite a slight paunch noticeable beneath his silk waistcoat. "To another Texican."

Hannah noted that Mariana seemed to manage a smile, but her mouth was taut with obvious tension as her trial preparation got down to the wire. Pushing her eyeglasses up on the bridge of her nose with one finger, she quipped, "Stoney, you may change your mind about working for our wild and woolly family. You have our permission to bolt from The Barony here and now."

"No, ma'am. I'm here for the long haul." He accepted the serving of Bourbon Pecan Pie Aunt Angel proffered. "Thank you, ma'am." He grinned. "I grew up in the Panhandle—on the JA Ranch near Amarillo, and that's pretty durn wild and woolly."

The light hum of the usual chit-chat resumed, but Hannah's gaze snagged with her mother's peek in her direction. Her mother and father shouldn't worry about her. She herself didn't.

To tell the truth, she simply didn't feel anything. Living in Paris, the city of light, it seemed ironic her own light had gone out. But Paris's charming energy held memories of Michael, and that was probably the only thing that kept her going these days. That and her work.

As if sensing her melancholy, Stoney turned his sloe-eyed gaze on her. "I hear you've been away, Missus Kraft, in Paris. You must miss the Texas sunsets."

All eyes turned sympathetically toward her. She took advantage of his comment to escape the claustrophobic net of concern her family was casting over her. "Sunset is still to come," she equivocated, "but I think Timmy and I would love to see first that calf you mentioned—if that's all right with you, Belle?"

With a pleased expression, she nodded. "Get your jacket, Timmy."

He popped out of his chair. "Whoopee!"

Hannah followed him to the entryway's hall tree and helped him into his small woolen jacket. "You know how to ride?"

"A horse?" His response was said indignantly, as if insulted she didn't know his mom was the Queen of the Cowgirls.

She had to smile. "No, a bicycle. I'm sure Aunt Giselle can scrounge up one somewhere around here." One of the first females to ride a bicycle at the 1893 Chicago's World Fair, Hannah's aunt still rode, even though she was nearing sixty.

Shrugging into a tatty sweater clinging to the hall tree, Hannah shepherded the kid out to the veranda. A sweat-stained Stetson covering his brown locks, with hands jammed into a dungaree jacket, Stoney was waiting for them.

"I had been monitoring the calf's mother until she up and died on me, but I'm still hoping to save the young'n."

They crossed the well-tended lawn to the nearest barn. Strange, here a life had been snuffed out, that of Emelda Bonaventure's. Yet, here, too, life was being given. The smell of musty hay and manure enveloped Hannah. Stoney led them to a stall lit by a warming lamp. Nearly obscured by the deep layer of straw lay the Santa Gertrudis calf.

"Can I pet it?"

Stoney nodded. "Especially its head, kiddo."

She leaned on the top wooden slat and watched Timmy drop to his knees besides the calf. Next to her, Stoney propped his booted spur on the stall gate's lower rung and braced his forearms on the upper one. "The calf was wedged in the pelvic canal too long, and her head is a little swollen."

"So, the petting actually helps the swelling?"

"Touching always helps heal—whether you're plant, animal, or human. We all need it, ma'am."

"Please, don't call me ma'am. Even if I am far older than you."

"What would you like me to call you?"

"Hannah. Just Hannah."

Beneath his hat's u-shaped brim, his eyes contained the lambent glow of quicksilver. "My pleasure, Hannah."

The way his muscles corded the sun-browned column of his neck, the easy way his smile lifted to fill his face, even the heady smell of him... she trembled, so hot she was, it was like a scorching flame ignited inside her. She was thinking how long it had been since she had been touched, and how pathetically needy she had become. "It's just about time to catch that Texas sunset."

She turned and promptly strode out of the barn. Once outside, she surreptitiously wiped the tears off her face.

15

The charismatic prosecutor was wrapping up his opening statement, now edging past the fifteen-minute mark. An eloquent and persuasive man, Herbert Godley played the philistine jury like a violin virtuoso. The bastard.

From the jacket pocket of his impeccable three-piece suit, a pipe-stem protruded, imparting intimation of genteelness. Hands clasped behind his back, he paused in prowling before the jurors to glance over his shoulder at Heath, sitting next to Mariana, then slowly shook his head as if incredulous that a person of such depravity could actually exist.

"...and, therefore, I contend that Mister Paladín has lived a life so accustomed to having every woman on film he wants that he identifies his personal life with this image as well. The superstar status created by one's professional image does not bestow privilege in one's private life."

Godley had a soft, mellow voice that beckoned the jurors' attention. "And having his advances refused by Missus Emelda Bonaventure," Godley continued, "Mister Paladín took away from her the right to refuse ever again. The State will prove that Missus Bonaventure was cold-bloodedly killed by Hollywood Handsome Heath."

Heath inclined his head next to Mariana's. "When I'm fat and flabby, will you still love me?"

Her love-struck heart tripped a beat. "I might find it in me to love your worthless ass," she shot back in a hushed voice. "That is, if you should live that long."

The courtroom's dusty windows shot a fuselage of the wintry morning's cold, gun-metal gray onto Heath's pale, chiseled face. He emanated that powerfully magnetic male energy that attracted one and all.

But most of the spectators watched the drama with something akin to blood lust in their expressions.

How she admired his aplomb in the face of disaster—and that was what this trial was mounting to be for her client and the love of her life.

Godley was presenting Hollywood as a modern-day Sodom and Gomorrah, with Heath as the orchestrator of its immorality, while painting Bonaventure as a philanthropist and his young wife as dedicated to her husband and her horses.

The prosecutor waved a hand toward the local and national flags behind the judge's bench, which stood like a mahogany altar. "When the time comes for deliberation, your job is to make sure justice is done."

Justice might be due process of law for one—and the satisfaction of revenge for another.

"And I plan to prove that justice would be putting Mister Paladín in the electric chair," Godley continued. "Justice will be stopping this monstrous murderer from ever again taking advantage of his celebrity position."

She shot to her feet. "Objection, your honor! My client has never been found guilty of murder."

"Sustained."

Godley seemed unfazed by the sustaining of the objection, only smiling smoothly. His stirring presentation was reinforced by newspaper and radio blitzing both Bonaventure's philanthropy and Godley's prestigious profile as a prosecutor.

"To the criminal defense attorneys and crooks," wrote one newspaper editor, "this meticulous and fair-minded litigator embodies their worst nightmare. He can go toe-to-toe with the best of the defense attorneys. When, at last, the referee holds aloft the winner's hand, the defender is usually the one on the floor, and his client is headed either to the slammer or to the electric chair."

Wedged within the various articles was usually a single sentence sympathetically mentioning Godley's deceased wife fighting a brave but losing battle to tuberculosis.

In contrast, Mariana had no track record, and being one of the few female attorneys practicing law in Texas did little to lend her credence. Female attorneys faced the resistance of the public, determined opposition from the bar, and actual hostility from the bench.

Add to that Mariana's Hispanic surname, anathema to the KKK in Texas, one of the nation's most active groups. Some of them could even be seated in the jury box. But, even worse, she was a Paladín family member, and that linked her, at least in Texan minds, to unbridled power.

At her advice, none of the Paladín family were in attendance today. The last thing she wanted was the presence of the potent Paladín clan to add further intimidation to the jury. Heath's legendary stature could just as well work against him in the form of resentment.

Yes, the odds of her saving Heath's hide were slim.

The black-robed judge, with his mane of flowing white hair, could have been a latter-day Moses. He nodded at her now. "Miss Cordova?"

Feeling very small, she rose, straightened her simple tailored dress of navy wool, and went to stand at the foot of the bench. Behind her, the courtroom was standing room only, with would-be spectators spilling outside into the freezing weather. Only the Scopes Monkey Trial four years before had more people in attendance.

Two rows of hardback benches had been set aside for the AP Bureau, journalists who had come from all over the United States, and even several foreign journalists.

While Godley's opening statement was masterful, hers was woefully flat and to the point. She wanted to get the grandstanding over as mercifully quick as possible. She knew the opening statement could be the most important time during the entire jury trial, because it was the only time when an attorney had the jury's complete and undivided attention.

She glanced at her notes, which swam before her eyes like foreign script, then drew a fortifying breath.

"Ladies and gentlemen of the jury," she began hesitantly, "on the morning of December 27th, 1927, at approximately ten a.m., the stable boy Manny Ayala entered The Barony's main barn to clean the stalls. Missus Bonaventure was waiting there for my client." Personalize it, Mariana. "Heath Paladín was not lying in wait for her. On the contrary, Heath abandoned Hollywood because of the females lying in wait for him."

"Objection," Godley spoke up, rising from his chair. "The Defense is improperly suggesting Missus Bonaventure was lying in wait for him."

"Overruled."

She cleared her throat, finishing her opening remarks. "I plan to prove that Heath did not intentionally, nor recklessly, kill anyone—other than during the Great War, when he nobly served our nation. I ask that when y'all adjourn to the jury deliberation room," she finished in a deliberate folksy drawl, "y'all keep in mind that Heath is a victim himself of Hollywood hysteria."

Less than a minute…. So much for her opening statement.

THE TRIAL WAS WELL INTO the third day, with no actual witnesses linking Heath to the crime. So, this put the trial on a "he said/she said" testimony. Bonaventure's against Heath's, and the decision of the jurors would proceed on the strength of credibility.

"Mister Paladín, as a product of Hollywood's celluloid, might quite likely have a difficult time distinguishing fiction from reality." Godley's statement—along with much of his defense—undoubtedly reduced Heath's credibility factor with the jurors.

As a rebuttal, she could put him on the witness stand. He was articulate and riveting. But he was losing his affability. In addition, Godley could damage Heath's story on cross examination by merely questioning him on the number of men, women, and children he had killed in combat.

Her nails were bitten to the quick with jagged nerves. The Tums she had purchased at the pharmacy around the corner did nothing to smooth the painful grinding of her stomach. And the raccoon's mask of dark shadows around her eyes testified to her lack of sleep. How could she sleep, when her dreams were haunted by the image of Heath swinging over and over again… his broken neck jacked awfully to one side, as Dan's had been.

That afternoon, as a desperate resort, she called the stable boy, Manny Ayala, to the stand. The eleven-year-old was wearing a jacket too big for him—obviously a hand-me-down—and his coal-black hair was slicked down with Brilliantine.

He lifted his right hand to be sworn in on the witness stand, then took his seat in the witness chair, also too big for him. His little sweaty hands, their nails pared and immaculately cleaned, twisted together in a washing fashion.

After thanking him for coming, she said smiled reassuringly. "Manny, did you see Missus Bonaventure the morning of her death?"

"*Sí*… yes."

"Tell me about it."

"I was cleaning stalls. She—*Señora* Bonaventure—came in."

"Did she say anything to you?"

"No."

"Was that man," she pointed at Heath, "was he there?"

"No."

"What happened after Missus Bonaventure came in?"

"*Nada.* She walks. Back and forth." He shrugged his thin shoulders. "Then she puts on—"

His hand gestured to his lips and Mariana supplied, "Lipstick?"

"*Si.*" He nodded vigorously. "With her *espejo compacto.*"

"Her compact mirror? Then what happened?"

"*Señor* Heath, he comes in the barn."

"And then?"

He shrugged again. "They talk about horses, I think. I leave."

"Did Heath tell you to leave?"

"No, *Señora.* I finished."

She turned to the judge. "I'm finished with the examination, Your Honor." She could only hope she instilled, at least, a shred of doubt in the jury's minds as who was lying in wait for whom.

The judge nodded at the Prosecutor. "Mister Godley? You wish to cross-examine the witness?"

"Yes, Your Honor." He crossed to the witness stand and flashed Manny a fatherly smile. "Good afternoon, son."

Manny's head bobbed.

"Would you please describe Missus Bonaventure—as you remember her."

The little hands lifted in a vague gesture. "*Bonita*... like the Madonna, like the *Virgen de Guadalupe.*"

Silently, Mariana groaned. The child could not have replied better had he been coached.

Godley smiled beatifically. "Thank you, son. That will be all."

The judge wrapped his bony Moses fingers around the gavel and tapped it. "The court is recessed until tomorrow morning."

———————

"The State calls Frederick Bonaventure to the stand."

Heads craned to see the esteemed newspaper tycoon and horse breeder make his way to the stand. The snowy haired gentleman settled gingerly into the chair on the raised dais and smiled with crinkly eyes.

Mariana's own eyes studiously surveyed the ceiling's ornate scrollwork. One would think Bonaventure didn't possess enough strength to kill a cockroach, much less his wife.

"Mister Bonaventure, I would ask your occupation, but I think everyone in the courtroom could attest that you are famous for your media ventures, among other things. So, I'll merely ask how long you have been a professional horse breeder."

A smidgeon of chuckles trickled through the jammed courtroom, and the frail-looking man accepted the homage with a diffident smile. "Nearly thirty years."

"The public knows you are the founder of the impressive newspaper, the *Los Angeles Clarion,* but for those of us who aren't as well informed, would you please share some of your charitable activities."

"Well, I'm on the board of Community Chest, Catholic Charities USA, and several service clubs, fraternal organizations—those sorts of things."

"And it was at a fundraiser for Catholic Charities USA that you met the victim, your late wife, Emelda Bonaventure?"

Again, Mariana mentally groaned. Practically the entire population of Nueces County was Catholic.

"Yes."

"How long ago was that?"

"Approximately thirteen years ago."

"That would have made her—" Godley glanced down, appearing to check his notes, "thirteen at the time."

"Twelve, actually."

"What were the circumstances of the meeting?"

"I was in the El Paso area—one of my horses was competing at the Juarez

Race Track—and I had coordinated attending it with the opening of the new Catholic convent and orphanage in El Paso's Second Ward. Emelda's kitten had escaped. It was perched atop a high bookcase. I retrieved it for her. After that, when I made my yearly appearances for the orphanage's fundraiser, Emelda and Whiskers—that was the name of her cat—would greet me."

Just grand. An orphan and a pussycat. All Bonaventure needed to do was well up with tears, and he'd have the jury's sympathetic vote hook, line, and sinker.

"And when did you marry your wife?" Godly continued.

"Five years ago, when she turned eighteen."

"I know this is very difficult for you, Mister Bonaventure, but will you describe what took place the morning your wife was murdered."

Bonaventure rested his chin on his clasped hands for a moment—a long, too silent moment—as though he were gathering the stamina to go on. Then he raised his narrow, ascetic face and his rheumy eyes glistened. "Mister Paladín had—"

"Pardon me, Mister Bonaventure, but *which* Mister Paladín? Is he in this courtroom, and, if so, would you please point him out for us?"

The elderly man nodded and then lifted a trembling, accusing finger in the direction of Heath and Mariana. "There. Heath Paladín."

"Go on, then."

"Mister Paladín had invited us to The Barony to breed our stallion Comeuppance with his mare. My wife is… *was*… highly experienced at this and handled that aspect of our operations. The morning Paladín killed her, we had—"

Mariana shot to her feet. "Objection! The defendant has not been found guilty of the murder of Missus Bonaventure."

"Overruled." The judge sighed and looked down at her. "The witness was asked to recount his recollection of that day—in his own words. Please keep that in mind, Counselor."

Her feigned look of contrition barely made it into her expression. "Yes, Your Honor."

Bonaventure clasped his veined hands in his lap. "Just before my wife was to meet with the Defendant, she was pacing the floor of our guest room. One of The Barony's guest rooms. Anyway, it was obvious she was agitated. I asked her what was wrong, and she told me that, given Paladín's reputation with women, she was worried about how best to handle any potential unwanted advances without antagonizing him. I told her I'd go with her, but she wouldn't hear of it. She worries so about me and my blood pressure… worried, I suppose."

He paused, took a steadying breath, then went on. "After she left, I got to thinking about it and decided I had better make sure she was all right. As I entered the barn, I could hear Paladín shouting. He called her a bitch. Said something—something threatening—about her being sorry. I couldn't hear all of it. But that's when I saw them, made them out. He had grabbed up a pitchfork. Instinctively, I ran at him. Tried to grab it out of his hands. But he was stronger."

Bonaventure paused, gulped, and lowered his head.

"No further questions, Your Honor."

"Miss Cordova?" asked the judge.

She crossed to the witness stand. For a moment, she fingered one pearl earring, as if puzzled where to take up the questioning, doubtlessly reinforcing the media's portrayal of her as an inept attorney.

"Mister Bonaventure, what is the name of the orphanage in which you found your wife?"

"The Sacred Heart Orphanage." He gave a soft, wheezing sigh.

"And did Missus Bonaventure reside at the Sacred Heart Orphanage the entire time—until your marriage, five years ago, I believe you stated?"

"Of course." His reply was just a tick off, not so much that most people would take note.

"I'm finished with the examination, Your Honor."

Murmurs of surprise ran through the audience. Clearly, they were dismayed that she had failed to follow through and pursue the line of questioning directly related to the time of the murder.

The Judge nodded and rapped the gavel. "Court dismissed for the day."

———————————

"YOU SAY SHE TOLD YOU she was selling her body on the streets of Juarez when she and Bonaventure met, right?"

Heath nodded.

"You look like Death warmed over."

"Thanks." It was close to seven o'clock that evening. His squared-off jaw wore a beard-stubbled shadow. Only the two of them sat in the Nueces Courthouse's Visitation Room. The Hispanic guard yawned, clearly ready for his shift to be over and to go home.

She squeezed Heath's hand, so much larger it could break every bone in hers. "Keep the faith. I've put in a call to Aubrey. With her experience working for French Intelligence, I feel like she can establish whether or not Bonaventure perjured himself. She's checking out that Sacred Heart Orphanage morsel."

When Aubrey's call came through the next morning at the Nueces Hotel's lobby switchboard, her investigative result was a difficult morsel for Mariana to swallow.

"Mariana, a little over five years ago, the order of the Sisters Servants at Sacred Heart completed the convent's move from the Second Ward to land they had purchased on Tobin Place in the outskirts of El Paso. Whatever records they kept before the move... they no longer exist."

"What about the Sister Servants? Do any of them recall Emelda?" Between Aubrey's French accent and the static on the line, Mariana was having trouble following the conversation.

"Their order was actually founded in Mexico in 1885, and, after the Mexican Revolution in 1917, the Sister Servants were given sanctuary in the El Paso Sacred Heart Convent and Orphanage. The Sisters, they were to care for the children and orphans of Mexican refugees from Villa and his revolutionaries."

"But since then?" Mariana asked, trying to curb her impatience. "Any record keeping?"

"*Eh bien,* later, after the orphanage moved to the Tobin Place location in El Paso, the original Sisters were dispersed to isolated locations throughout the Southwest, with no records here in the United States to trace either them or the orphans. I'm so sorry."

"So am I." And so would Heath be. Mortally sorry.

MARIANA PONDERED THE PROBLEMATIC DAY ahead, as, brief-case in hand, she briskly walked from the Nueces Hotel, a good ten minutes from the courthouse. In those ten minutes, the sidewalk iced over, a rarity in Southwest Texas. Shivering, she drew her side-wrap coat, with its fur-collar, more tightly against her.

By the time she settled into the courtroom antechamber, sleet stung its windowpanes. Not a good sign. Beyond the antechamber door, she could hear spectators filling the rows and buzzing like disturbed, angry bees. They wanted justice meted out—and punishment.

She found herself doodling on her notepad. A crude representation of a cannon slowly took shape. After the verdict was in, Texicans in high power, like Roger and Brighton Clarendon, would be figuratively—if not literally—waiting to gun her down next for taking on one of their detested enemies, the Paladíns. The fact that she belonged to the clan made her a post office's most wanted poster candidate.

Hopelessly, she looked once more at her scribbled notes. At least it was a cut-and-dried case that shouldn't take long—and would look good on the prosecutor's record when it was over. Yet even though she felt she knew the outcome of the verdict, her nerves were vibrating in anticipation… this was the sentence that would rip her love from her.

Newspapers and radios had already tried Heath and were readily providing reminders to any who might have had a lapse of memory in the nearly two years Heath had been incarcerated, pending trial.

Now they demanded a stake be driven through his sybaritic heart.

The uniformed bailiff opened her antechamber door, ushering in the noise of the audiences' clamoring, and nodded at her. It was time for the shootout at the O.K. Corral.

———————————

TO THE SIDE OF THE crowded courtroom, Roger Clarendon sat in his wheelchair. This day would be one of particular delight. Killing two birds with one stone. Heath Paladín and Mariana Cordova were but two of his targets. In time, when the dust finally settled, he would finally prostrate the entire damn Paladín clan.

Today, they occupied the courtroom's entire three hardbacked benches in the back row. Like scurvy roaches, they had gathered from all corners of the state—Dallas, Galveston, Houston, El Paso, The Barony, of course—and even as far as France.

His mouth crimped into a smile at the thought of the old minstrel song. "Ten little Injuns standing in a line, one got executed then there were nine. Nine little Injuns…." And eventually, there would be none.

Everyone but Roger swiftly stood as the judge lumbered to his seat. The defender and prosecutor took their seats behind their respective tables. Roger thought his father—alas, in D.C.—would be pleased with Godley's performance. He had thoroughly demolished the defender. At the next vacancy on the Texas Court of Criminal Appeals, the Governor, an ass-kisser of Roger's father, would most assuredly appoint Godley to serve out the judge's term.

Up front, a young female, slant-eyed with black bobbed hair, was conversing in whispers and rapid hand gestures with the Cordova woman.

The judge glared at the defender. "I trust, Miss Cordova, that there will be no surprises before we proceed to closing arguments?"

Mariana Cordova came to her feet. "Well, as a matter of fact Your Honor, I do have another witness to call." She circled her table and approached the bench to confer with the judge. The judge's grizzled brows climbed his patriarchal forehead, but he nodded grudgingly.

She returned to her table. "Your Honor, with the Court's permission, I would like to summon to the stand an unlisted witness."

He turned to the prosecutor. "Mister Godley?"

"No objection," the prosecutor replied, but his expression was wary.

A murmur of speculation as to what this development might mean filtered through the audience.

"The Court calls Rosa Ramirez as a Witness for the Defense."

Roger leaned forward in his wheelchair better to see a small, thin Mexican woman make her way down the center aisle. Her head was ducked, and two thick, black braids bobbed on her flat chest.

After she was sworn in, Mariana Cordova turned to face her. "Missus Ramirez, can you tell me how you know the defendant, Heath Paladín—the man sitting at that table?"

Rosa Ramirez darted a glance at Heath. "I don't know him. But I know him." With that, she pointed at Bonaventure, who had taken a seat on the front row behind Godley's table.

"Mister Bonaventure?"

The copper-colored woman nodded.

"How do you know him?"

"My husband, he worked for him. My husband was a jockey."

"*Was?* Is your husband dead, Missus Ramirez?"

"*Si.* He was murdered."

Smothered gasps flitted throughout the courtroom.

"How?"

"He was…"—her small hands groped for the right word—"…his head, it was cut off."

Outright gasps followed.

"Why was he murdered?"

"Objection, Your Honor,"—Godley started to stand—"the nature of the Defense's question is leading."

"Overruled."

Goddamn Godley, get your act together! The courtroom reporter's stenotype machine clicked away annoyingly. Stress grinding in his gut, Roger's hand slipped inside his jacket to feel the reassurance of the leather holster.

"Why was your husband murdered?" Mariana prompted again.

"Porque he was going to tell about Missus Bonaventure. About how she often tried to... to make sex with him."

Mutterings of astonishment reverberated throughout the spectators. The jurors stared with bewilderment, waiting for some kind of signal from the bench as to exactly what effect this sensationalism would have on their deliberations.

The judge rapped his gavel and declared sonorously, "Court is recessed! I'll see attorneys in my chambers."

———————————

THE JUDGE'S PRIVATE OFFICE WAS located adjacent to the courtroom. He shoved a blue-veined hand through his white mane and glared at Mariana and Godley. "Off the record, you two with your highly irregular tactics are making a three-ring circus of my courtroom. And I won't tolerate much more. In fact, I want you to wrap up your summations now. Make it short and sweet, understand? My patience is at an end."

Both she and Godley nodded, and she thought that though she was falling apart inside, he looked visibly rattled—and furious.

When court was resumed, Godley paced before the jurists and delivered in five minutes, admittedly a sound-proof summation of all the evidence pointing to Heath's guilt. She, on the other hand, could barely stand before the jury box, so wobbly were her knees. She was desperately afraid her voice would crack from the many months of accumulated strain, that she would break down weeping like the stereotyped female so many of her male colleagues scorned.

Frazzled, she could only finish her summation with the weak last resort. "…and I remind you, that if you have the slightest doubt of the charges against my client, then you must find him not guilty."

She wanted to weep then and there at her ineptness. She couldn't bring herself to look at Heath, afraid to see his stricken face, as the bailiff led him away. And as soon as the judge sent the jury to deliberations, she grabbed her coat and galoshes and fled outside.

She paced the slick sidewalk. Her arms wrapped about her, as though this way she could hold herself together if Heath was found guilty.

Fifteen minutes later, Betty, bracing her small-boned body against the wind, joined her. Shaking her head, Betty crimped her mouth. "The verdict could come in soon, within fifteen minutes, Mariana—or it could take days."

"It's not like I'm going to miss sleep, since I don't anyway." She sighed. "Let's go back in."

When she entered the courtroom, electricity vibrated the air. The bailiff was bringing Heath back in, and the sequestered jurists had already returned to the jury box.

She hurried to resume her seat next to Heath at the counselor's table. The judge entered, and everyone immediately stood. Sudden panic gripped her. Had she done everything she could? But it was too late now to do anything more. At her side, she could feel Heath's solid presence, hear his steady breathing. What was he feeling? Just relief, either way, that the long ordeal was over?

Once the court was called to order, the judge requested the foreman read the jury's verdict. Her heart was throbbing in her throat.

"Your Honor, we, the jury, find the accused Heath Paladín… not guilty of the charge of first-degree murder."

She collapsed then, and it was Heath's large hands which caught her, supported her, and drew her against him. All around them, it was chaos. Camera bulbs flashed as people shoved and yelled. And he kissed her tear-wet lips. Her first kiss from the love of her life. Never would she have imagined it would happen like this. But, of course, life with Heath could never be any other way but on-the-edge exciting.

16

ROSWELL, NEW MEXICO
MAY 1929

In the cramped bathroom's tarnished door mirror Edna squinted at the reflection of her ungainly, naked body. It looked like a flagpole with a basketball mask taped to it. She couldn't imagine what Byron had found appealing enough to lust after her.

Best friends, confidants, colleagues… these might possibly justify why the handsome and imaginative Paladín heir would consider marrying her—her, a nobody, one of five daughters of a hard-scrabble dairy farmer outside Roswell. But to be randy enough to bed her with the same loving lust over all these years… well, given that and his charming sockless obsession, he had to be as eccentric as most people probably thought him.

The stench from the cattle pens had been enough to convince her to get a higher education to support herself and move on. After all, with her lack of looks, she was anticipating being the proverbial Old Maid for the rest of her life. The strange sight of an immense balloon drifting above the dairy farm and a human leaning from the balloon to wave pointed the direction her studies would take.

She ran a doting hand over her mounding stomach with its faintly pink stretch marks and outie belly button—and gasped at the sudden pain thrusting through her. She collapsed to her knees, her head braced on the commode lid, her arms cradling her knotting stomach. Contractions so soon?

For days, a lower backache had plagued her, but the baby wasn't due for another three weeks. Byron had driven in to Roswell to pick up ordinary machine parts for a combustion chamber he had designed and wasn't due back for hours.

Drawing a steadying breath, she waited for the pain to pass, then levered her heavy body upright. Probably just a false labor pain, but best to gather supplies, just in case. Towels, tissues, a sheet, scissors, and hydrogen peroxide for sterilizing. She had to smile, thinking how ironical it was that Byron used the same chemical in his rocket fuels.

When she finally managed to open the linen closet, her smile faded abruptly, and she gripped the edge of the shelf for support. Her teeth clenched as she doubled over, feeling the fluid soaking her loose knickers. Looking down, she saw the bloody mucous on the chipped linoleum floor between her legs. Dear God, the baby was coming.

She grabbed a couple of shabby towels and toed off her sturdy oxfords. Moaning when another sharp jab fired through her, she shed her cotton stockings and underdrawers, then eased herself into the clawfoot tub.

With each round of pain, she shoved her feet against the tub wall. She tried timing between the contractions and realized they were mere minutes apart. The baby had to be coming soon. Oh, Jesus, and let Byron be coming soon, too. Sweat blossomed on her temples and upper lip, and the contractions continued. One upon the other—waves of pain crashing against her.

Where the hell was Byron? And where the hell was the baby? Groaning, panting, she pushed, trying to move her baby on into this world. Yet there were still the bouts of debilitating pain that left her gasping and had her sweating all over now.

She suspected what was wrong. The baby was stuck in the birth canal. And, for the umpteenth time, she cursed her broomstick frame. But, she didn't really begin to worry until she saw the pink froth pooling at the tub drain. At some point, she could hear her shrieks, coming as though from a distance. As what surely had to be an hour passed, she could feel herself growing weaker.

Oh, God, the continuing pain was more than any human could possibly tolerate. Screams—and shouts that weren't hers—reverberated against the bathroom walls. Through tear dampened lashes, she made out Byron leaning over the tub's rim. His hands were pushing, massaging her hard stomach.

"Push, Edna, *push!*"

"Goddamnit, Byron… I have been."

Then he was in the tub with her, jamming her legs up against her stomach and thrusting his hand inside her, feeling around. Her head tilted back in a shrill howl that went on forever. When she found her breath, she gasped, "Let… me… die… but our baby… help… help it."

"Listen to me." He was gasping, too. "I've got to cut you."

"No!" she shrieked. She wouldn't live through a cesarean. Couldn't. She was delirious with the pain. She kept pushing past it. "Oh, God… just don't let our baby… die."

He moved away, climbed from the tub, and she barely heard his answer. "…an episiotomy."

Pain after pain roared through her body, leaving a wreckage of bones and flesh. Her raw throat got out little more than a feeble yell of protest.

Then he was back, crouching in front of her, hunting knife in one hand, hydrogen peroxide bottle in the other. His steely focus of determination distorted his features into a gargoyle's face. "Look at me, Edna."

She tried to pay attention, but it required so much strength.

He began talking in a steady, reassuring tone he might use to gentle a nervous filly. "So, here is what we'll do. What I'll do will be quick—just enough to widen the passage. All that you need to do is breathe slowly and—"

With that, his knife ripped through her, and a never-ending scream ripped through heaven and hell to make its way through her sternum. She thought for a moment she had passed out, then she heard him sobbing. She lifted her head, peered through bleary eyes, and saw the tiny thrashing, mucousy limbs he cupped between his huge hands. "We've added another male Paladín to the old Baron's peerage pole, Edna!"

––––––––––––

THE BARONY, TEXAS
NOVEMBER 1929

Pierce opened the door to The Barony bedroom he and Aubrey had been assigned for the week's Thanksgiving and wedding festivities and stopped short. His mouth opened, shut, and opened again. "What in the hell have you gone and done?"

Aubrey, scissors in hand, stared at him in the vanity dresser's mirror. Her glorious dark Victorian locks lay strewn about her stool. *"Eh bien,* you took notice, *n'est-ce pas?"*

He planted his fists on his hips and eyed her hair, shingled *a la* Claire Bow. "Just what does that mean?"

Swishing her white silk dressing gown out of the way, she swiveled on the stool. Her large, almond-shaped brown eyes, over-emphasized by curls framing her gamine features, stared back unflinchingly. "You take no notice of me… except those nights when your need for me overcomes your…." She paused to select the best fitting word in English. "Your *guardedness.* But I see it. I see the want in your eyes sometimes, *ma chérie."*

Shutting the door behind him, he went to her, step-by-purposeful-step. He cupped her upturned face between large splayed hands. "I want you all the time. The haircut doesn't do your beauty justice."

Her lips worked. She waited, wanting from him what he was unable to give—his absolute trust, his willingness to be vulnerable.

He dropped a kiss on her forehead. "Put the scissors down, my love. You might hurt yourself."

Her fathomless eyes searched his. "Or you?"

He turned away and, hobbling toward the bathroom, began shrugging out of his V-neck sweater. "You had best start getting ready or we'll be late for the wedding procession."

The scissors thudded against the bathroom door and clattered onto the Saltillo tiled floor. He paused and looked over his shoulder. She was standing, facing him, her hands clenched at her sides. "You have a bad aim, Aubrey."

Her eyes glistened, but her tone was as sharp and steely as her scissors. "Oh, I think not. I did not do so badly with a surgical knife ten years ago, did I?"

He shut the door, bracing his hands on the washstand edges. Staring into the shaving mirror, he did not like the beard-shadowed face he saw. Could he and Aubrey go on for another decade like this, pecking away at each other's hearts until there was nothing left in their chest cavities?

From among his toiletry bottles, he grabbed the jar of shaving cream and razor. When he exited the bathroom, showered and dressed, she was sitting on the bed's edge, dressed for the evening and waiting for him.

He opened the bedroom door and, in silence, she rose and crossed the room. She paused in the doorway to look up at him with a small, tight and angry smile.

He returned it and indicated for her to proceed him. She was undeniably beautiful in an ivory jersey dress with pearls that draped down her nearly bare elegant back. Her shingled auburn hair exposed her long, graceful neck and nape, a spot he found most erotic, more so even than a woman's breasts. It was all he could do to refrain from bending his head and kissing that exquisite spot.

The parlor was spilling over with Paladíns who stood elbow-to-elbow in the arched corridor, all waiting eagerly for Mariana to descend the wrought-iron staircase.

As a marriage between first cousins was still considered a felony in Texas—with a ten-year prison sentence for having sex with one's spouse, an incestuous act—no formal announcement had gone out to the public. But beginning with the biblical Isaac taking his cousin Rebekah for a wife to as recently as Prince Albert wedding Queen Victoria, with none of the offspring the worse for it, popular opinion was growing less condemning.

Heath, in a black cutaway and looking as dashing as his screen image, waited at the bottom and talked in restive gestures with his father and Byron and Darcy, as well as the father of the bride. Uncle Nicolás looked both happy and misty-eyed. Darcy's stepson Timmy shifted from foot to foot, plainly bored.

Pierce spotted Rosa Ramirez, reticently standing off to one side of the corridor. With Aubrey, he wedged through the press of people to join Rosa and her three children, the youngest no longer a babe in arms but now a toddler with a thumb jammed in his bud-like mouth.

It had been Aubrey and Betty who had made a last-minute desperate and persuasive reattempt to get the widow to testify. With only hours to spare, he had flown them from El Paso to Corpus Christi.

"Are you getting settled in, Rosa?"

She smiled shyly. *"Sí, Señor* Paladín." Her soft voice was almost lost amid the hubbub of conversation of the waiting wedding guests. Her braids were wreathed atop her head like a crown, and she had on a pretty, pink calf-length dress.

After the trial, Uncle Drake had given her employment at the *hacienda* and sanctuary at the *Paladíneños'* villa, *La Baroncita*—just in case Roger and his father decided to seek reprisal following the Not Guilty verdict that had been brought in. The Clarendons were sure to be in a rage to revenge upon losing this battle in their ongoing war against the Paladíns, though in Pierce's mind, the Clarendons were worth little more than target practice.

The State had yet to file any kind of charge against Bonaventure, and Pierce suspected an under-the-table exchange of money would ensure the matter would disappear into obscurity.

Aubrey was already leaning near the two eldest children to chat animatedly with that charming way she had with her hands. Both grinned bashfully.

Her longing for children was almost tangible, and it knifed him with guilt. It was not for lack of trying. Rather, he suspected nothing could be created and nourished by their antagonism.

"You wish to learn to ride like your father?" Her smile encompassed the girl who appeared to be about eight or nine. "You have met Manny? He can tell you about The Barony horses."

Her younger brother, Pablo, cried, "I want to ride, I want to ride."

Also crying at that moment was Byron and Edna's six-month-old, Jack. Naturally, Aubrey's face lit up as she turned to Edna, who was trying to shush the infant. Aubrey's soft cooing clearly worked her magic with the baby.

Suddenly, the corridor and parlor went silent. Pierce followed the direction of the guests' uplifted faces. Mariana stood at the top of the stairs, poised momentarily like the glorious tawny-orange monarch butterflies that migrated through Barony lands each autumn. Behind her hovered her mother, Pearl, and Aunt Angel. He supposed the two were performing the last-minute miracles demanded of fairy godmothers.

Mariana had shared with Aubrey that she considered herself too old at the ripe old age of twenty-seven for virginal white. Keeping with an autumn theme, she chose a floor-length gown of beige lace over old gold silk and carried a bouquet of bronze chrysanthemums. Flouting the tradition of a wedding veil, she wore a large brimmed picture hat of brown and cream velvet that gave a peekaboo glance of her inky black hair.

Pierce glanced back at Heath, waiting at the bottom of the stairs. His cousin's face was a study in joy and deep contentment. How Pierce envied him. He thought of his own youthful excesses, of making choices without heed to their consequences.

In the mellow afternoon, the wedding guests followed the bride and groom up the zig-zag incline of the rocky bluff behind the *hacienda*. At the crest, as they took their positions, fallen leaves of the enormous live oak crunched underfoot.

Here, in 1763, a Paladín had first stood and surveyed his royal Spanish land grant. Here, too, were buried the Paladíns that had followed. And here, beneath the live oak, the widower Alex Paladín had taken the Frenchwoman Therese to be his bride.

Theirs had been a blend of frenzied passions and fiery temperaments that coalesced into deep, abiding love. Pierce sincerely doubted if, in marrying his own Frenchwoman, he had any hope of a similar outcome.

Where once beneath the oak a rotund padre in cassock had awaited the arrival of Alex Paladín's wedding party, a rawboned priest in roman collar now stood, awaiting Heath and Mariana.

The beaming Father O'Donnell began with an impish smile. "Along with baptism and burial, marriage is one of the three grand events in a person's life, and the only one at which he or she can fully appreciate the full glory of being the center of focus."

Chuckles turned to sniffles as the vows were exchanged. Hannah and Betty as bridesmaids played at vying for the bouquet Mariana tossed over her shoulder, then it was back down the bluff to the *hacienda* and the all-night festivities.

Except, Pierce didn't make it more than a few yards back down the slope. With a small yelp, Pablo slipped on loose shale and tumbled to his knees. "Hold on, son, I'll piggyback you."

But when, with his less-than-smooth gait, he went to circumvent a rocky ledge protruding on the narrow path, Aubrey shoved him. Shocked, falling, he looked up into her eyes for what seemed an eternal second—and saw their grim determination.

After all those years of relying on his instincts, he should have known better.

THE ANXIOUS GUESTS GATHERED IN twos and threes, scattered throughout the parlor, dining room, kitchen, and the stair steps—most within distance of Drake and Angel's bedroom, where Aubrey had been carried. Stoney—who, as a vet, was the closest and most immediate access she would have to an M.D. for the snake bite she had suffered pushing Pierce out of harm's way—examined her cautiously as Pierce gripped her hand in his own.

Outside the bedroom door, hushed voices drifted around in idle conversation, talking about other things to take their minds off their concern for her. "I fear the worst is yet to come for the banks—and for our country," Hannah's Uncle Nicolás was saying, one sleeve braced on the staircase's wrought-iron newel.

"Well, the market has nowhere to go but up." Father O'Donnell shook his head. "Just look at the considerable recovery in the past weeks since the panic selling."

Politely listening, Hannah struggled to contain her boredom. Besides, of everyone present, Nicolás Cordova, a broker, would have greater inside knowledge about the stock market crash the month before. Or even Preston, who was said to have the largest savings and loans in Houston.

Restless, she took her mug of brandy-laced coffee and wandered through the house. As she passed the kitchen, she overheard concerned feminine voices, softened to discreet murmurs, expressing their concern for Aubrey. In the parlor, several people were huddled, only half listening to the radio, its volume lowered.

She sighed, feeling she fit in nowhere and roamed out to the veranda. At one end, Preston and Byron hunkered on the railing with Hannah's father, David. From the other end, ensconced on the veranda swing, her mother's dulcet voice and that of Aunt Angel's vied with the creak of the swing's gently swaying chains.

Hannah circled back through the house, passing Uncle Griffin and Uncle Drake in his study. The sweet cherry blend of cigar smoke drifted through the doorway, and she unintentionally eavesdropped on their talk of baseball— that Babe Ruth had hit his 500th homerun against the Cleveland Indians.

The memory of that electrifying meeting with Michael, at the World Series held at the Polo Grounds, snatched the breath from her. It was like that, even after all this time, when she least expected it—a word or a glimpse or a sneaky reminiscence would twist a dagger deep into her heart.

Stunned, she turned away, sloshing her coffee. However, her new route took her past Heath and Mariana, locked in one another's arms beneath the stairwell's dim alcove. His hands roamed possessively over his bride's shoulders, back, and waist. Making little mewling noises, Mariana looped her arms around his neck, arching her slight body against his.

At that erotic glimpse, Hannah bolted out back of the *hacienda,* heading for the refuge of the old gazebo. The night was chilly, but she didn't want to brave the crowd inside to find a wrap.

Settling down on the bench that ran the perimeter of the octagonal gazebo, she leaned back against a post and, setting down her mug, tried to steady her breath. The pang of passion's loss was sometimes more than she could bear.

Blindly, she gazed at the frosty stars twinkling low on the horizon. How could she still be grieving over Michael after all this time? It wasn't as if she didn't go out on occasional dates, but they were cosmopolitan men with effete good looks and none of Michael's driving force.

"Your coffee's getting cold."

Surprised, she almost overturned her half-drained mug. Looking over her shoulder, she saw Stoney directly behind her. Trailing his blunt fingers along the cedar railing, he strode around the gazebo to its opening and ambled toward her. With each step, his boots thudded on the old boards.

He took a seat a little away, flipping back his black corduroy denim jacket, stretching out his stovepipe, jean-clad legs, and cupping his palms behind his nape. "So, you had to get away too?"

"I had hoped to catch the sunset." Not a complete lie. She leaned slightly toward him. "How is Aubrey?"

He heaved a fatigued sigh that rustled his black satin string tie. "She's going to make it. It was a big rattler—its head as large as a child's hand. It'd been sunning itself on the rock, most likely. When she shoved Pierce out of the way, the diamondback clipped her instead. On the forearm with one fang—the other hit the rock."

She shivered and set the mug aside, rubbing her upper arms. "One less puncture wound, at least."

"True, less venom. And she's young and healthy. As far as long-term health problems, it's difficult to say. Things like phlebitis, arthritis, nerve pain. But I seriously doubt there will be any lingering issues."

Hannah had been farther along down the trail when the incident happened. "I hope someone smashed the damn snake's head flatter than a pancake."

Laced fingers still bracing his neck, he turned his head slightly to peer at her through the darkness. Beneath the sweep of this brown mustache, his lips twisted in a half smile. "Amazingly enough, vipers have been reported to bite humans even after being decapitated."

"You're kidding me!"

He shifted his gaze back out to the starlit shrubbery and trees. "No, ma'am."

"Remember, I asked you call me Hannah."

"And you can call me Stoney."

"Where did you get the name, Stoney?"

He straightened up, dropped his clasped, capable hands between his spread knees, and turned to fix her with one of his corner-hitched grins. "Stonewall Jackson. And if you laugh, I swear I'll take a switch to you."

Her mouth twitched in an effort not to grin. She held up two fingers. "Boy Scout's honor, I won't."

"My turn with the questions. I heard about your husband's assassination."

"Four years ago, last month." She was somewhat dismayed at the sound of her monotone voice. It was if she were discussing the best way to fry an egg.

"Your puncture wounds, to the heart," he murmured. "Have they healed?"

She started. "Why are you asking?"

"Just wondering if you miss Texas sunsets enough to come back permanently."

Oh God! She grabbed her mug and rose. "You're too young for me."

At that he grinned broadly, flashing those pearly whites. "I was thinking more along the lines of hooking you up with my father. He's a friend of your Uncle Drake's."

It was all she could do to refrain from tossing her coffee on him. "Of course you wouldn't know,"—her withering tone enunciated each word— "but Paris is famed as the City of Light. I much prefer its night-long brilliance to a two-minute paltry Texas sunset." With that, she made the most dignified exit she could muster.

———————————

LOOKING DOWN AT AUBREY'S FRAIL form, struggling to cope with the poison in her system, Pierce was overcome by his love for her. He sat at her bedside, holding her right hand. Her left, cleansed and covered by a loose, sterile bandage, lay at her side... ringless.

Dr. Jackson had immediately told him to remove the wedding ring. He'd told him the most important thing he could do at this point was to keep her calm, with her heart rate down, so the venom didn't spread farther.

And so, smoothing back the damp tendrils of hair from her temples, he spoke in a quiet, soothing whisper, telling her what he knew her heart, her soul, most wanted, most needed, to hear from him.

"Aubrey, can you hear me? Do you know how much I love you? How much I have always loved you? So much, so greatly in fact, that I was afraid of losing myself. But isn't that what love really is? The complete surrendering of oneself for the other?" Tears welled in his eyes as he murmured, more to himself, "As you have for me."

He could feel the walls he had carefully constructed falling away and knew that, at last, his heart had come home to stay.

———————————

PUFFING ON HIS PIPE, BYRON sat mesmerized in the upholstered chair as he watched Edna nurse their son. An enthusiastic Jack nuzzled her breast like a hungry piglet. Her breasts were no longer flat as a washboard, and

Byron had to grin. Her hips had expanded from beanpole size to that of a voluptuous starlet. Her face glowed with a beauty that Hollywood paint could not reproduce. He sure hit the jackpot when he married her.

And he had almost lost her—both her and the baby. It made his heart shrivel like a raisin every time he thought about that afternoon he found her bleeding in the tub.

She squinted at his oxfords. "If it isn't Buck Rogers, wearing socks!"

"Now, don't go getting ideas, old girl." He took the pipe from his mouth. "I spruced up for Heath's wedding only. Once we get back to Roswell, I am retiring the socks."

As if mention of the New Mexican town summoned alchemy, a rap came at their bedroom door, followed by his mother's voice. "Byron, your father says the switchboard operator has an urgent call for you. From Roswell."

Byron exchanged a glance with Edna, puzzled as to whom would be calling that late in the evening. Angel, her glasses perched atop her head, led him down the corridor to Drake's study. "Drake says the call is from a Robert Goddard."

Byron and Edna hadn't heard from Goddard in three years—not since the Guggenheim Foundation agreed to fund his research. So, what the hell was he doing in Roswell?

Drake passed him the telephone receiver and discreetly left, his arm around Angel's shoulders. "Byron here."

"Byron, it's Goddard. I'm calling from NMMI."

"Yes." He recalled the military institute was in an hour earlier time zone and, of course, they would have his father's telephone number. "What are you doing in Roswell?"

"Hell, with the stock market crash, Guggenheim has cut my funding. And I refuse to work with the CalTech scientists. Roswell seems the perfect place for Esther and me to hide out and work. Does you offer still stand?"

"Sure, you and Esther are welcome to join us." A man of Goddard's rocket wizardry would be a boon to his own astrodynamic research. "Why don't you motor on out to the place? Old Hector down the road has the key—he's feeding Fritz for us—and he can let you in."

"Uhh… well, that's another reason I'm calling, Byron. We were just out at your place and… uhh… Byron, it looks like someone has been here ahead of us. The front door had been broken in. I don't know what all, if anything, was taken. But, uh… Esther found Fritz in the entryway. Dead. He'd been shot."

He gulped, trying to get a word past his throat and cleared it again. Fritz… smart, devoted, Fritz had been like family. "Listen, would you mind burying Fritz for me? Beneath the old bois d'arc tree behind the house. I'll start back at once."

When he told Edna, she buried her face in her hands in a silent weeping that tore his heart out. They made their excuses to the rest of the family and started back that night. Late the next day, Goddard and Esther met them out on the porch. "Come on into the kitchen," she told a worn-out Edna, giving her a warm hug. "I've made a meatloaf and chicken salad sandwiches. And here, let me hold the baby while you eat."

"Go ahead," Byron told them. "I'll join you all in a few minutes."

But Goddard knew what Byron was about and followed him back to the tiny second bedroom that served as an office. Byron glanced at the papers strewn on the desk, the piles in both wire-frame baskets, then crossed to the crates that served as bookshelves. He counted his notebooks, then frowned.

"Is something missing?"

He shook his head. "Not one page, not one notebook. Everything is here."

"But…?"

"I'd swear on the old Baron's grave… these pages, my notebooks, Edna's records—they're not in the same order, the same place, as when we left."

17

This was one Barony Thanksgiving no Paladín wanted to celebrate but was forced to attend. Drake had designated the date for the family conclave. The last such war council had been called by his father during the Panic of 1893.

The difference in this one was that President Hoover wasn't calling it a panic or crisis but rather a depression—perhaps to soften the impact of thirty billion dollars vanishing into air in a single day.

But following that Black Tuesday of October 29, 1929, when investors had committed suicide by jumping from windows, unemployment had begun to soar, and poverty and starvation became real possibilities for everyone. Governments seemed powerless against the worldwide economic collapse. Fear ruled. The United States was closer to crumbling than it had been at any time in its history since the Civil War.

The Great Depression had begun.

Apart from Drake and Angel, ten people stood, lounged, or sat in his office—six men, Claire and Pearl, and their daughters, Hannah and Mariana. All Paladín heirs and The Barony Enterprises's Board of Directors, with Mariana serving as legal counsel.

Drake propped his scuffed and spurred boots atop the massive desk that had been his father's and bit back the protesting groan of his old bones.

In one of Angel's sassy, chiding looks, her eyes narrowed, their crow's feet fanning out.

He rolled his own eyes but took his boots off the desk. Hard to believe that he had won her, a child of seven, in a poker game. Like a leach, she had latched onto him and wouldn't let go until he married her a decade later, thank God. What a *pendejo* he had been, until she had made him see the light—and, for that matter, literally see. At least, see *better.*

He leaned forward, his clasped, weathered hands braced on the desk blotter. "In view of the bottomed-out economy," he stated in the same no-nonsense, gravelly tone of his late father's, "I called this meeting. Barony Enterprises is on shaky ground."

He bit off the end of his cigar and spit it into the spittoon next to the desk. "Before we address this issue directly, just one item I'm required to put on the floor that has an indirect bearing. The Texas Highway Department wants to traverse Barony domain with a Hug-the-Coast-Highway. The recompense is paltry, but it's money much needed. Thoughts?"

"Hell, no," Heath's arms folded. He stood with his usual casual grace, slightly behind him as his right-hand man. "Grandfather Alex would turn over in his grave. Didn't he always say 'Land is everything. Buy land and never sell?' We are the second largest ranch in the world, and if I have my way, it'll stay that way."

"Anyone else?" Drake inquired.

"I still have colleagues in Austin." The gray that had thoroughly invaded Griffin's red hair imparted a trustworthy look that matched his character. "I do know highway commissioners have moved quickly to allocate hundreds of thousands of dollars in federal money to road projects to create further economic benefit in Texas. I'll see what I can do to get this particular project taken off the table."

Griffin flicked a glance at Mariana. "Can you check on any legal barricades we may be facing?"

"Sure thing, Uncle Griffin." She jotted on the notepad braced on her lap.

"Show of hands for Heath's position?"

As he had known all along, the motion carried unanimously.

"All right," he continued, "next. My plan for stabilization of Barony Enterprises. Survival tactics are required. Simply put, it calls for funneling all surplus income from the various Paladín companies—including Angel's Lone Star Smelter—into Barony Enterprises, which is everything any Paladín worth his salt holds dear. It's our land itself."

Between his father, his Uncle Niall, and Uncle Karl, who had served as legal counsel back then, the three had architected The Barony into a tightknit fabric of financial support, and for that, Drake was grateful.

He paused. "Any dissension so far?"

Byron was the first to speak. "Well, apart from the patent from my tri-cone rotary rock drill, which isn't worth a hill of beans right now, Edna, Jack, and I are living on beans, you might say." He rubbed his beard-scruffed jaw. "But Barony Enterprises is welcome to Paladín Tool's dwindling revenue."

Hannah, seated on the cracked leather old sofa, spoke up. "I have only a third interest in Dallas Emporium, but count mine in, Uncle Drake."

"And my third of the Emporium, as well," chimed in Claire, wedged between her daughter and Mariana.

Mariana glanced at Heath and nodded her assent. "We're in," Heath said. "Mariana's practice has escalated since the trial, but who knows, as time goes on, if people will be able to afford legal representation."

Drake struck a match off his boot bottom and lit his cigar. "Everyone here understands, of course, that Heath, as head of The Barony Ranch, is forfeiting his salary for now?"

General nods of agreement passed through the office.

Pearl added, "Barony Enterprises is welcome to whatever proceeds my share comes to."

Griffin's well-groomed hands, accented by gold cufflinks, made an expansive gesture. "Paladín Builders is behind your plan, Drake, for whatever it's worth. Other than the Empire State Building, construction across America is dead as a doornail."

Pierce tunneled fingers through his tawny-gold locks. As general manager of Lone Star Smelter, he was managing to keep afloat the company Angel had inherited while the national economy sank. "Paladín Aviation may go down the tube as well, but as long as I can keep its aircraft in the air, The Barony's got its profits."

"As the bearer of good news, at least for now," Darcy shrugged, "Double Take Studio Productions is well into the black. Bad times for the public is good times for Belle and me. You can bank on us."

That left only one hold out—the one who had invariably held out all these years. And yet, Drake felt himself a kindred spirit with his renegade grandnephew. He turned his focus on Preston, who stood at the far back of the room, slouched against one corner wall.

Dressed in Levi's, his hands, all but his thumbs, jammed in the pockets of his old bomber jacket, his dark red hair badly in need of a haircut, no one would suspect one of Houston's skyscrapers belonged to him, as well as an ornate theater, a grand hotel, and a savings and loan. Rumor had it that he was a love 'em and leave 'em rogue, much as the old Baron was reputed to have been before Fiona Flanagan's smile cut him off at the knees.

"And you, Preston?"

"Loving poker like I do," Preston drawled, at last, the toothpick in his mouth bobbing, "I'd advise The Barony—and the U.S. government—to raise its bid. Increase its spending by borrowing rather than cutting back. Capitalizing on creative credit, I like to call it."

Word was that when there had been a run on two Houston banks after the stock market crash, which jeopardized all the others, Preston had called the city's leading businessmen to his office to work out a plan that would allow his savings and loan and their businesses to rescue the two faltering banks, for the time being anyway.

A savvy businessman, his grandnephew, stabilizing the other two banks so his own didn't sink with the national debt's ship. But even high-stakes gambling wouldn't have produced the kind of money needed for skyscrapers and grand hotels.

"Preston, your poker methodology is all well and good, but banks have already lost their depositors' savings. Whatever banks still do have funds, you can bet your creative credit they are already charging sky-high interest rates."

"Not my bank."

"Meaning what?" Mariana paused in her scribbling and frowned. "That your bank isn't charging sky high interest rates—or that your bank, and your other investments, aren't included when discussing a coalition of family businesses?"

"Both."

The office air temperature plummeted thirty degrees.

"Well that makes sense," she turned her face back to the notepad in her lap. "You never did need family, did you?"

His narrow-eyed gaze swept the room. Silence pervaded a beat too long for Drake's peace of mind. "No."

"Being a gambling man," Pierce asked his twin in an obvious attempt to ease the tension in the room, "exactly why didn't you lose any money with the crash?"

Preston removed its toothpick. "Hell, when I overheard even the shoe-shine boys speculating on stocks, I knew the stock market had to be in a bubble. I sold out early and kept the profits."

"Hot damn!" Drake laughed and slapped his palm on the desk blotter. "So, you won't throw in your lot with us losers. If we do take your sage advice and borrow, Preston, what would your bank offer Barony Enterprises in terms of an interest rate?"

Preston pushed off the wall with his wiry strength and headed for the door, then paused to look over his shoulder. His eyes, fanned with squint lines, surveyed once again the family members, one by one, then settled on his father before returning to Drake. A cocky grin nicked the ends of his mouth. "An interest rate? What interest rate?"

NOW THAT THE SPEED LIMIT had increased to thirty-five miles per hour, the forest green DeSoto sedan fairly flew up the newly constructed Highway 2 between San Antonio and Dallas. But after wild darting and dashing of Paris taxis, Hannah's father's sedate driving seemed excruciatingly slow.

Her mother, appearing unaware of the snail's pace, was chuckling at the jingle on a series of Burma-Shave signs they were passing.

Within the vale...
of toil...
and sin...
your head bald...
but not your chin. Use...
Burma-Shave.

Despite her sour mood, Hannah had to smile, though it soon faded from her lips.

As she had done yearly, she made the transatlantic voyage for The Barony Thanksgiving festivities in conjunction with her own annual office conferences at the Dallas Emporium.

This year had been different, of course, with the emergency calling of The Barony's Board of Directors in response to the stock market crash. She was certain she would have to address that same issue when she got back to Dallas and met with her father and mother's Emporium officers.

In buying for next year's fashions, she had not anticipated the radical drop in hemlines following the crash. The trade shows she had attended had given no indication of the coming trend. Her flair for color and design could not counterbalance the drastically narrowing profit margin.

The radical change in women's clothing styles affected not only inventory but catalogues now featuring outdated fashions. Worse, few could now afford Dallas Emporium's upscale merchandise.

But it was not the Paladíns' admittedly dire financial straits nor that of Dallas Emporium's that perturbed her. True, the face-off with Preston had been disturbing. She hated dissension in the family. Thankfully, and astonishingly, he had offered Barony Enterprises a percentage-free laissez-faire at his bank.

So, she shouldn't be aggravated, but she was—with Stoney Jackson, of all people, damn him. He had pricked her pride.

A year had passed since last she had seen him, there in The Barony gazebo. A year filled with meaningless affairs with Russian royalty, Italian counts, French playboys, Latin adventurers, and German diplomats. All in an effort to forget a man who had never even held her hand. A man who had only hurt her Paladín pride.

When her mother pressed, she merely replied she was "keeping company" with this gentleman or that. She navigated through European *haute société's* pretentious emptiness with ease, because that was precisely what she was— pretentious and empty.

And Dr. Stoney Jackson, the simple and honest animal doctor he was, saw through her facade.

But did he have to show up at The Barony this Thanksgiving with his father in an obvious effort to foist the widower on her, making a sour point that she was an older woman?

The forty-six-year-old Dobie Jackson was a mature version of Stoney. Same virile good looks but with graying hair, he was confident yet humble, observant and intelligent—and short and bow-legged and boring.

Stoney was trying to persuade his father to move from Amarillo to San Antonio, where Stoney provided his veterinarian services to surrounding ranches—though he was on call at any time for The Barony. Uncle Drake and

Aunt Angel considered him like family, and Heath depended on his superior veterinarian skills above those of other vets the ranch employed.

Seeing through her as Stoney did, she had been unconvinced that he would actually want her for a stepmother.

At the Thanksgiving dinner that followed the Paladín war council, Stoney had the brashness to lean forward and, catching her eye, smile. "Hannah, my father is going to be in Fort Worth this coming March for the stock show. If you're in the country, I would be much obliged if you would show him around Dallas."

Conversation around the table had ebbed. Dobie had cleared his throat, his fork midway to this mouth. "I apologize for my son, Missus Kraft. I realize what an imposition he has placed on—"

"That would be no imposition at all." She stabbed Stoney with her most charming smile. Surely, the vile man had to have been aware that she was in the country only a couple of times a year, at that, and neither of those coincided with Cowtown's stock show.

"You know, Hannah," her father interrupted her fuming reverie, "when I kidnapped your mother, we made the trip from The Barony all the way to Dallas by buckboard."

"You kidnapped her?" She had never heard this version of her parents' get-together.

The common story went that his and her mother's grandparents, long-time friends, thought it would be a good match. Sort of an old-fashioned marriage of convenience.

Lamentably, Grandfather Buck hadn't seen it that way, and another family feud had been precipitated.

It was difficult to imagine this distinguished older man, her father and one of the founders of Southern Methodist University—despite his being a Jew—doing such a rash, romantic act.

Her mother reached across and tweaked his earlobe affectionately. "You most certainly did not kidnap me, David Solomon. If you had not have asked me to go with you, I would have stowed away among all that merchandise you were hauling."

He grinned and slid her mother a look that, after all those years, still communicated distinct desire. "Claire was only sixteen, Hannah, and the same week I met her, I asked her to marry me. In an instant, I knew she was the only woman for me."

She knew what was forthcoming and tried to forestall it. "I've been going over the Emporium's numbers, and I think if we begin by cutting back on our high-end items, we ca—"

"Hannah," her mother broke in, half turning in the front seat to face her, "you're almost thirty. Do you never think about remarrying?"

So much for avoiding the inevitable. "Why should I, Mom? I have everything I want. Friends. Family. Career."

"But you don't have children," her father chimed in.

"One less worry. Especially now, with the crime and poverty all around us."

"It has been and always will be." Her mother shook her head. "And you were never a worry. You were our richest blessing."

"You're worrying about me now, are you?"

"What about that nice young veterinarian—Doctor Jackson?"

"Mom, he's eight years younger than me."

"Oh, that does seem like an insurmountable age difference." Her father smiled wryly.

"You may jest, Father,"—her tone was dry as the desert—"but try the age difference between me and his father. It's his father Stoney's trying to pair me up with, not himself."

Over his shoulder, her father shot her a glance of dismay. "For all your pseudo sophistication, Hannah, you are hopelessly naïve. I think it's time we recalled you from Paris—at least for a while."

"Oh, no you don't, Dad. You're not going to bring me back to pair me up with Stoney Jackson. I'm not leaving Paris."

Even if her parents ordered, she had far too many contacts to ever be adrift in Europe without resources. Its cosmopolitan cities were like second skin to her. Comfortable. No, Europe was the only place where her heart most found respite, insulated as she was by memories of Michael.

ROSWELL, NEW MEXICO

With one-year-old babbling Jack sitting atop his shoulders, Byron strode from his jalopy toward the launching tower. As much as he loved seeing the family and The Barony at Thanksgiving, he was glad to be back to work.

And glad the Goddards had watched over the place while he and Edna were away. Since the break-in and the loss of Fritz, he was uneasy. Fortunately, because of Edna's own uneasiness, all his research papers since then were kept in a trunk that went with them whenever they were away.

Ahead of him, despite the cool day, a gust of wind whipped the red sand into a dust devil, rare for that time of year. Jack squealed with delight and yanked on Byron's shaggy dark locks. "Whoa big guy." He loosened the tight little fists of hair. He had volunteered to watch Jack while Edna played bridge in town with Esther and some others.

Goddard, who had bought Old Hector's ranch, was already waiting for him at the launching tower. He had towed the latest version of their liquid fueled rocket from their workshop in an old hay cart. Nearly twelve feet in length with fins, it was already installed in the steel-frame tower.

He noted Goddard wore a look of misgiving. "You ready for the test flight?"

The small, thin man had taken to wearing ten-gallon hats to protect his pate. He frowned. "Me and the Soviet Union Secret Police."

"What?"

"While you were away at The Barony, we had a visit from the Secret Service. Seems the Soviets managed to plant a spy in the U.S. Navy Bureau of Aeronautics. A stenographer. She gave the Soviets a report of our tests, flights, and research work."

"What the hell was the Navy doing with our papers?"

"Probably took photographs of them during your break-in last year."

Byron's mind automatically connected the dots between the U.S. Navy Bureau of Aeronautics and the Supreme Court's far reaching tentacles.

"The only good thing to come out of this," Goddard growled, "is that your research material back then was in its early stages."

"Yeah, but it may have given the Soviets and the Germans a leg up."

He swiped from Goddard the Brownie metal camera the scientist had brought along just for this special occasion. If all went well, their rocket would reach 500 mph and 2,000 feet in altitude. "Here." He passed Jack over to the older man. "Watch your godson. I'm going to take our own photos before the Navy or the Soviets or the Nazi's can beat us to it, damn it!"

Quickly, he began to scale the fifty-foot steel ladder. He was excited, so excited he didn't notice the loosened rung near the top—until it gave way in his hand. He tottered, arms flailing as the Brownie plunged out of sight. Despite the cool day, sweat immediately beaded his skin. He grabbed desperately for the ladder's rail, just as another dust devil whirled through.

With no rung to support him, he clung to the side rails, waiting for the winds to whip past—but his was not the slight body of a gymnast with only an upper muscled body. He was a strapping man, and his hands were sweating to support his weight.

The ripping wind roared in his ears. Sand stung his eyes so that he could not see where to grab next. The ladder wobbled, its top section bouncing a few inches either way against the platform, swinging him like a trapeze artist—only there was no secure trapeze bar coming his way. His hands started to slip... and then, at once, all was quiet and still as the wind blew on past. All except for his heart. It was a kettle drum, reverberating in his ears.

18

Francine Bagby, on the cover of *Life* as 1921's debutante of the year, was the ultimate good-time-girl clotheshorse. Not to say that she wasn't intelligent. Her name, her breeding, her civic standing, and, most importantly, her intellectual curiosity could not be overlooked. Flawlessly stylish, the poor little rich girl was high profile, which was what appealed to Preston foremost.

A socialite in the international limelight would not be as likely to be eradicated as had Darla Ridley, the daughter of a boom-and-bust oilman. Even the mafia—or the Clarendon's, for that matter—would think twice before taking that kind of a chance.

She was related to Alexander Hamilton on her father's side and Sam Houston on her mother's. Her father was one of the heirs to the famed Mallory Steamship lines and railroad interests, based out of Galveston, and her aunt, Lady Grace Farnsworth, was the original English snob.

Yes, Francine would be safe with him. He had learned to be extra careful with his heart for fear the Clarendon's would rip a beloved from his grasp.

Preston had met her at the grand opening of the second Waldorf-Astoria on Park Avenue, the first having been demolished to make way for the Empire State Building.

President Herbert Hoover, in a radio broadcast from The White House, had saluted the new hotel, the tallest and largest one in the world. *"This Waldorf-Astoria marks the measure of our nation's growth in power, in comfort and in artistry... an exhibition of courage and confidence to the whole nation."*

All palaver to allay a nation seized up by financial fear, a nation in which former tycoons were selling pencils on street corners and people were dying of starvation. Meanwhile, no social inequity could stop high society. Celebrities, socialites, and aristocrats were losing themselves in the glitter of disregard.

In the largest of the Waldorf's ballrooms, every woman, from the most prominent actresses to the least significant debutante, ogled him. Well, not him, but his wealth. Of course, his good looks hadn't hurt. While the male guests wore a tuxedo, bowtie, and top hat, he had worn a black suit, Western string tie, and his Stetson.

He knew he had erred in violating his vow to never leave Texas. Texas was unrestrained, unbridled, and untamed. It was where he belonged—not at some damned peacock parade. But the Waldorf-Astoria was the granddaddy of them all, and it needed a rival in Texas. He wanted a hotel with a pool you could water ski on and a golf course and full-service spa and—hell, he wanted out of the Waldorf-Astoria and New York right at that moment.

Drowning in perfumed flattery and come-hither eyes, he withdrew to the mezzanine's view of the ballroom. He was supposed to connect with William Wrigley, Jr. in the hope he could interest the industrialist in forming a limited company to develop a hotel-resort on Galveston Island the way Wrigley had developed Santa Catalina Island. But Wrigley was ailing and had missed the *soirée*.

Glamorous, sophisticated, and twice-divorced, Francine had found Preston alone on the mezzanine and had not left him alone since that night.

Not that he was complaining. After all, she was from Texas—as unrestrained and unbridled as her home country, at least in bed. Untamed, well he would see about that.

They lay entwined on her bed's rumpled and soiled silk sheets in her home in Houston's glitzy River Oaks. Some of its houses were monstrosities, but many displayed refinement and elegance.

He should have been delighted with what he had made of his life, but there was a restlessness that would not be appeased by wealth or women. He felt like the legendary ghost ship, the *Flying Dutchman,* that could never make port and was doomed to sail the oceans forever. Except, he was determined his vagabond soul would never leave American soil again.

If he was challenged to pinpoint a reason for his choice to remain unfettered, he supposed it could be that he wouldn't settle for less—that foolish concept of the mythical soulmate spitefully teased the back of his mind.

Besides, did anyone ever really stay in love... after the luster wore off? His parents, Heath's parents—Mariana's and Hannah's—they appeared to get along well with their mates. Or was it merely toleration? Were there behind-the-scenes scrapes that left the heart bleeding? Emotional manipulations that bound one tighter than any marriage contract could?

None of this was evidenced in the couples he had known—except for the person closest to him, his twin. When Pierce had brought Aubrey back with him from France, it was obvious to Preston, who knew Pierce as well as he knew the lines in his own palm, that something had been amiss.

Granted, the little time he had spent with them last Thanksgiving at The Barony, he had observed that their relationship evidently had been transmuted. Her selfless courage in saving Pierce from the rattler's bite had to say something in favor of marriage, didn't it? Pierce looked more at ease, contented even, than he had since their holy terror days as youths, and Aubrey positively radiated.

Francine's fingers snuggled in the mat of Preston's chest hair, and her lips brushed a moistened trail up his neck. She was five years older than he but didn't look it and was an expert at social maneuvering. "Your mind is somewhere else, sweetcakes," she whispered at his ear, "but I bet I can bring it back to this bed and me—as well as that decadent overconfident mouth of yours."

Her fingers deserted his chest and headed south. He captured them and brought them to his lips, licking each one separately. "Actually, I was thinking about us. I think it's time we let the world know we're getting married."

THE BARONY, TEXAS
NOVEMBER 1931

That Thanksgiving, while the families played Mahjong, Parcheesi, and Canasta in the parlor or horseshoes and croquet outside, Mariana and her uncles, Griffin and Drake, closeted themselves in his office to strategize.

Over the Thanksgiving feast, Mariana and Griffin had informed the family members of their plan to toss both their hats in the ring for next November's elections—Griffin for governor of Texas and Mariana for U.S. Senate.

The hoopla over her victory in the Bonaventure/Paladín trial, plus the fact that she was not only a female attorney but also a Paladín, had helped gain her national attention.

"We just have to capitalize on that," Uncle Griffin had said.

Naturally, the entire family was behind it, each jumping in to offer support—all but Preston, of course. Since he rarely attended the traditional Thanksgiving gatherings, his absence raised few inquiries. His recent engagement announcement did, but none of the family knew any more than what made the headlines.

Mariana had felt lower than a worm after her confrontation with him last Thanksgiving, especially after he had come through with the percentage-free loan for Barony Enterprises. But did he have to distance himself from the family?

The two of them, plus all their other cousins, had ridden horseback, fished in the Nueces, and swum in The Barony's tank ponds together. She would never forget the Thanksgiving Preston had played a prank on her by tipping over the old outhouse in which she had been hiding. What a stench!

Seated at Drake's desk, she worked on a political campaign, along with Uncle Griffin and Uncle Drake, that was aimed at May's primary. The present governor was facing impeachment due to indictment for misappropriation of funds. Griffin, reinforced by his multi-terms as Galveston mayor and his father's own multi-terms as governor of Texas, should make him a shoe-in.

On the other hand, Mariana, who had no political experience, was running against Joseph Fuller, a railroad commissioner and a candidate backed by Roger Clarendon no less.

Hands behind his back, head lowered, Uncle Griffin paced the room slowly, thoughtfully. "Get prepared to travel, Mariana, to speak to voters and raise campaign money at various functions from quilting bees to spelling bees. West Texas has an untapped Hispanic vote that needs to be addressed. Your Hispanic ancestry will be a plus."

Uncle Drake straddled the chair next to her. "The cost to run is going to be high," he warned. "Only people with lots of money and connections stand a chance, and that would be James Fuller. His connections are of a higher suit—they go all the way to the national level."

She frowned. "According to a rumor I heard, state highway contracts are only going to companies that advertised in Fuller's newspaper, *Fuller's Forum*. A House committee investigated the charge but, of course, nothing has come of it."

"Nor will it," Uncle Drake grunted, wearily running calloused fingers through his still-dark hair. "Despite what Griffin pointed out—the untapped Hispanic vote—the deck is still stacked against you."

"I'm having campaign literature delivered to my office this week." Griffin turned to face her. "Meanwhile, be prepared to be the Great Mediator of problems that Texas faces—rural electrification, farm foreclosures, and prohibition. These will be the hot issues of this campaign. You must be prepared to counter Fuller with solutions and answers."

She was not nearly as worried about countering Fuller as she was Heath. They were both strong-willed, passionate, and goal directed. That night, as she readied for bed, he shucked his boots into a corner, then slumped in the overstuffed chair, his hands clasped behind his head. He appeared to be relaxed, but she knew better.

She shrugged out of her navy cable-knit sweater and tossed it on the wide bed. Wearing only her brassiere and her wide trousers, she sashayed across the carpet to him. She snuggled onto his lap and looped her bare arms around his neck. "All right, my love, exactly what is bothering you?"

"As if you didn't know."

She did, but she knew he needed to get it out of his system. "Hmmm, is it because I didn't bring you your cup of Mexican coffee this morning?"

"Try again, sweetheart."

She twirled her fingers in his hair, as black as a bat out of hell. "Then, is it because you lost to Darcy at poker last night?"

He snatched her fingers from his hair and planted a hot kiss on the inside of her wrist. "Washington, D.C. is too damned far away. You won't be spending nearly enough time in our bed."

"It won't be that much different than when I'm in San Antonio." Although she kept an office in nearby San Antonio, with the efficient and capable Betty Chan running it in her absences, she was often called away by clients as far off as Austin or Dallas or Houston. "The Senate will meet in December and be done by May or so. Maybe Pierce could fly you up to Washington every so often. Besides, I have yet to win the Senate seat. So, let's not argue over it."

His eyes pinned her as surely as any lepidopterist did a butterfly to the board. "So," he parroted, "you'd leave me to follow your dream?"

Her mouth pressed into a thin line. "You knew what my vision was from the day my friend Daniel Jarvis was hanged!"

"And a dead Daniel is more important than our lives together?"

She sighed and bent to kiss him, but he positioned her wrist between them. His stormy eyes drilled into hers. "Don't you understand that by going to Washington, you're going into the lion's den?"

"Like I said, I may not even win the—"

He shook her wrist so that her hand wobbled. "Listen to me, Mariana! The Clarendons are going to bring out all their guns at the primary. That means they'll use our marriage against us—firing off a salvo of incest charges against you at every public meeting."

Her eyes fired back their own barrage. "I can hold my own!"

"With words, ideas, maybe. But accidents? In Washington, you'll be too far away from me to—"

He broke off, leaned his warm forehead against her palm. "God, Mariana, I can't lose you."

EL PASO, TEXAS
DECEMBER 1931

Pierce peered down the dust-blown street of Chihuahita, hoping for sight of Byron's jalopy.

Sirocco-like winds were howling in from the Southwest and drifting sand into dunes along fencerows and bar ditches and the municipal airport's runways. Not that the year's continuing dust storms could reduce Paladín Aviation airport operations any more than the Depression was already doing.

Sometimes the dusters, with their eerie silence, could last as long as three days, and the erosion the dusters were causing was becoming terrifying.

Byron and Edna, along with two-year-old Jack, were motoring from Roswell with Robert and Esther Goddard. Pierce was concerned they might be caught in today's violent turbulence, springing up suddenly from nowhere, as they were doing more often these days.

Pierce was already concerned enough after Byron had shared with him at Thanksgiving about his close call on the launching tower.

"I think someone had cut the rung away," his cousin had given a grim shake of his shaggy head. "I worry more for Edna and don't like leaving her alone, even with the Goddards just a couple miles off."

The two couples were coming to El Paso both to discuss Pierce's collaboration with Byron and Goddard and to observe the colorful pageantry that evening across the Rio Grande in Juarez—*Dia de la Virgen de Guadalupe.* It appeared to Pierce an outlandish combination of Mardi Gras, Halloween, and High Mass.

The aroma of spicy chicken tantalized his nostrils, drawing him from his vigil on the stucco's veranda to the tiny kitchen. Aubrey, so talented with her French cuisine, was preparing the twelfth of December's traditional spread— Spinach soup with macaroni, *frijoles negros,* stuffed *tortillas,* and *Mole Poblano,* Mexico's national dish.

He came up behind her and, reaching around, dipped his finger in the sweet flan simmering on the stove.

She whacked his hand with her wooden spatula. *"Non, non, non."*

Wisps of damp hair had tumbled loose from the clasp of slightly longer hair at her nape. He couldn't help himself. He brushed his lips over her exposed nape. She stilled and dropped her head for his further pleasuring of her.

Since the day she had thrown herself between him and the rattler, their love had evolved into something breathtakingly beautiful, something he would have never imagined. Her selfless act had set his tortured spirit free. His hands grasped her narrow hips and turned her around to face him. "What about *oui, oui, oui?"*

Her lips curved in that smile that still enchanted him after fifteen years. That, and the way she carried herself. It was more than gracefulness, though she radiated grace. She was an iron butterfly. "I think ooh-la-la."

"Turn off the stove. I'll grab the *mezcal,* and we can adjourn to—"

She flicked off the gas but placed her fingertip on his lips. "This *mezcal.* I think it is better I do not drink it."

"Then the cognac," he laughed, tugging her from the kitchen.

She held back, smiling mischievously. *"Non.* Not even the cognac, *mon amour."*

He stopped mid-step. There was something about her smile. Puzzled, he canted his head. What was going on?

She stood on tiptoe and kissed him softly. "I was saving this for *Noël,* for Christmas, but I think, now is better." She blushed, ducked her head, and, taking his hand, splayed it on her concave stomach. "I am carrying your baby."

Elation surged through him dizzily. He had all but abandoned hope. Not that he didn't love the life the two of them had created, solely focused on bringing the best to the other. Bending, he scooped up her legs to cradle her against his chest, and she giggled.

With but the slightest limp, he carried her easily into their bedroom, where he stretched out beside her on their bed. "When?"

"July."

His forefinger traced the sweeping curve of her cheekbone, the bow of her upper lip, the delicate arch of one brow. "I love you so," he whispered, totally at a loss at expressing his overwhelming happiness.

Her lips curved upward. "Show me."

His breath caught. He knew this wanting of her would never grow old, though his body and hers would.

"I would be most delighted, Madame Paladín." Even as his lips claimed hers, his fingers worked dexterously at the buttons of her housedress.

The front door slammed open, and Byron's baritone voice called out. "Hello? We're here!"

"Damn!"

Aubrey laughed lightly, the knuckle of her forefinger nudging him beneath his chin. "Tonight," she promised.

19

"Darcy Paladín looks as elegant on horseback as Fred Astaire does on the dance floor," the gossip columnist Walter Winchell had written in the *New York Daily Mirror* that morning, much to Darcy's chagrin.

Heath had called to goad him about the comment, and Belle was even teasing him, threatening to dance on his back.

He grabbed her waist, thickening with their child, and drew her against him. While Mae West was certainly winning fans with her ribald wisecracks and statuesque figure, Belle's adoring fans remained loyal to her upbeat, fresh, and saucy screen presence.

Yet, the birth of their child could very well put an end to the career for which she had worked so hard—and he suspected she was apprehensive about what the change would mean, not only in her career but also between them. So was he.

"You are just lucky," he growled, "that there is a *piñata* on the set for me to take out my frustrations on."

Her eyes widened in feigned fear, but the dimples beneath her cheeks gave her away. "Oh, what would you do to me if there wasn't, Mister Paladín?"

"Well, Miss Belle...." He nuzzled her neck, "If I had the time, I'd take my lariat here and tie your hands and bend ya over the hitching post and then I'd yank up—"

"I'm glad you don't have the time," she laughed.

Indeed, even at that moment, the sound stage door slid open, and Charlie Chaplain wedged through onto the closed set with his guest of honor just behind him.

"Delivered, just as I promised." Charlie called out.

With his hand at the small of Belle's back, Darcy circumvented the ox cart and *cantina* facade and crossed the cable-strewn set to shake first Charlie's hand, then that of Albert Einstein's. "Good to see you again, Mister Einstein. I'd like for you to meet my wife and leading star, Belle Bevins."

His grizzled broomstick mustache twitched with his smile. "Surely a star that eclipses all those in the heavens, Darcy."

She grinned. "I had heard you were a ladies' man, Mister Einstein."

"What you may not have heard is the latest in Berlin," Charlie's voice was glum. "In Germany's election held earlier this week, the Nazis won 230 governmental seats, making up over half of the *Reichstag.*"

"Each time I leave Germany, I fear it will be my last." The scientist traipsed along with them as Darcy led them outside to the dusty backlot of his movie ranch, blistering under the afternoon sunlight.

Einstein and Chaplin were pronounced pacifists. Darcy's own aversion to war had led to a close friendship with Chaplin—and Darcy's giving a studio tour to Einstein, in the U.S. on another two-month visiting professorship at the California Institute of Technology.

"We bought the 500-acre ranch," Belle was explaining to him, "and built that two-story Spanish *casa* you see on the ridge—to use both for our current film *Mexicali Rose* and for our own personal use afterwards."

"Just beyond is the *Mexicali Rose* mission set, where Belle and John Wayne marry," Darcy added. "And back of it are the corrals and pens and stables for whatever stock we use in filming."

Hands jammed in his pockets as he skirted a pile of cow chips, Chaplin eyed the set pieces strewn about. *"Hollywood Reporter* claims you are planning on filming a couple of war movies here."

"You know me better than that, Chaplin," Darcy shot back, avoiding a donkey, chomping on rabbit weed. "The closest we'll be coming to a war movie is Fu Manchu firing off a cap pistol at Charlie Chan."

"You need to get Disney and his story department on your lot," Einstein grumbled in his heavily accented English. "People want to know more about Mickey Mouse than they do quantum theory."

Belle chuckled. "Our son Timmy is fourteen, and he likes both."

"He knows about quantum theory?" Einstein asked, clearly startled.

"Well, maybe not quantum theory," she conceded, "but his Uncle Byron has him terribly interested in rocket dynamics."

From there, the conversation drifted to German Expressionism in the film industry with the four eventually adjourning for dinner to the Brown Derby.

Arriving home late, Darcy slumped into the bedroom's wingback chair and tugged off his boots. Belle peeked in on Timmy and returned, grinning. "Our son's fast asleep, if you can discount his protest of mumbles and yawns when I kissed him."

She was divesting herself of the metallic lamé skirt and butterfly-sleeve top that artfully concealed her pelvis's small bump. He set down a boot, watching her expression carefully. "If your screen popularity fades, will you be content chanting mindless nursery rhymes?"

She put her hands on her hips. "I missed out on Timmy's childhood. What do you think?"

"I think," he drawled, "you are a wonderful mother, Belle Bevins Paladín."

Her eyes misted. "Well, I think, my Prince of the Paladíns,"—she sauntered slowly toward him, her hands still on her hips—"that we should be practicing making more babies."

His hands caught her and drew her down into his lap, cupping her head against the hollow of his bare neck. He didn't want her to see his fear. His fear of losing her—either through childbirth or some "accident."

He had grown too complacent. The day before, the set's wagon-wheel candelabra had come crashing down only seconds after he had called for an early lunch break, at the spot where Belle had been standing, delivering her lines.

Making certain first that she was all right, that none of the shattering glass had cut her, he then charged up the twenty-foot scaffolding. As he navigated the complex of catwalks, the prop man was on his heels. "I swear, Mister Paladín, I secured the candelabra tightly yesterday—and rechecked it just this morning."

Darcy knelt, fingering the cable's ends. Not frayed ends but ones snipped neatly, discounting two dangling ends that had most likely kept the candelabra temporarily suspended. Barbed wire could not have been cut any better. And in the ceiling's dimness, no one else was in sight.

He didn't like this, waiting for what could happen next, when next the Clarendons would strike. He felt as if the Sword of Damocles hung over his family's heads. Maybe peaceful means didn't always settle disputes. Maybe, he was out of step with today's militant attitudes. Maybe it was time he changed, did whatever ruthless act was called for to protect what was his.

THE BARONY, TEXAS
NOVEMBER 1932

Hannah made it home for Thanksgiving that year—early, in fact, so that she could vote for Mariana and Uncle Griffin in the November eighth elections. At least, that's what she told the family—and herself.

That Tuesday morning, a car caravan made the trip from The Barony to the nearest Nueces County precinct. Stoney's sin-red pickup joined the convoy. Hannah was already ensconced in her parents' DeSoto. Darcy and

Belle had acceded to the pleas of Timmy, who had taken to dogging the vet's footsteps, and let him ride with Stoney.

Silly to be jealous of a fourteen-year-old kid. After all, Timmy, was about as close in age to Stoney as she was... only she was at the other end of the spectrum. Jesus Christ! The end that was already edging toward death.

Journalists, cameramen, and radio reporters were waiting outside the Nueces precinct when Griffin and Mariana stepped from their automobiles. They, as well as the rest of the Paladíns, were mobbed on sight.

Emerging from the DeSoto, Hannah stared in astonishment at the pandemonium. What must Mariana and Griffin be experiencing, so close to the eye of the jostling reporters?

Amidst the shoving and flashing of strobes, Stoney's brick-like body interposed itself between Hannah and the reporters. His hand gripping her elbow, he strong-armed a cleared path inside for her.

Breathless, she looked up at him. "Thank you!"

He gave her only a cursory nod.

Quickly, the Paladíns eligible to vote cast it and made their escape. Late lunch found the family at the Lighthouse Café on Corpus Christi's bayfront. The restaurant, expanded around the base of the converted lighthouse, was crowded. The tangy smell of frying fish and potatoes assailed her.

A radio had been turned up, and the high-powered, radio-blaster transmitter XER, out of Del Rio/Villa Acuna, promised listeners they would receive bulletins of the latest election results.

Of course, Southwest Texicans recognized the Paladíns on sight. The waiters scurried to assemble several tables into a single long one to accommodate all the family members. The family was larger now, increased by the birth of Pierce' son—Julian, a namesake for Audrey's father.

After ordering, talk soon turned to the election. She eavesdropped, not really participating.

"...that the Clarendons run the political machine controlling the electoral choices...."

"...because of his corrupt activities—voting in graveyards—we'll be damned lucky if...."

Across from her, Stoney delighted Timmy by ordering him a Dr. Pepper and all but ignoring her.

Once the platters of oysters and shrimp and hot, buttery rolls were pillaged and the family settled in to listen more intently to the latest election result broadcasts, Hannah made good her own escape up the lighthouse's spiral staircase to the widow's walk.

It was a perfect autumn day, with the breeze brisk and a little cool. She braced her hands on the rusted railing. Nearer the shoreline were the masts of shrimpers and funnels of steamships, but further out, in the Gulf's blue horizon, an orange blaze of sun was edging toward it.

The sound of steps echoing on the staircase reached her, and she couldn't help but hope that they would be those of Stoney's.

They were—but also along with those of Timmy's. "Aunt Hannah, Stoney told me that Corpus Christi used to be a pirates' lair! Did you know that?"

She glanced from the good-looking fourteen-year-old to Stoney. He was smiling congenially. "Did he now? Seems I've heard something about pirates in the vicinity."

"Do you think they buried a treasure?"

She ruffled his hair. "They could have. Somewhere out there." Her hand made a sweep of the area.

Timmy began edging his way around the circular railing, as if hoping to spot some tell-tale signs of prior digging.

She turned to Stoney. "Well, aren't you the popular one? Adored by animals and children alike."

His mustache twitched. "But obviously not by Miss Hannah Solomon."

"With so many admirers, would my affections make a difference?" Instantly, she realized her *faux pas*—interposing the word "affections" in lieu of admiration or adoration.

At that moment, Timmy completed his circling of the widow's walk, coming upon them once again. "Timmy." Stoney placed his hand on the boy's shoulder, never taking his eyes off her. "I want to talk to your aunt alone."

"Yes, sir." The authority in Stoney's command was enough to send the boy scampering down the stairwell.

Stoney reached out and brushed from her cheek a swath of hair the Gulf's salty breeze had whipped from beneath her hat. As he tucked the wayward strands behind her ear, she stood still, not even seeming to breathe.

"Yes, your affections would make a difference." He grazed her lips with his thumb. "My question for you would be if your affections would make enough difference for you to give up your career in Europe?"

Happy tears backed up in her throat. She captured his thumb before it could desert her lips and lingeringly kissed its callused pad. His lids flared, his breath inhaling sharply. Gazing up at him from beneath damp lashes, she managed to dimple a smile. "Until we are alone, that part of my answer will have to do for now."

He gave her one of his slow, sure grins. "That part, maybe. But not our engagement. I want that part of the answer now. Is it official then?"

"I'm yours, Stoney Jackson. Signed, sealed, and delivered." She stood on tiptoe to kiss him, and the wind seized her hat, tumbling it over the lighthouse railing. Lost in his kiss, her heart tumbled, too.

WASHINGTON, D.C.
DECEMBER 1932

Bread lines might be wrapped around the block outside, but Washington society was once again kicking off its dazzling election season, meaning new faces to replace the stodgy old ones—at least, according to outspoken Ettie Garner.

And Ettie ought to know. Her husband, Cactus Jack Garner, had served in Washington since 1902 as the Representative from Texas. At a time when women weren't even allowed to vote, Ettie had actually run against him for county judge because she didn't see eye to eye with him. Two years later, they had married—and now, in three months, Cactus Jack would be sworn in as Vice President of the United States under the president-elect Franklin Delano Roosevelt.

Mariana had just barely edged out James Fuller, the Clarendons' protégée, for the senatorial victory. Foolishly, Fuller had miscalculated and raised the issue of her incestuous marriage to Heath, and a legion of Heath's romantic fans, females who had only recently been accorded the right to vote, had rallied behind her.

Officially, the election season had kicked off two weeks before with President Hoover hosting at the White House the diplomatic reception, a gleaming fête of gorgeous uniforms and gowns.

This was followed days later by the Cabinet Dinner, the Judicial Reception, the Speakers Dinner, a morning musical, and, of course, a myriad of private parties.

To Mariana—newly elected senator from Texas and one of only two female senators—Washington society was hopelessly bewildering. Her calendar was already full of dinners, debuts, breakfasts, receptions, luncheons, and teas.

"It's a caviar carousel." Ettie was explaining at one such function, as she adjusted her long, white opera gloves. "And there are rules. An invitation from the White House is a command—only death is an acceptable excuse for failure to attend. As for cocktails at the Ceylon legation, you may stay at home and darn your husband's sock if you should so choose."

Mariana chuckled, swallowed her champagne wrong, and had to cough.

Ettie went on in total disregard. "Some social or charity work is absolutely *de rigueur,* my dear. Repay calls promptly. Acknowledge invitations, whether accepting or declining. Never leave an affair until the guest of honor has prepared to depart. And as for the rules of precedence, an ambassador is a representative of a ruler, so a senator must call upon him. However, a minister is representative of the people, and he must call upon the senator."

Mariana found the protocol mind boggling. Even more mind boggling knowing that outgoing President Hoover had nominated Roger Clarendon to fill the vacant seat of Associate Supreme Court Justice.

But, then, wasn't that why she was in Washington, to get justice for Dan Jarvis, even if it meant confronting the Goliath, Roger Clarendon? Especially if it meant confronting Roger Clarendon.

Below a blue and white bunting, an orchestra was playing, "Happy Days Are Here Again," the unofficial anthem of the Democratic Party, and a tall, plain-looking woman in a fussy brown hat approached her and Ettie.

"I understand you are Mariana Paladín." She assessed her, from her open toed shoes to her perky Cossack hat.

"I am," she replied somewhat uneasily.

The rather dowdy woman's toothy smile was both rascally and impossibly charming. "*Life* described you as a spicy conservative who stands for money-making, oil derricks, prairie skyscrapers, and $100 Stetsons."

"*Life* also said I was hardboiled and overbearing."

"Just my kind of woman." She stuck out her hand. "Eleanor Roosevelt."

Mariana was stunned. "You're... you're the President Elect's wife!" She couldn't believe the controversial wife of the governor of New York knew who she was.

"I can tell you now, being First Lady of New York state wasn't worth a pail of warm piss, but as First Lady of the United States, I plan to start with an empty pail. Things will be different."

Mariana managed to get out. "We share the connection of my long-time family friend, Teddy Roosevelt."

The deal was sealed. From that point on, Eleanor and Ettie took her under their wing. Like her Aunt Giselle, Eleanor was also a feminist and racial activist, well informed about the events of the 1917 hanging of the thirteen colored soldiers.

Between her two mentors, Mariana learned to navigate the back corridors of political maneuverings. Naturally, there was the usual petty jealousies, and daily, she faced discrimination by the male congressmen who resented her presence mightily.

Hell yes, they were a sticker burr in her butt, but she treated their resentment in the same fashion as she treated them—as trivial politicians—and ignored them.

Then, going into 1933, things turned out not to be so trivial when Eleanor Roosevelt came to her with a dangerous proposal.

20

Only the rich and privileged rendezvoused at the Ritz. The hotel was synonymous with opulence, service, and fine dining. Along with Parisian socialites, Hannah and Mariana ate that afternoon on the Ritz's fabled garden terrace.

Hannah's smile was politely fixed, but she sat, stunned. She thought Mariana had chosen merely to take a French holiday during Congress's spring recess, though it seemed strange her cousin would leave Heath back home. Hannah wondered if perhaps there was trouble on the home front.

But apparently, there was trouble on the home front—not The Barony's, but America's.

"Did you know that recently, while Albert Einstein was in California with Darcy, his home outside Berlin was raided and all his research stolen?"

"No, but then everybody knows much of the news here is censored." This was part of the reason for the Nazi book burning. The new German government had also passed laws barring Jews from holding any official positions, including teaching at universities, and Jewish students had been barred from schools.

Mariana speared an olive with her salad fork. "Then you probably didn't know Einstein has been put on a list of enemies. There's a $5,000 bounty on his head."

Hannah shook her head. The once flavorful asparagus tasted like cardboard.

"So, you see," Mariana said softly, her face plastered with a smile, "It's grim. We couldn't even take a chance of sending this request by diplomatic courier or mail."

"Request?"

Mariana leaned closer, taking a piece of a baguette from the wicker basket next to Hannah. "I am passing along an unofficial request for you to help bring Jewish scientists out of Germany. Look, Hannah, when Eleanor came to me with the proposal, I tried to beg off, but she emphasized this should be entirely up to you. I'm only the messenger. Even though I hate it."

So, the "unofficial" request went that high up in the government. "You said scientists. Plural."

"At this point, the Nazi's are detaining in 'protective custody,' as they call it, only two—notable scientists, both of them."

"Why me?"

"With your popping all over Europe at a moment's notice—and having been married to a German and familiar with the country's language and customs—the War Department felt you were a good risk and that fewer questions would be asked. But I think it's too damned risky and hope like hell you turn them down!"

"Does the rest of the family know about this?"

Unable to meet her gaze, Mariana stabbed almost viciously at the foie gras. "No. This is classified as Top Secret. If you agree, and I hope you don't, the War Department wants to pair you with Leo Gunther Von Rosch as a cover. You know who he is?"

"Von Rosch? The German-American tennis player?"

"A.K.A. Baron Berlin to his many detractors here in the U.S."

Hannah knew of him—arrogant, autocratic, aristocratic—and a woman-izer on both continents. His "von" with a capital "V" underscored his egotism.

"He's in Europe right now, playing some tournaments. Posing as romantic interests, you two would travel together. You would, of course, appear at a few of his matches, but mostly you two would operate out of the hornet's nests, there in Berlin. Final details for each "recovery," as the War Department terms it, would be filtered through Von Rosch to you only in the final stage. That way, I would imagine, there'd be less possibility of slip ups."

Stoney would not be happy with this. She had agreed to wrap up the fall buying season, close her garret and Paris office for good, and be back at The Barony in time for a Thanksgiving wedding. They had compromised, with his relocating his veterinarian practice to Dallas, where—upon her parents' retirement—she would run the Emporium.

She sighed, laid down her fork, and carefully patted her lips with her napkin. "Mariana, I am happier than I have ever been in my life. I'm engaged and getting out of Europe while the getting is good—remember, I'm Jewish. Why would I risk it? Tell the War Department I am sorry, but the answer is an unqualified 'No.'"

Why should she risk it, Hannah asked herself over and over again, as she and Mariana waited at the Gare Saint-Lazare station for Mariana's Paris-Le Havre train. She was catching Hannah up on the family and what was going on back home in the States. "…FDR has created a Civilian Conservation Corps to combat unemployment and pover—"

She broke off at the sound of the collective scream from the waiting pas-sengers and the even shriller blast of the train screeching along the rails to a spine-grating halt. Neither Hannah nor Mariana could see what was going on through the press of people, but word quickly spread that a man had fallen from the quay onto the path of the arriving train.

The next day, *Le Temps* reported in dry details the accident at the Gare Saint-Lazare. The fatality was identified as Otto Neumeyer, a noted Berlin professor.

Reading the small article, buried on page three, and recalling the grizzly scene of the mangled body lifted from the tracks, it became obvious to Hannah the answer as to why she should risk the War Department's proposal. It was not just because the scientists were Jewish, as she was. If she turned her back, she would hate herself. She would face not physical death but, at least, a spiritual death.

Immediately, she laid aside the newspaper. Crossing to the wall phone, she picked up the mouthpiece and asked the exchange to ring through to Mariana's hotel in Le Havre. The American-bound steamer which she was booked on would not sail until the following day.

While Hannah waited for the call to go through, she tried to think of the message she would leave with the hotel's front desk. The wording had to be circumspect, just in case.

With tears cascading down her cheeks, she had to repeat it to the desk clerk twice. "Mariana, please tell Stoney I'll have to postpone the wedding. And tell him don't believe what the news stories may say."

The desk clerk went to read it back, but Hannah hung up and, doubled over, she cried soundlessly.

PARIS, FRANCE,
MAY 1933

Yes, the tall and vigorous Leo Gunther Von Rosch was arrogant, temperamental, and demanding—but he was also defiant, daring, and gutsy.

Casually—and boldly—he draped his arm on the back of Hannah's front row seat in the Stade Roland Garros, named for the French flying ace of the Great War.

While two competitors battled out the fourth round of the men's quarter-final singles on the clay courts of the French Open, Leo occasionally inclined his fair head near that of Hannah's in the appearance of some flirtatious exchange.

The crowded, noisy stadium made it difficult for anyone to eavesdrop. This was to be their first publicized date. God only knew how Stoney would feel when he saw the AP photos in the *San Antonio Light*. She couldn't take the chance of writing him with the behind-the-scenes covert operation but would have to depend that Mariana was able to get word to him.

"Stanislaw Gould," Leo's adoring gaze focused on hers, "is a scientist engaged in the study of nuclear fission—he's being held at Columbia-Haus in Berlin. Report is, he's being tortured."

As she had with Mariana, Hannah smiled back while her mind filtered the appalling information. She leaned closer, her fashionable, wide-brim straw hat shielding her face against the fierce sunlight—and spy cameras. "What's required of me?"

"I have an exhibition match in Berlin at the *Mommsenstadion* on the eighteenth of June," Leo continued. "You are to be in the stadium to watch me win. Afterwards, it is up to us to get Gould out of Columbia-Haus."

She peered up at Leo. He had a strong nose and jaw with impassioned hazel eyes. He might be termed irregularly handsome, but his features were too bladed for her taste, as was his narcissistic manner. "That's it?"

"That's it."

The sun was beating down on her pale skin as she swished her fan to cool herself. She felt eyes on her and Leo and could only pray the attention was focused on their seeming budding romance and not their covert purpose.

Four or five minutes passed, then, during a break in the match, he leaned toward her again. "I want to pleasure you. I can do this tonight or anytime between now and June eighteenth."

She was sure her mouth dropped open. She smiled for the sake of any gawkers and whispered between her teeth, "You overestimate your charm, Leo."

His gaze settled on her lips. "You have yet to experience the full force of my charm."

HANNAH AND LEO WERE SEEN together gambling at Longchamp Race Course, dining at Maxim's—it didn't hurt that both the famed playwright Jean Cocteau and the Prince of Wales were there at the same time, which meant greater publicity for her and Leo as a couple—and partying at the Moulin Rouge Cabaret, where everyone who was anyone was seen.

Indeed, she found it difficult to discount the self-proclaimed charmer. Charismatic, Leo seemed oblivious to besieging tennis fans and focused his fierce energy solely on her, much as he did when trouncing an opponent on the tennis court.

His long, dexterous fingers found countless ways to graze her skin—from her earlobes to her collarbone and the back of her arms. And, of course, the intimate act of handholding was a given. But the way he thumbed the inside of her palm or raised the inside of her wrist to his lips was difficult for her body's auto responses to ignore.

She and Stoney had found time to exchange only a handful of impassioned kisses before she had to return to Paris. There was no doubt in her mind or heart that she loved the gentle yet strong-willed veterinarian.

What worried her was that he would find doubt in his mind or heart, despite whatever information Mariana may have been able to relay to him.

Hannah had heard nothing from him, but, really, what could he reply? That he approved of her covert undertakings? Of course not. Not only would he not approve but he could not express his disapproval and risk alerting German intelligence.

"When cornered by a *Paris-Soir* journalist about dallying with Von Rosch while reportedly engaged to a Texican veterinarian, she had shrugged and flashed a jaunty smile. 'As you French say… it is okay to stray.'"

Dear God, what the American news reporters would do with that outrageous response. Worse, what would Stoney do?

Whether he understood that the romantic photos captured of her and Leo were merely staged was highly doubtful. Anyone glancing at the photos would think otherwise. There was no mistaking Leo's passionate, predatory expression.

If she had her own private doubts about the mission she was undertaking—and, of course, she did—those doubts were squashed one afternoon, when strolling the Champs de Elysée with Leo. Her arm linked in his, they were forced to pause for a parade of protestors. They were all fascists marching in paramilitary garb… campaigning against the Jews.

ALTHOUGH LEO WASN'T SCHEDULED TO play the exhibition match in Berlin until June eighteenth, he and Hannah caught the first train out for Berlin on the morning of the seventeenth in order to give him time to rest and warm up. This would also give them time to lay plans for secreting Professor Gould out of Columbia-Haus.

Leo had reserved a first-class private compartment, replete with bed and washstand. Since the trip's duration was eight and a half hours, there would be no need for traveling overnight, for which she was vastly relieved.

She stood uncertainly just inside the compartment's sliding door. He turned from stowing his suitcase and tennis bag, along with her suitcase and hatbox. He beckoned with steely fingers. "Come here."

She managed a friendly smile. "Are you accustomed to having your orders complied with so easily? Come here… go there… do that?"

He smiled sardonically. "I am accustomed to having a woman anytime I want one. I want you to want me. So… I wait, no? Now turn around, so that I can help you with your suit jacket."

As she slipped out of her jacket, his hands lingered on her shoulders. She paused, alarmed by the heat of his touch, then forced herself to briskly move away. Officiously, she seated herself a little apart from him, crossed one leg over the other, and began removing her gloves. "I think we should begin formulating some kind of plan regarding Professor Gould. Now fill me in on the details, please."

He lit up a Gaulois Bleu, a symbol of both high status and French patriotism. Shrugging, he blew a helix of smoke. "The Columbia-Haus was original a military police station but has been empty since 1929. Only recently, since the Nazi party came to power, has it been made into a prison. But its operations are rather lax. Getting in should present little problem."

"But getting out will be, I presume." She tucked her gloves into her purse. With nothing to occupy her hands now, she was forced to give him her full attention.

He flicked an ash inside his trouser cuff. "The building contains 134 cells, ten interrogation rooms, and a guardhouse."

Interrogation rooms? The image made her shudder. "What about papers for him?"

"The War Department has taken care of that. While I'm playing the match tomorrow, you will be sitting, watching. There will be a gentleman in the seat next to you. I haven't a clue who he is, but he will have Gould's papers and instructions."

She exhaled audibly. "All right."

He stabbed out his cigarette in the arm's ashtray and rose. "Let's eat lunch, have a drink, and relax." He frowned. "Tomorrow will be stressful enough—both on the court and off."

Over chicken *à la chasseur, château* potatoes, and a buffet of desserts in the dining car, they discussed lighter, U.S.-related topics—the delivery of a singing telegram, the radio's *Lone Ranger,* and the movies.

She took a sip of her wine. "Last year, Fay Wray tried out for a part in a film my cousins' studio was producing. That was before she landed her role in *King Kong.*"

"You are close to your family, are you not?"

"Yes." Her fingertip traced the rim of her wine glass. "I don't think they would be happy if they knew what I was doing."

"And Doctor Stoney Jackson? What does he say?"

She looked up sharply. "How do you know Stoney?"

"I don't. But I know *about* him. More than just what the tabloids report. I went into this demanding to know everything about you. After all, you hold my life in your hands. As I hold yours."

He took the wine glass from her and set it aside. "Come. We return to our compartment. We have only a few hours before we arrive."

She tried to hold herself apart from his seductive charisma, but he was there, so close, steadying her, as they made their way back through the noisily swaying and vibrating coaches.

Shutting and locking their compartment's sliding door behind him, he drew her over to sit beside him, his arm across the seatback. "Understand me, I don't like mixing pleasure with business, Hannah, and I have never gotten involved with anyone I have been paired with before. But with you, it is different."

"How long have you been doing this—been working with our War Department, I mean?"

"I was recruited almost four years ago. But you are stalling. I want you to tell me you don't feel the strong current—the chemistry—between us."

Her gaze met his in that smoky moment. "If you know about Stoney, then you know I'm engaged to him."

"You have yet to go to bed with him. Am I right? As sophisticated as you are, that cowpuncher-turned-doc will have you yawning within the year. If you still want him after you and I have—"

Suddenly, the train rounded a sharp curve, lurching the coach and slamming her into Leo. Somehow, she was in his arms, and his lips were brushing along her throat. A helpless, startled sigh of pleasure escaped her. But when his hand dropped to her knee, hiking at her skirt, panic jerked her back to reality.

Sensing her wavering, Leo murmured, "Give in to me, Hannah. Give in to what I know you want, too."

Fortunately, the brusque knocking at their compartment door halted Leo's skillful fingers. He swore softly. Quickly, she pushed herself erect and straightened her skirts.

He opened the door to greet the German conductor, making the requisite collection of passports for review.

With relief, she dipped into her purse for hers. She had been saved from making an egregious mistake.

After the conductor departed with her and Leo's passports, he turned to her. "Well, the mood has been spoiled." He slipped an arm around her waist. "Shall we play a game of strip poker?"

She slid free of his clasp. If they were to continue to work together, she had to keep this light, friendly. She smiled. "No, but I'll play you a game of pinochle."

He gave a Gallic shrug, as if conceding she had won for the moment. "You're on." He fished a deck of playing cards from his tennis bag.

They were evenly matched. She kept score, and he smoked intensely. Occasionally, she drummed her fingers when stumped, and he would goad her. "Come on. Take the chance."

The remainder of the journey passed pleasantly as they played cards, with a view of the beautiful countryside provided through the compartment's large picture window.

But when the train began to slow, and Berlin's rural outskirts came into sight, she began to worry. The conductor had not returned with their passports. This was not the time to have them go astray. "Should we ask for them?"

He took that trick, laid aside his cards, then raised a brow. "If you're that worried, of course. I'll check with them while you get your things together."

By the time she had donned her suit jacket and collected scattered items, the compartment door slid open and she turned, relieved.

It was not Leo who stood there but two plain-clothes men bearing semi-automatic pistols. *"Gestapo,"* identified one rigid-faced man. "Your passport?"

Chilling fear zippered up her spine at the same time that her skin flushed with prickly heat. "I… the conductor has our passports."

"You have no passport?"

Her mouth went dry. She swallowed. "I told you the—"

"Then you are under arrest."

21

THE BARONY

JUNE 1933

"I think Hannah was betrayed." Through her horned rimmed glasses, Mariana's grimly serious gaze moved from one family member to the next, pausing only on Preston in the back of Uncle Drake's office.

Doubtlessly, she was mildly surprised to find he had attended this calling of the clan. So was he. But family was family. When push came to shove... well, nothing got in the way of that. And clearly Hannah had been shoved— right into Spandau Prison.

When Mariana had called him early yesterday morning, tersely imparting only the barest of details and requesting his presence at the hastily summoned meeting, he had done some research on Spandau Prison. He hadn't found much, but what he did find was a punch in the gut. The prison was notorious. Pedestrians strolling outside could hear screaming from inside.

Formerly a military detention center, Spandau held up to 600 inmates. Regulations were so rigid that every other cell was left empty to avoid prisoners' communicating in Morse code. Newspapers were banned and diaries forbidden.

"…Von Rosch was conveniently out of the train compartment while the *Gestapo* were there?" Mariana shook her head. "And why was Hannah the only passenger arrested? These are questions the War Department is trying to find out. But that could take weeks, months. Meanwhile, Hannah is… well, meanwhile, high level authorities have given us informal clearance—and I stress the word informal because all knowledge of us will be disavowed—to get her out of Spandau."

Stoney, who had been pacing a narrow strip of floor at the back of the office, not far from where Preston stood, halted abruptly. "I'm going for her."

"Not without me." Uncle David had one fist pounding into his other palm. At sixty-one, his dark face glowered with all the potent fear and impotent fury he had to be feeling.

From behind his desk, Drake drawled, "David, no insult intended, but at our age, you could slow things down a mite. And I know you love her, Stoney, but first we gotta figure out the most expedient and safest way to get her out."

"Then that would be me."

All heads in the packed office craned around. Preston levered his lanky frame off the paneled wall and edged past the overstuffed chair where his mom cradled her grandson, Julian. Hunkering a hip on the edge of Uncle Drake's desk, Preston surveyed his family. Of them all, Mariana looked, perhaps, the most stunned by his volunteering.

He began ticking off on his fingers as he spoke. "First, I'm single and have no spouse or children." At least, Francine had informed him of none at the same time she had told him through clenched teeth that she was tired of waiting for a wedding date to be set and had forthwith hurled the four-carat diamond engagement ring he had given her.

"Second, I was based in France during the Great War and imprisoned in Germany. I know my way around, both geographically and linguistically. Third, I'm the only soldier to have ever escaped from the Karlsruhe prisoner-of-war camp."

He paused to stare directly at Stoney, who stood with arms folded and a defiant expression. "Lastly—and most importantly, Stoney—Hannah needs someone to come back to."

———————————

Preston had sworn he would never leave Texas again—except when the Grim Reaper came to take him to Hell. But Hell would have been a much better place to be condemned to than France and Germany, returning to the sights that had held only horror—of bloodbaths and mudbaths—where dying had been far better than living.

He would never forget the gagging stench of dead horses, the coppery smell of human blood, and the ghastly sweet odor of rotting human flesh that had been the Great War.

He must have lost all reasoning powers, but it didn't matter. Come hell or the Grim Reaper, he would complete his two-fold personal agenda—rescue Hannah and exterminate the unassailable roaches infesting the U.S. legal system, Brighton and Roger Clarendon, in that order.

Closeted with Mariana an hour later in Drake's office, Preston quickly laid out his plans. "Keep the War Department out of this. Brighton Clarendon, as retiring Secretary of State, was head of the U.S. Foreign Service—he had to have been informed about Hannah's mission."

Mariana nodded, shoving a hand through the heavy mass of her ebony hair. Tension was etched in the tight lines of her mouth and her narrowed eyes, as if squinting against glaring light. But glinting there, too, was shining admiration for him.

"I can't tell you how shitty I feel." She drummed her pencil against her pad like a funeral dirge. "I should have been on to Brighton Clarendon. I hear he's planning on being a presidential candidate for the next election. At least half a dozen times, a Secretary of State has gone on to become President of the United States. Scary, isn't it?"

"Damned scary." He flexed his fingers, surprised to find they were rigid with their own tension. "That's why we're keeping this in the family. I'm all for bringing Pierce's wife in on this. Aubrey was with French intelligence and has contacts in both France and Germany."

"But it's been fifteen years. Times have changed. Maybe people she knew have died or moved away."

As it turned out, Aubrey's father was still alive. Although nearing sixty-five, Jules Clermont was still active in community affairs—espionage affairs included. In a Metz beer garden, he rendezvoused with Preston and appeared to talk jovially over their steins.

"You must rely on a young student from the University of Munich," Jules said quietly. "She is with the Nazi Resistance. She will meet with you at Wannsee Terrace Restaurant. The Strandbad Wannsee is an open-air lido on the eastern shore of Wannsee Lake."

"How will I know her?

"Oh, she will know you."

BERLIN, GERMANY

The largest inland lido in Europe, Strandbad Wannsee's beach had been expanded with sand from the German shore of the Baltic Sea. It was in southwestern Berlin—not far from the Spandau borough. Its famous beach provided an area for sunbathing, including a promenade, thatched pavilions, facilities for canoeing and kayaking—and a sign forbidding Jews to access the premises.

Preston sat at the small table wedged against the terrace's stone balustrade. The terrace overlooked the sparkling lake. He and Fabienne Allaman were meeting for lunch so they could have a preliminary chat.

He couldn't help himself. He kept staring at her.

She was wearing a classic collegiate black-striped shirt with white duck sailor trousers. Fresh faced, she wore no make-up, but there was something else about her. Something different from the others. Just what, he couldn't say, but she was wholly enchanting, and he feared with this exceptional female, he could easily become besotted.

She stared back at him, open-eyed with what he suspected was a vulnerable heart. Of medium height, with a well-honed body, she had long, sun-streaked brown hair clasped at her nape. Above a dusting of freckles, intelligent eyes in a bright blue studied him.

"Jules Clermont told you about me?"

She gifted him with one of those dancing-on-sunshine smiles. *"Non,* I have known you long before this. Since 1918."

"What?" His fork paused in spearing the beer-glazed bratwurst on its bed of red cabbage.

She smiled and shrugged. Her teeth, as white as baby powder, were delightfully uneven. "A schoolgirl crush."

Her English was nearly perfect, with the barest of accents, though it was difficult for him to decide if it was French or German. "We have met before?"

She laid aside her fork, and he noted she had long fingers with very short nails. "Only on paper." Her eyes twinkled, but they were, also, watching him carefully. I was one of the correspondents who wrote to you through *'Les Marraines de Guerre,'* the Wartime Godmothers."

His breath constricted, then rushed out. "Oh, my God... Fabienne, the twelve-year-old!" His bratwurst, red cabbage, and Lyonnais potatoes went untouched. "I remember your letters. They were... I felt as if you had some kind of uncanny pipeline to my brain." What a dunce he was—to blurt such an admission like a schoolboy. He, the so-called Casanova of the Paladíns.

He tried to cover his *gauche* remark. "But what are doing here in Germany?"

"My father and mother came here to study, so I was born and grew up here until we were forced to flee back to France. Come," she laid her linen napkin aside, "let's go canoeing."

She charmed good sense and rationale right out of his mind. In a role reversal, she rowed the skiff. He drenched his fill of her, the way the sunlight and water glinting off the golden skin of her honed forearms and the scimitar sweep of her cheekbones.

"Spandau Prison is located on Wilhelmstrasse," she told him. "Originally, Wilhelmstrasse was a wealthy residential street, with a number of grandiose palaces belonging to members of the Hohenzollern royal family. Recently, the Reich confiscated them and turned them into the Ministries of Transport, Finance, Public Enlightenment, and such. From one of those palaces, the President's official residence at Wilhelmstrasse 73, the *Führer* was sworn in as German Chancellor and addressed cheering crowds from a window."

Preston was having trouble paying attention to what she was saying. His attention was riveted on how she was saying it, her captivating accent and her bright, brisk beauty.

"Now," she went on, "Hitler regards his residence and Chancellery inadequate and not representative of Nazi architecture. He has ordered a reconstruction of impressive architecture for the baroque strip of buildings on Wilhelmstrasse. I am minoring in Neo-Classical Architecture at the University for just such a purpose—and this will be our ticket into Spandau."

"And our ticket out of Spandau?"

She grinned. "That will be your project."

"I have one more project."

She paused in her rowing, the water dripping off her arrested paddles. Her head canted, and the lake breeze captured strands of her hair to unscroll them across her intent face. "What?"

"I also need to get a Professor Gould out of Columbia-Haus."

"You don't make it easy, do you?"

He stared back into the drowning depths of her blue eyes. "No, but you will."

––––––––––––

WILHELMSTRASSE 23 TOWERED LIKE AN old fortress. Access to the prison was through a guardhouse, which itself formed part of a fifteen-foot inner brick wall, topped with electrified wire. Twenty-eight yards of dead space in which even the guards were not allowed was followed by a wall of barbed wire. Some of the sixty soldiers on guard duty manned six machine-gun-armed towers twenty-four hours a day.

Barking orders at Preston, a step behind her and carrying rolled blue-prints, Fabienne strode through between the baroque prison's twin turrets to the guardhouse. Her forged identification papers and passes were carefully examined by one of the soldiers in an ash-gray tunic and peaked cap. He motioned another guard over and pointed at something on her set of papers.

"The Ministry of Justice will not be at all happy about this delay," Fabi-enne snapped.

It was all Preston could do not to stare at her with an open mouth. Her bold and commanding persona was different from the engaging, ingenuous young woman of the afternoon before. Had he read her wrong? Was he, too, being duped as Hannah had been by Von Rosch? Was Fabienne a double op-erative? Luring him into the prison only to incarcerate him? His gut knotted.

At once, the guard directed her and Preston to Complex Three. Obvious-ly, Fabienne was convincing in whatever guise she chose. Today, she wore low heels, an A-line twill skirt, and a short-sleeved blouse of non-descript brown.

Workmen engaged in Hitler's reconstruction plan plied a confusion of corridors. "Hannah Kraft is Prisoner 1069 in Cell thirty-five," Fabienne whis-pered beneath her breath.

Still suspicious, he eyed her warily. "How do you know this?" His German was good enough to understand the guard had said nothing about Hannah.

Fabienne glanced askance at him and grinned. "My friend Rudy is a janitor at the Ministry of Justice. At least, for the past couple of weeks he has been."

Preston, who had never known the meaning of jealousy, felt its sting and didn't like the resulting pang of insecurity one damned bit.

"We're here to check for load-bearing walls of Complex Three, if anyone should ask. But try not to talk, Preston. Your accent will not stand the scrutiny."

The interior of the military prison was devoid of color in all gray. In total, the dungeon's complex held 134 cells with tiny, barred windows set into the steel doors. Cell number thirty-five was on the left, just past a guarded exit to the exercise yard/garden. Preston glanced over his shoulder, paused at the cell door, and called Hannah's name softly through the barred window.

Within seconds, she appeared at the window, her fingers wrapped around the bars. "Preston!"

He heard the break in her voice, saw the astonishment on her face, and noted her forefingers—both blood-crusted and nailless. Rage corked in his throat. "We're getting you out," he promised, more to himself than to her. "Tomorrow. Be ready."

She nodded rapidly. Before any passing workmen or guards—positioned at either end of the corridor—could notice, he swung away. He fell in behind Fabienne as she sauntered on, appearing to inspect walls and ceiling, jotting notes.

Once they were back outside, he gasped at the fresh air. Fury roiled through him. "What all did they do to her?" he demanded of Fabienne.

"De-nailing is most likely the extent of it. After all, she has been imprisoned less than two weeks. You notice they extracted only two nails from their beds. She is in possession of solely limited information. They know it. They do it to establish fear and, thus, obedience."

He stared down at her upturned face, her features so strong-willed, so fearless. "Why do you do this?"

"Because, like you, I lived through the Great War. I don't want France and my people ever to experience such a holocaust like that again. Never, ever, will I cease fighting for my country."

Illogically, he felt a sudden fierce tenderness toward her. And something else—a craving riding him that was too potent to deny. Worse, he wanted her too much to settle for a quick bout between the sheets.

FABIENNE'S SPARTAN, MINISCULE APARTMENT WAS located

near the University in the Mitte district, the center of Berlin, along the Spree River.

Up until May of 1933, the University has been home to many of Germany's greatest thinkers of the past two centuries—among them, Hegel, the Romantic legal theorist and famous theoretical physicists, Albert Einstein and Max Plank. It even housed the founders of Marxist theory, Karl Marx and Friedrich Engels.

But in May, some 20,000 books by degenerates and opponents of the Nazi regime were taken to be burned.

Preston sat on Fabienne's lumpy couch, his long legs sprawled across the nubby carpet. Fabienne sat with her lithe legs folded beneath her in a tattered armchair. With a teacup in hand, she laid out her plans.

"Tomorrow, it will be up to you to get Hannah out of Spandau. You know her cell's location now. You two are to meet me at the Berlin-Spandau train station, Platform sixteen by five o'clock. I shall have your passports and travel papers. If you do not show by that time, I will know we have been compromised."

He rubbed his forehead. "I suppose I can dynamite Hannah's cell door."

Fabienne grinned, displaying those dazzlingly white, uneven teeth. "That will not be necessary." She held up what looked to be two wires and a chunky lock, which looked like it could have been fabricated in the nineteenth century, when the prison was built.

"The lock is spring-loaded—an old lever-mortise box," she explained. "To pick a lever lock, you will first use this." She held up a hooked wire. "It's a piano string. Put pressure on it—just so—and lift the spring lever. Still maintaining the pressure, you take this stiffer wire here, inserting it just underneath, and slide the bolt forward."

She made it sound so simple—picking a lock in a matter of seconds with guards at either end of the corridor apt to glance his way and catch him. Then there was the matter of parading Hannah past not only the interior guards but the guardhouse itself, when the guards knew exactly the number of people entering and exiting at any given moment.

"That's all there is to it," she finished.

"Easy enough." Sighing, he pushed himself out of the chair and crossed to kneel alongside her chair. "Show me how to insert the wires—precisely."

She clasped his hand, resting on the arm of her chair, and pressed his fingers against the old metal lock. "Do you feel the slight vibration when I twist the wire and the bolt is lifted?"

What he felt was the foolish pounding of his heart in its own rusted metal box—along with a powerful surge of desire. The desire, mixed with some other unidentifiable feeling, took him by surprise. The puzzling feeling might have been akin to the recognition of a kindred spirit.

He intertwined his fingers with hers and brought them to his lips. Her skin smelled faintly of peaches. Above their conjoined knuckles, his gaze sought out hers. Her bright blue eyes flared with the soulful passion that matched his. He rose, drawing her up to him. Standing on tiptoe, she looped her arms around his neck.

He slipped one arm around her waist. With his free hand, he captured her dimpled chin. He grazed his lips over hers, tasting her sweet mouth and its fresh, mint flavor. "Tonight, then, Fabienne, is all we have."

"Fifteen years ago, I wrote you that you had courage and confidence, but I wondered if you had a heart. We have tonight for you to show me, Corporal Preston Paladín."

That night, he made love to her with all the passion in him. But he wondered, as she did, if he had a heart in him—for surely, a heart couldn't contain murderous rage such as he felt.

Impossibly, she seemed to understand him, to draw forth from him his venom as he haltingly spoke of Roger Clarendon's vendetta against the Paladíns.

By dawn, holding her sleeping body nestled against his length, he knew he—the Paladín holdout—had met his match.

WEARING OVERALLS, A DIRT-SMUDGED shirt, sleeves rolled at the forearms, and a work cap, Preston pushed the large, unwieldly wheelbarrow toward Spandau's fortressed entrance. With a rolling arm motion, the guard indicated for Preston to wheel aside the deep-sided wooden cart for inspection.

Prickly heat popped beads of sweat across his upper lip. In the mounded wheelbarrow, he toted large red bricks. Not unusual, if searched. Not even what he had immediately beneath the bricks, the wood chips, would be likely to arouse questions. Unless one dug deeper and found Fabienne's Beretta pocket pistol. He hoped he wouldn't have to use it. It might be a man-stopper, but it wouldn't hold its own against several machine guns.

And, if he personally was searched… well, there were the two lever wires concealed inside his cap band.

With the barrel of his clunky Italian-made Breda machine gun, the soldier prodded aside some of the mounded bricks. A couple toppled over the wheelbarrow's edge. Brusquely, he motioned with his machine gun for Preston to pick them up. He took his time retrieving them, bumbling and dropping one even before tossing it back into the wheelbarrow.

Impatient, the soldier scowled and waved Preston on with his machine gun. He needed no prompting. Briskly, he entered between the twin turrets and took off down the corridor for Complex Three and Cell thirty-five. Keeping his head lowered, he passed a tool-belted workman and two joking guards.

Upon reaching Hannah's cell, he softly called her name. At once, she was at the small barred window. He grinned. "Ready to ride the choo-choo train?"

Tears glistened in her dark brown eyes, but her tremulous smile was pure bravado. "Only if you're the engineer."

"I'm working on engineering you out of here. Give me a moment, cuz." Checking to make sure he was not being watched, he whipped off his work cap, swiped the two wires from its band, and set to work with the antediluvian lock.

Moments passed. The piano wire slipped between his sweaty fingers. He lost the pressure on the bolt. If his heart hammered any louder, the guards would hear.

Yet again, the tried, inserting the wire while carefully applying tension on the lifter. He felt the click of the spring lever and quickly slid the stiffer wire in. Breath held, he moved that wire so that ever so slowly, the bolt shifted forward. He heard the click of the lock's release. Another second and he was shoving the wheelbarrow through the door.

Without a word to Hannah, he rapidly began to unload the bricks, piling them on her bunk. She picked up on the urgency and began helping him. The sight of her mutilated fingers gingerly clasping the bricks threatened to rob him of his direly needed focus. "You're a real trooper."

"Of course," she murmured, "I'm a Texican."

They reached the layer of wood chips. "Get in. Burrow beneath the chips."

She didn't question him. Within seconds, she was climbing in to curl in a fetus position. The large wheelbarrow tilted with her weight. Hastily, he covered her with the woodchips. Now began the most dangerous part of the escape.

Though, as it turned out, it was the easiest—thus far. He simply fell into the exit line behind two official looking men and a couple more workmen and was passed on through without even a glance from the guard.

Once within the safety of Spandau's forested park opposite the palaces on Wilhelmstrasse, he hurriedly scooped Hannah from her entombment of wood chips, sifted below them to find Fabienne's pistol and grinned. "The conductor's waiting for us to board."

Perhaps he should have said, "Waiting for you to board." For he could not leave until he secreted out Professor Gould as well—according to reports, a somewhat easier task than his rescue of Hannah had been.

But was time on Preston's side?

Waiting at Platform sixteen was Fabienne with a plump elf of a man, a St. Nicholas look-alike. The old man chuckled merrily. "Never thought I'd see a woman again, at least not one like Fraulein Allaman. But here I behold, not one but two beautiful women." He executed a slight Old-World bow to both Fabienne and a rather disheveled looking Hannah.

Questioningly, Preston looked to Fabienne. "Professor Gould, late of Columbia Haus," she said, by way of introduction to Preston and Hannah.

Even as Preston acknowledged her introduction, the conductor's warning whistle of departure shrilled. The train hissed a white cloud of steam. With no time to spare, Preston hustled the two fugitives aboard the coach.

Then he turned to Fabienne, who appeared to be edging away from her charges—having performed her mission, she was returning to her dangerous double-life. After their night of shared passions and souls, he sure as hell was not was not going to let her depart.

The works of Wagner, the German composer, may have glorified the heroic Teutonic nature that Hitler so vociferously perpetuated, but, for Preston, Wagner's greatness lay in his operatic portrayal of romantic fate— Tristan und Isolde.

And Fabienne was Preston's fate, for better or for worse.

Oblivious to the many onlookers, he grasped her upper arm and pulled her against him in the narrow aisle. Already, the train was beginning to chug slowly away from the platform, and she glanced uneasily out the window.

His pulse roared at his temples, but he attempted a moderate tone. "Look, I know how committed you are to France, how unwaveringly you love your country, but I'm not going to pretend I'm okay with leaving you."

She stared up at him with tears glistening in those luminous eyes and bit her trembling bottom lip. Despair sweated the back of his neck.

Still, though he knew it was useless, he urged, "Come with me to the States."

22

ABOARD THE ILE DE FRANCE WITH HANNAH <STOP>
WILL DOCK IN NEW YORK JUNE 29 <STOP> PRESTON

In preparation for landing, Stoney refolded the cable and shoved it in his jacket pocket. Pierce was easing down the twelve-passenger T-32 Condor twin engine, fully loaded with Paladíns, onto one of the runways of New York's Newark Airport—the busiest commercial airport in the world.

Stoney was aware that Eastern Air Transport and American Airways were crushing Paladín Aviation with court injunctions being filed that continually delayed Pierce's expansion efforts.

Not that Paladín Aviation would have been monopolizing commercial flights anyway. With the Depression, passenger interest in flights in and out of West Texas—the gateway to Enchanting Mexico, as Paladín Aviation promoted it—had dropped perilously close to zero.

It was obvious to Stoney and the rest of the Paladíns that a certain some-one was wielding power behind the scenes in a masterminded plan to destroy them. Not only was Roger Clarendon following in his illustrious father's foot-steps by becoming a Supreme Court justice, but he was the Master Puppeteer, now pulling his father's puppet strings.

At the hangar, the Paladíns split up for taxi rides to the Waldorf-Astoria. Stoney squeezed his strapping frame into the red cab's front passenger seat, settling his Stetson on his lap. Hannah's parents were ensconced in the back.

"Drake wants us to rendezvous tonight for dinner," Claire Solomon was saying, "and we'll go over the agenda for Hannah's arrival tomorrow."

Stoney glanced over his shoulder. Fatigue warred with relief on her face. The strain of the last three weeks had etched lines into patrician features that looked forty-five-years old rather than her fifty-seven years.

"Give everyone my regrets, ma'am. I've made other plans for tonight, but I'll be back in time for *Ile de France's* docking. Wouldn't miss being there to greet my girl, even if I have to stop time."

A frown furrowed David Solomon's high forehead. At sixty-one, his thick, nearly gray hair was receding from the temples. Well, that was too damned bad if the man was upset that Stoney was not participating in the family gath-ering regarding his daughter's rescue and return to the States.

What Stoney had in mind was of far more importance—at least to him.

He figured he could handle the melting pot of the nation, with its team-ing millions, though he was there to manhandle only a single person. After checking into his room and cleaning up, he headed back down to the Wal-dorf's Art Deco lobby, with its potted palms and marbled floors and columns.

As he strode toward the revolving bronze doors, a hand latched onto his shoulder. His head spun around to find Hannah's father at his side. "Out for a night on the town, son?" David inquired.

Stoney's eyes narrowed, and his mouth below his handlebar mustache flattened. What could Hannah's father want? "Hardly. Business to attend to."

"It can wait. Join me for a drink."

Something was afoot. The terseness in David's invitation betrayed his casual tone. "All right, sir. I can spare half an hour."

With Prohibition, the Waldorf had been forced to make up for loss of revenue and had instituted a kid's meal—but it was not pabulum Stoney needed. He had a difficult night ahead of him.

To his surprise, David bypassed both Waldorf's Peacock Alley and its tea service, as well as Broadway's bright lights. They wound up entering the wrought-iron gates of the 21 Club speakeasy, an oasis for the city's elite aristocrats. A girl in an abbreviated maid's uniform took Stoney's Stetson and seated them.

After a round of Tom Collin's were ordered, David sighed heavily, rubbing the bridge of his aquiline nose. "Were you thinking of catching the late train to Forest Hills and the West Side Tennis Club?"

Stoney tried to cover his surprise. "How did you know?"

"It was what I would have expected of you."

"I won't let Von Rosch get away with it." A muscle flicked in his jaw, and he forced his teeth to relax their clenching. "Whether he intentionally compromised Hannah or not, he abandoned her."

"You know, son, the Von Rosch home—a mansion, really—is as closely guarded as the White House."

He shrugged shoulders that stretched his jacket. "Yup." He took a drink of the Tom Collins. "Doesn't matter. I'll find a way to beat him senseless. When I'm finished with him, his remains will spread like jelly over bread on his damned indoor tennis court."

David smiled. "Well, that won't be necessary."

He cocked a brow and demanded, "And why is that?"

"Because of the Jewish community in New York. I heard back from an acquaintance of mine just before I came down to the lobby to wait for you. It seems Von Rosch had an accident, trying to change a flat tire on his Duesenberg earlier today. Somehow, his coupe rolled back and forth over his trapped hands."

Stoney simply stared, flabbergasted by what David imparted so casually.

David paused to take a swig from his glass. "A puzzlement, really, but alas, if Von Rosch ever plays tennis again, he'll be severely hindered by his injuries. I doubt he'll even file a report of the incident."

At that, Stoney drained his own glass and reached across to finish off David's in one gulp. He wiped his mustache with the back of his hand. "I say we take a tour of the city's speakeasies tonight."

A serious mistake, because when Pierce rudely awoke him the next morning, he had one hell of a hangover. Struggling to sit up in the rumpled bed, his head felt like a bag of cement was flopping around inside.

"Here," the blond Adonis smiled, thrusting a Bloody Mary at him. "Try the hair of the dog that bit you."

He groaned but downed the drink. "How is David feeling?

Pierce grinned. "His hangover is heaven compared to Claire's ire."

By the time Stoney had showered, shaved, and dressed, he was relatively sure he was going to live. And by the time he and the Paladíns arrived at Pier Fifty-Nine, he felt exhilarated—for there was the *Ile de France* pulling alongside the dock.

He had waited so long, so patiently, for Hannah to realize that there was no other but him for her. He had not given up on her then, and he would not now. Nor ever.

He shouldered through the hundreds of people assembled to greet the ship, with the Paladíns crowding behind in his wake. It seemed like hours before the passengers disembarked and practically an eternity before he spotted Pierce's tall, redheaded twin.

Then he sighted, alongside the glum-looking Preston and the pressing passengers, a pale Hannah, a changed Hannah, shuffling down the gangplank, her mutilated hands concealed in summer eyelet gloves.

Finally, Stoney reached her. He swept off his hat and swept her into his arms. He wasn't sure if the sob of breath was his or hers. Her body was trembling violently, like the small pet rabbit he had treated earlier that week. What

Hannah had endured at Spandau…. If she could endure and survive and thrive, then he could.

When at last he released her, she stepped back, held up her bandaged hands, and bestowed him with a dazzling smile through her glistening tears. "I think I need a doctor. Are you up to it, Doctor Stonewall Jackson?"

AS FATE WOULD HAVE IT, President Roosevelt in one of his Fireside Chats would be broadcasting the next day from the Presidential Suite of the Waldorf-Astoria, where the Paladíns were holed up.

The broadcast covered the actual swearing-in ceremony of Roger Clarendon as Associate Chief Justice in conjunction with the State of New York ratifying Congress's proposed amendment to repeal Prohibition.

Surprisingly, Brighton Clarendon had agreed to meet with Drake downstairs, in the Waldorf's Bull and Bear clubby men's bar. Magnificent bronze statues of a bull and a bear, representing Wall Street patronage, stood guard near the entrance.

Only tea and coffee were being served. Weak coffee compared to the varnish remover The Barony served up. He withdrew a cigar from his vest pocket and offered it to the recently retired Supreme Court Chief Justice.

Beneath a majestic shock of silver hair, Brighton's features were as hard as flint. His perfectly even teeth, however, were yellowed with age. "Let's forgo the pleasantries, Paladín, and get down to business. What is it you want?"

Cigar nestled between thumb and fingers, Drake's lips moistened its end. Then he lit it, puffing slowly. Only then did he reply. "I want to put this feud to rest, Clarendon."

In his youth, Drake had been impulsive, not seeing the long-term consequences of his actions. Now, both he and Brighton Clarendon were old enough to know better… and perhaps wise enough to prevent disaster barreling down on both their families like a runaway train.

"Your irresponsible actions diminished my son's life. And, if his retribution means his diminishing the lives of your family members, so be it."

He blew a smoke ring, watching it eddy. "What if that means more than diminishing lives. What if it means taking lives?"

"Are you threatening us?"

"No. I'm only warning you. The whole Paladín clan is hot tempered as hell. But my nephew Preston is a redhead—a sure sign of a fiery nature. And I can tell you now, he's 'bout ready to detonate."

"That's your nephew's problem."

"And your son's problem is obsession for power and control with no empathy to balance it. I guess that's my point, Clarendon—your son, whether you want to admit it or not, is unbalanced."

Brighton blanched, then he shot to his feet. His eyes blazed the blue of a flame's center. "I can take care of my family without your interference. And you and the rest of your Paladíns can go to hell."

NATURALLY, THE WALDORF-ASTORIA HAD achieved worldwide renown for its glamorous dinner parties and galas, often at the center of political and business conferences. Even former President Hoover had a suite on its thirty-fourth floor. After all, it was the tallest and largest hotel in the world.

What most of the world did not know was the special train that ran on Track Sixty-One, ending beneath the Waldorf-Astoria at a private elevator. Always wishing to conceal his disability as a paraplegic, President Roosevelt used the secret entrance that afternoon.

From Waldorf-Astoria's Presidential Suite that evening, FDR would be broadcasting his Fireside Chat. Immediately afterwards, a spectacular celebration would be held in the Waldorf's Grand Ballroom. Several floors above the Grand Ballroom, Preston sat in his suite with Darcy, who had stayed to cover the newsreel filming of the evening's gala.

Of course, Mariana and Heath had also stayed due to her political commitments and friendship with Eleanor Roosevelt, but the rest of the family had gathered around Hannah and headed back home with her to The Barony that morning.

And Preston had his own reasons for staying—to finish off, once and for all, the slime that relentlessly threatened his family. A quiet deadly rage had been mounding in him since he had beheld his cousin behind the dungeon bars. The acidic fury had eaten away at him. He had tried to contain it until he had gotten Hannah back to the States safely, but there was no stopping him from spewing now.

After the swearing-in as Associate Chief Justice, Roger Clarendon was due to appear at the Grand Ballroom festivities. In less than half an hour, he was to make his acceptance speech.

Preston glanced at his wristwatch. Thirty minutes. With each pace across his suite, another second of erupting fury built inside him.

Heath, standing near the sideboard, corked its crystal stopper in the cognac decanter and passed a sniffer to Mariana. Hollywood Handsome Heath had become her dark archangel, his wings enfolding her and shielding her with his love.

And Preston was envious of that deep, committed love they shared. He had hoped Fabienne could be as committed to him as she was to France. Without her, he felt he would lead a bleak, soulless life.

With a glaring ache, he remembered his first sight of her there at the Strandbad Wannsee's beachfront. He might as well have been struck by lightning, the breath vaporized in his paralyzed lungs, his heart incinerated. And then, when he realized that she was the one who had written him those engaging Godmother letters during the war, he had felt like bursting into laughter at the whimsical workings of the gods. Of all the women he had known and loved, only she had been his match, reaching from back in time to find him again.

"Look, Preston, I know what you're thinking—because I'm thinking the same thing. It's Clarendon, isn't it? The son-of-a bitch would rip the wings off a butterfly."

Preston flicked him an acknowledging glance but, hands locked behind his back, continued to stride the lengthy room. He, Pierce, and Heath had fought through the Great War together, but he doubted Pierce or Heath understood how strongly he resented that time of being the pawn of someone else's power, of having no control.

He had shed his tuxedo jacket and wore only his white tuxedo shirt and midnight blue cummerbund and trousers. His forefinger tugged inside his bowtie, loosening it. He glanced at his Rolex again. Twenty minutes. Once the Master of Ceremonies took the podium, the White House Police would close the ballroom doors. This was one function Preston had no intention of missing.

"We all want to stomp the shit out of Roger Clarendon," Darcy was saying. He stood near the decorative fireplace, drink in hand.

"Like someone stomped the shit out of Leo Von Rosch," Heath rumbled. He wrapped an arm around Mariana's waist The raven-haired beauty wore a slinky gold gown that would have made Gloria Swanson look dowdy.

"But killing Clarendon is something else," Darcy continued, ever the pacifist. "So, let's take that off the agenda's possibilities."

"Maybe it's something other than just killing Clarendon," Mariana's shrewd gaze followed Preston as he paced.

Heath arched a brow. "Just, sweetheart?"

She threw her husband an exasperated glance, then stepped in front of Preston, blocking his restless tread. "I think it's also Fabienne Allaman. You're in love with her, aren't you?"

His mouth screwed in a dry smile that was more a scowl. "I take the Fifth."

He was determined to put all thought of her behind him. But that image of her, reclining on her apartment's narrow, lumpy bed, her tawny hair spilling across the pillow... the image of her merely turning and walking away from him on the train... those two images were burnt onto the back of his eyelids indelibly.

Mariana gave him one of her mistress-of-magic smiles. "Fabienne is wait-ing for you down in Peacock Alley."

"How did she—"

"Let her tell you, because I...."

But he was already grabbing his jacket.

"We'll meet you two in the ballroom," she called out after him as he strode toward the elevator and the Waldorf's bar below.

Peacock Alley was frequented only by New York's crème de la crème. That evening, a few people were already imbibing, despite the obvious fact that the U.S. Congress had yet to ratify the repeal.

Fabienne, wearing a simple two-piece white linen suit and wide-brimmed hat tilted saucily to one side, sat in a rounded booth in a corner. A crystal chan-delier sparkled light that transmuted her freckles into shimmering fairy dust.

He slid into the leather-padded booth beside her and took from her the flute she lightly clasped. He breathed in her faint peach fragrance. He longed to take ownership of her lush mouth, ownership of her, there and then. Somehow, he managed to get out matter-of-factly, "How did you get to the States so quickly?"

Her smile displayed those endearing, irregular teeth. "I chartered a flight to Southampton the next day and sailed out on the RMS *Aquitania*. Much quicker. The champagne here is *atroce.*"

"That bad, huh?" He took a sip and made a face. "You're right. It is atro-cious. What changed your mind?"

He had to know, had to hear her say that the transatlantic trip she'd made was not merely a romantic escapade for her. She was younger than he, still full of idealism. He had to know that she wanted him enough to stay in the States. Because in a short time, Europe would be unsafe for anyone.

She took the flute back from him, drinking from the rim's side. "To get back my Beretta you took with you."

"Is that all?" He tapped his jacket pocket. "It's right here."

She frowned. "In your pocket? Why?"

"A keepsake to remember you by."

Her lips made a moue. "I understand you better than you realize, Corporal Paladín, and I do not like it when you lie to me."

It was uncanny, this potent magnetism between them. And the bond she shared with him… a bond fashioned of fascination, admiration, and, yes, contentment—something that had been missing in his life. "Well, that is partially the truth."

"But not the whole truth, as you Americans say."

"The whole truth is that"—he glanced at his wristwatch yet again—"in less than ten minutes I intend to persuade Roger Clarendon that confession before dignitaries and cameras is better than a hole in the chest."

She stilled. "Your American revolution inspired my country's revolution. What you are about to do—to kill instead of using your democratic system of justice—is no better than what the Nazis are doing."

"Even in the best of societies, justice sometimes go astray."

She frowned as he leaned over, one hand cupping her neck, and pulled her to him. Her soft lips tasted piquant—of champagne, youthful energy, and a siren's song. Gradually, she yielded. Her arms slipped beneath his jacket to encircle his waist and, pressing her glorious breasts against him, she slanted her mouth over his and parted her lips in a soft, sighing moan.

A gesture of concession, at least in this one instance, that offered the promise of something more substantial than mere silk and steel.

At last, quite unwillingly, he released her and stood. Time was pressing. "Wait here for me. Finish your champagne."

Mouth open, she stared at him as he dropped a wad of bills on the table and slid back out of the booth. He knew she would be there when he got back, but would she be there forever?

FINGERS KNOTTED BENEATH HER CHIN, Belle paced before Darcy

as he dressed for the evening's stellar political event at the Waldorf Astoria's Grand Ballroom three floors below. She was both furious and terrified. "This goes against everything you believe in, Darcy. What you've campaigned against your entire life."

Standing before the suite's wall mirror, he adjusted his tux's bowtie. His image reflected a tall, strikingly handsome man. What it didn't reflect was his overly confident mouth and his overly loving heart. "Be that as it may," he mumbled, one gold cufflink tucked between his lips, "there are exceptions to every rule."

In a clipped paced, she crossed the plush carpet and plucked the cufflink from his lips. With agitated fingers, she quickly fastened the link to the starched cuff with which he was now wrestling.

"And you were one of them," she mumbled angrily. "One of those rules. My rules. Never get involved with a cowboy." She reached up to straighten his collar over his bowtie band. Even the expensive men's cologne she had gifted didn't distract from his own natural, wonderfully fresh, woodsy scent. "They'll break your heart every time and strike out for the freedom of the range."

But, God help her, she had. From the first, she'd never been able to get the lumbering cowboy out of her mind. She'd wanted him in her arms, in her bed. Hell, she had become so vigilant, so distrustful of the motives of the male species. But he had been steadfast, had declared he intended to spend the rest of his life with her. And had proven her trust in him time and again. How could she not love this Rider of the Range?

He quirked that arrogant yet guileless smile that often drove her nuts. "Just proves my point." He held out his other strong-boned wrist for its cufflink. "That rules are meant to be broken. Even my own staunch rule of nonviolence. Because the Paladín's motto is greater—family is everything. Now, give me the gun, sweetheart."

Tears spilling over her lids, she took the pistol from her purse and passed it to him. Instead of taking it right away, his hands framed her beautiful face. "It's a just-in-case thing, Belle. Believe me, you're my everything."

She latched onto his hand. "Then, don't take it. Please, Darcy!"

He pocketed the gun and patted it. "All these years, you've trusted me. Trust me now, sweetheart."

———————————

FROM THE THIRD FLOOR, SOARING four stories high, ruled the magnificent Grand Ballroom. Most of the thousand or more guests were already seated, but a few latecomers were still filing in from the Silver Corridor.

Flashing the two White House Policemen one of the VIP invitations—procured from the First Lady by Mariana—Preston slipped through the invitees still stringing in. At the long, damask-draped head table, the guests of honor were taking their seats. He scooted into his chair beside Heath.

As usual, Eleanor and FDR had already been seated in order not to display his disability. The First Lady was chatting with Heath, seated to her right. Off to one side, Darcy was finishing the setup of camera and cables.

To the President's left sat a self-confident Roger in his wheelchair and, next to him, a pleased-looking Brighton Clarendon.

Why wouldn't the father and son be pleased? Over the years, time after time, they had sabotaged the Paladíns.

Mariana leaned over and whispered, "Where is Fabienne?"

"Waiting for me in Peacock Alley."

"Then you aren't planning on staying? We were hoping you would bring her with—" She broke off as the famous humorist Will Rogers rose to stand behind the microphone as the evening's Master of Ceremonies.

He looked out over the diamond-and-pearl crusted guests, grinned and wisecracked, "Lord, the money we do spend on government, and it's not one bit better than the government we got for one-third the money twenty years ago."

Chuckles rippled through the room, and he went on to say that he was running as a candidate of the Anti-Bunk Party. "My only campaign promise is that, if elected, I will resign." Now laughter filled the ballroom. With the audience warmed up, he gave the floor over to FDR.

The President, speaking into table microphones placed before him, addressed briefly his New Deal program, then introduced the newest Associate Justice and slid the table microphone to him.

Amidst thundering applause, Roger Clarendon projected a humble smile. "Thank you... thank you. The Supreme Court is the highest court in the land. It is the final judge involving laws of Congress and the highest law of all—the Constitution. No freedom, even one specifically mentioned in the Constitution, is absolute. Even words themselves may pose a clear and present danger to the well-being of our country. That is why it is so important—"

"Just as you pose a clear and present danger to the well-being of our country?" Preston interrupted Clarendon as he rose from his seat.

Roger's lids, unsynchronized, blinked crazily. "I beg your pardon?"

"I have in my pocket proof—a signed confession by Leo Von Rosch—that you have been collaborating with the Reich." Actually, he had no such admission in his pocket, only Fabienne's Beretta.

"Get him out of here," Roger shouted, motioning at the back of the ballroom entrance for the two White House Policemen.

"No, let him speak." President Roosevelt's characteristic open-mouthed smile was in place. "As far as I know, the First Amendment is still in force."

But Darcy, off to one side, was fiercely shaking his head. He knew Preston's intent.

Preston ignored him. "Not only with the Reich, but our illustrious new Associate Court Justice also collaborated with Galveston's mobsters to murder—"

"That's enough!" Brighton Clarendon rose from behind the table, drawing all eyes to him now. "Those are absurd allegations about my son. A pack of ridiculous lies!"

Surreptitiously, Roger's hand slid beneath his jacket, his hand going for his shoulder holster, exactly what Preston had counted on provoking. It was the icing on the cake—kill Roger in self-defense and he'd rid the Paladíns and the world of a piece of shit, and he himself walk away a free man.

But never free of his conscience, the thought of cold-bloodedly killing another gave him pause, even as instinct bellowed at him that now was the instant to go for the Beretta.

His great-grandfather, Alex Paladín, had turned his back on a duel. Could he do any less?

Roger managed to extract the pistol from its hampering holster and raised the gun to fire point blank. Screams erupted throughout the room.

Preston watched the glacially slow drama of his own death unfolding within blinks of the eye. So, this is what it's like to face a firing squad. What a fool—to lose a chance of the happiness he might have known with Fabienne.

The room reverberated with the gun blast. Astonished, Preston saw Roger crumple forward in the wheelchair. From there, Preston's gaze alit on Fabienne. Wide-eyed, trembling, she stood with her Beretta in her hand, its muzzle still aimed at Roger.

His hand went to his jacket pocket. *Empty!*

Pandemonium raced through the room. The White House Police were shouldering through the crowd to reach the President.

At the same time, Heath and Darcy were circumventing the end of the table to reach Preston, but he was already heading for Fabienne. She stared, astounded, at her revolver, clutched in her hand. Stunned, she looked up at him. "I did not have the chance to fire it, Preston."

"What?"

His eyes flicked to the nearby commotion—a heartsick and subdued-looking Brighton Clarendon was being handcuffed by the two uniformed White House Policemen.

THE BARONY, TEXAS
NOVEMBER 1933

That Thanksgiving was one of those perfect, crisp autumn days, and the entire Paladín clan celebrated the holiday dinner in The Barony gazebo. Twinkling electric lights circumferenced its eaves, and within the gazebo, a savory feast mounded the tables strung together.

Naturally, the main topic of discussion was the recent Grand Jury's decision not to indict Brighton Clarendon for the murder of his son. "He's a broken man." Drake passed a basket of butter-glazed rolls. "Even if he does run for President, it's doubtful the votes are there."

"Well, if you don't mind my changing the subject." Heath stood, wineglass in hand. As usual, The Barony's Thanksgiving dinners served as an occasion for the announcement of important family events, and all heads turned toward him expectantly. He grinned down at Mariana, then his pleased-as-punch gaze swept the table. "I'd like to announce the addition of another Paladín, coming this March, as close as we can figure."

Congratulations, claps, and yelps of joy rang out.

Preston wanted to make another addition to the clan. His hand sought beneath the table that of Fabienne's. She glanced quizzically at him.

Amidst the confusion of delirious babble, he pulled her away, tugging her outside into the night. A harvest moon lit his way.

"We should not have left like that," she protested.

"That's exactly what we should have done." He managed to temper the raw, primitive part of his voice that was harshly masculine with tortured desire and wanting.

Once past the lawn's carpet, yellowing with fall's weather, he took her elbow and guided her up the incline's graveled path toward the sentinel that was the large oak tree. Almost protectively, it stood vigilantly not only over the graves of past Paladíns but also The Barony itself.

Hands on her supple shoulders, he backed her against the tree's rough bark. His knee anchored between her thighs and his blood surging to his groin, he took possession of her mouth. Her hands cupped his jaw, and she returned his kiss with a life affirmative passion his broken soul needed.

Would this wanting of her never be assuaged? He had the feeling that, like his twin and his great-grandfather, he was destined to fall in love with a Frenchwoman.

Dazed, gasping, he dragged his mouth from hers and lifted his head. In his ears, his voice sounded as rasp as a farrier's file. "I need to know, once and for all. Your letters to me all those years ago... you wrote that you thought I was so self-sufficient that I would find that people intruded upon my space. You wondered if I had a heart. I gave you my heart, there in Berlin. Will you take my name now?"

Her perfectly white and uneven teeth gleamed in the moonlight. "I was beginning to think I might have to use my Beretta to persuade you to propose. My ferocious lover, I have been spellbound by you since first I saw your newspaper photo. It breathed virility. It whispered you preferred recklessness over caution. I believed then, and I do now, that a reckless love trumps a cautious one. So, I too have sought the reckless side."

He couldn't suppress his cocky grin. "Does that mean you love me and will marry me?"

Her clever fingers slid up his jawline to frame his face. With a supremely feminine smirk, she lifted her sweet mouth close to his. *"Bon dieu,* but you Texicans are tough ones to convince."

AUTHOR'S
NOTE

I WANT TO ACKNOWLEDGE USE of *The Falcons of France* by Charles Nordhoff and *The Greatest Air Combat Stories Ever Told* by Tom McCarthy, as well as, "The Secret History," *Texas Monthly,* by Don Graham.

PARRIS AFTON BONDS IS THE mother of five sons and the author of more than forty published novels. She is the co-founder and first vice president of Romance Writers of America, as well as, co-founder of Southwest Writers Workshop.

Declared by ABC's *Nightline* as one of three best-selling authors of romantic fiction, the award-winning Parris has been featured in major newspapers and magazines, in addition to being published in more than half a dozen languages.

The Parris Award was established in her name by the Southwest Writers Workshop to honor a published writer who has given outstandingly of time and talent to other writers. Prestigious recipients of the Parris Award include Tony Hillerman and the Pulitzer nominee Norman Zollinger.

She donates spare time to teaching creative writing to both grade school children and female inmates, whom she considers her captive audiences.

Lightning Source UK Ltd.
Milton Keynes UK
UKHW040626250521
384341UK00001B/45

9 781633 736306